MORE THAN PANCAKES

By Christine DePetrillo

Cover design by Dar Albert of
Wicked Smart Designs
www.wickedsmartdesigns.com

Edited by Janet Hitchcock
www.theproofisinthereading.wordpress.com

Author Contact:

Website: www.christinedepetrillo.weebly.com

Facebook:
www.facebook.com/christinedepetrilloauthor

Dedication

To Mother Nature and her maple tree magic…

Chapter One

"Leave it, Poe. Quit fooling around."

Rick Stannard wrestled his glove away from his coyote. She was forever burying, slobbering all over, or chewing holes in his good work gloves. Ever since he'd rescued the abandoned, starving pup from the woods at the edge of his property, he'd been living with the eccentricities of having an animal meant for the wild living in his cabin. He'd trained her. Knew she wouldn't attack him while he slept, but now and then, her feral nature would flare up. Poe considered it playing, and most of the time so did Rick, but today he had to insert the taps on his maple trees and inspect the lines. The sap was about to run and that meant the Stannard Mountain Pure Vermont Maple Syrup Company—Rick's company—was all systems green.

"C'mon, you beast. We don't have all morning to waste. We've got work to do." Rick gave a final tug that freed his glove from Poe's jaws. He stumbled back, landing on his backside on the hickory floor of his small kitchen. "Brat." He swiped Poe's muzzle with his glove.

The coyote licked his hand and happily trotted beside Rick as he went into the garage to load his sled with the necessary tools. Clothed in his snow pants, thermal shirt, fleece jacket, knit hat, boots, and snowshoes, Rick was ready for a day out on his three-hundred acre property in the woods of Danton, Vermont. He'd upgraded his equipment, all gravity-fed lines, about three years back. The only assistance he accepted was from his aunt, Joy Stannard, and his cousins, Hope and Sage, who ran the bakery and book swap storefront of the business during the late winter and early spring months. Customers needed a cozy, friendly little shop from which to purchase their maple products. Rick didn't do cozy or friendly, but Aunt Joy and his cousins excelled in both areas.

Leaving the sled outside, he pushed open the door to the storefront and let Poe scurry in first.

"Morning, Rick! I was thinking if we arranged the tables this way, it would allow for more interaction between customers, and if the customers interact more, this place could become the social center of Danton. It would mean more sales, more book swapping, more action. Sometimes this place can be such a tomb, but with the tables like this, maybe some hot, interesting guys will come in and whisk me away to—"

Rick held up two hands to stop Hope from continuing her verbal assault. Too much. Too early.

"Sorry." Hope pushed in a chair at one of the tables she'd moved. "I forgot you aren't a morning person."

"Isn't much of an afternoon or evening person either," Sage, Hope's sister, called from behind the pastry case where she had been vacuuming the shelves.

Rick shot her a glare to which she responded with a snarl that ended in a grin.

"What brings you amongst the people, Grouch?" Sage gathered her long, blond hair into a ponytail then leaned against the pastry case.

Rick pointed down to his winter attire. "What does it look like I'm going to do?"

"Sumo wrestle with Bigfoot?" Hope offered, making Sage chuckle.

"If you weren't so busy turning this place into a dating club, you'd know what's going on." Rick pulled his glove off to scratch Poe between the ears as the coyote pushed her muzzle into his knee.

"I'm not turning it into a dating club, Rick." Hope gestured to the tables arranged in a tight little formation that made him a little claustrophobic. "It looks better this way, doesn't it?"

"It looked fine the old way." Rick shrugged.

"How is it that you're only six years older than me but seem as if you're *eighty*-six years older?" Sage asked. "Change is good, old man."

He knew Sage was only busting his chops, but it stung a little today. He didn't know why, which made him feel exactly like an old man.

"I don't care what you do with the tables, Hope, as long as there are tables and they're clean." Rick headed for the door. "Where's Aunt Joy?" *And why do I want her around? Because Hope and Sage are picking on me? Foolish.*

"She went into town to buy some fabric. Don't freak out, Rick." Hope grabbed his biceps and opened her brown eyes real wide as she stood on tiptoes in a useless attempt to look him in the eye. "She wants to make new curtains for these windows. Now I realize she didn't clear it with you first, O Master of Keeping the Status Quo, but I don't think a curtain change will destroy the world as we know it."

Rick growled at Hope, and she laughed along with Sage. Even Poe let out a few short barks that sounded like chuckling.

"Whose side are you on, mutt?" He nudged Poe with his knee, and the coyote let out a whimper of apology.

"You headed out now?" Sage asked.

"Yep."

"Take this." Sage placed a thermos on top of the pastry case and slid it toward him. "Minestrone like no other, Cuz."

For all her poking fun, Sage took care of him just as Aunt Joy and Hope did. They were his family, all he had. All he needed.

"Thanks." He took the thermos and held it out of Poe's reach as the coyote tried to climb up his leg for it. "Down. No meat in this one." He tapped her on the nose, and Poe sank to all fours. Even if the soup did have meat in it, he wasn't sharing. Everything Sage made tasted like heaven.

That was what made her a fantastic caterer when it wasn't sugaring season. She was busy cooking all times of the year. And her cookies? Off the charts tasty.

"I've got some website updates I've been working on." Hope gestured to her laptop on one of the tables she'd moved. She handled all their online sales, promotional materials, and website. She was awesome at it too, which was good because Rick didn't want to handle that stuff. Lots of people didn't want to handle that stuff, so Hope was busy with that work in the off season.

"Okay," Rick said. "Make them happen. I'm sure it's all good."

Hope patted his cheek. "I love that I have you trained to believe I'm always right."

"Except when you move my tables."

Hope stuck her tongue out at him then said, "Don't get lost out there."

"Have I ever?" Rick zipped the front of his fleece coat.

"No," Sage said, "but we can dream." She smiled sweetly and turned on the vacuum again.

He could still hear his cousins' laughter as he left the store with Poe on his heels. He put on his hat and picked up the cable attached to his sled. A day out in the tranquility of the woods stretched before him, and he couldn't think of a more perfect way to spend his time. The morning sky was clear, and a fresh snow had fallen last night making his property seem like uncharted territory, free from any indications of civilization.

On a whistle, Rick and Poe headed out. His snowshoes cut a trail across the blank white page of his land, and he fell into the easy rhythm of his work. He moved at a steady pace, covering more ground than he'd expected. The terrain was a bit hilly in this section of the sugar bush, but he pushed onward. He chewed up some of his time watching a moose and her calf at the edge of the still frozen Cassie's Pond. The cow's ears constantly twitched as she listened for signs of danger. The baby huddled beside her, its thick brown coat lightly dusted with snow.

When a hawk cried overhead, the cow nudged her baby and the two wandered deeper into the woods. Woods that weren't a part of Rick's property, but were tapped by him. When he'd first started his syrup business on his land, he'd cut a deal with his neighbor to lease and tap her trees. She received a specified amount of money per tap for the intrusion, which she didn't seem to mind, and Rick always supplied her with free syrup every year. She was a great neighbor. Not around much and as respectful of his privacy as he was of hers. A marvelous business arrangement if such a concept existed. Someday Rick hoped to own her land when she was ready to sell it and double his empire without having to go all big city and corporate.

He continued inserting spiles until the sun faded and hunger knocked on the walls of his stomach. He'd install the taps on his neighbor's trees tomorrow and spend tonight going through three boxes of donated books back at his cabin for the book swap. The bonus was he got first dibs on anything of interest in the donations, and he'd made some good finds in the past. An early edition Kafka. A leather-bound collection of Shakespeare plays. An autographed Jane Austen. Those finds were now displayed on the floor to ceiling bookcases that lined three of Rick's living room walls.

Anticipating the buzz he always got when surrounded by books, he pulled his sled around to head home, but as he turned he dropped the rope attached to the sled. He was on enough of a hill that the sled immediately slid away from him. Not wanting to have to chase the sled and his tools all the way to the bottom, Rick ran after it in his snowshoes.

No easy feat.

He started off all right until the tip of his left snowshoe got caught under a fallen branch hidden below the snow. His ankle made an unnatural grinding sound as his foot stayed wedged in one direction and his body fell the opposite way. He let out a howl of pain that had Poe darting over to sniff his face.

"Back, Poe." Rick pushed the coyote out of his space, but she circled around him, sniffing and whimpering.

The hurt in his ankle was a slow burning that got hotter as he tried to release his boot from the snowshoe. Every movement sent ripples of fire up his entire left leg. After too many minutes of struggling, he finally managed to unfasten the straps. His foot spilled off the snowshoe and when it landed in the snow, he hurled a shout into the arm of his fleece jacket. The muffled agony further agitated Poe who began howling. A few dogs replied, and Rick suddenly felt very Stephen King.

Not a great feeling.

Knowing it would be dark soon, he tried to stand. That went okay until he put his weight on his left foot and crumpled right back down to the ground.

Dammit. I don't need this now.

He grumbled under his breath as Poe ran a little ahead of their position and then galloped back to him. When she came close enough to sniff him again, he grabbed her. Pointing her toward the sled resting at the bottom of the hill, he said, "Go get it. Get it, Poe."

Poe barked once and shot down the hill toward the sled. She dug in the snow a bit and touched her nose to the ground. When she raised her head, the rope was in her teeth. She bounded back up the hill with the sled gliding along behind her, and Rick cursed over his stupidity.

What good is having a coyote if I don't know how to use her?

Poe continued past him with the sled until it rested on level land. The coyote stood by the sled and barked at him as if to say, "C'mon. Let's go."

"Would love to, Poe." As much as he didn't want to, Rick untied his boot and slid it off with a few grunts of pain. He removed his thermal sock and glanced at the instant swelling in his ankle. That was the last thing he saw.

When he opened his eyes again, the snow-covered canopy of trees had been replaced by the tongue-and-groove pine ceiling of his living room. He was still in the jeans he'd worn during the day and his thermal shirt, but a flannel blanket had been thrown over him. Good thing too, because he was freezing.

And maybe a little dizzy. Definitely tired as all hell.

"You awake, sugar?" Aunt Joy came in from the kitchen.

He attempted to sit up, but found he didn't have the strength.

"Easy, Rick. Take it slow." Aunt Joy stood over him with a smile on her face he knew was forced.

"How'd I get back here?"

"When nine o'clock rolled around and we didn't see this face," she bent to pat his cheek, "we knew something not good had happened."

Aunt Joy helped him wiggle up to a sitting position on the couch, and a plastic air cast spanning up to his calf stared back at him from the armrest on the other end. Rick let out a groan and flopped his head onto the back of the couch.

"Yeah, it's severely sprained. Doctor Reslin made a special house call so we didn't have to take you to the h-o-s-p-i-t-a-l." Aunt Joy whispered the letters, and despite his situation, Rick appreciated the woman's tenderness. She knew better than anybody how much he hated hospitals.

"The police found you in the snow, one shoe on, one shoe off, and out cold in more ways than one." Aunt Joy sat on the edge of the old chest Rick used as a coffee table and rested her chin in her hands. "Gave an old lady a good scare, sugar. I don't like when you do that."

He pulled his gaze from the cast and looked at Aunt Joy's face. Her brown eyes were watery, her nose a little red. He reached his hand over and tugged one of hers out from beneath her chin. Giving it a squeeze, he said, "I'm sorry, Aunt Joy. I tripped. It was stupid."

"It was an accident. Could happen to anyone." She placed her other hand atop his. "Just glad you're okay. You're a miserable hermit most of the time, but I kind of love you, you know?"

"I love you too."

"Of course you do. Nobody takes better care of you than me." Aunt Joy patted his cheek again and stood. "Okay, here's the scoop. Cast for a few weeks. Stay off the ankle for the rest of this week and keep it elevated, then Doc left you a cane so you can hobble around."

Rick opened his mouth to protest, but Aunt Joy waved him off. "I know. I know. 'Aunt Joy, how am I supposed to stay off my feet when there's so much to do?' Listen, kid, this is the way the cards got dealt this hand. Roll with it."

She made it sound like no big deal. No big deal that he was reduced to the functioning level of an infant during a key time for his syrup business.

"It doesn't hurt that much," Rick said.

"That's because you've got these in you." Aunt Joy reached to an end table by the couch and shook an orange bottle of prescription pills. "Wonder drugs. Once they wear off, you'll be writhing in pain." She leaned in close to his ear. "Here's a tip, sugar. Don't let them wear off."

Chapter Two

The Jeep Lily Hinsdale had rented hit every snow-covered crater in the stupid, one-lane, dirt road. Didn't Vermonters see the need for paved streets? Completely uncivilized. Not at all like lovely La Jolla, California.

And why the hell is it so dark? The headlights cut two narrow tunnels of gold into the night, but that night stretched on in an icy forever. No shops or restaurants lined the sides of the road with brilliant neon signs. Acres separated the few homes in the area, and those homes appeared unoccupied save for a single porch light here and there.

Lily had not wanted to stay at Grandma Gail's place, even if her recently deceased grandmother had bequeathed the Vermont property to her, but staying at a hotel meant being nearly an hour away from the land. Silly to delay talking to the neighbor—some backwoods maple syrup company owner—about the right of first refusal agreement her grandmother had made with him. Lily had to get this guy to refuse the land quickly so she could turn it over for development to Utopia

Resorts, the hotel company where she worked. She had no time to waste and being in the woods longer than was necessary made her stomach clench.

She slammed into another deep rut in the road and missed California, her office at Utopia Resorts, her Marilyn Monroe posters, her sunshine and balmy temperatures. Being Senior Hotel Designer for the world's most successful resort chain came with a constant flow of work, and she loved every minute of it. There was nothing she wanted to do more than design extravagant, themed hotels.

Except this time.

Utopia suddenly wanted to divert from its usual business plan of glamorous resorts and delve into projects catered to "regular" folks. Moms who drove kids to soccer practice in minivans. Dads who cut their own grass on Saturdays wearing baseball caps and stained jeans. Children who rode their bicycles, got dirt under their fingernails, and thought toads were pets. The entire notion of having a Utopia Resort dedicated to the average family made Lily nauseous. But if Utopia wanted something, Utopia got it. End of story.

She hadn't meant to suggest Vermont to Utopia either, but her father had basically struck her with lightning when he dumped Grandma Gail's property and this right of first refusal crap into her lap. Before she knew it, she was telling the vice president, Rita Davenbridge, about a log cabin themed resort idea she'd pulled out of her ass. Of course, Rita loved it. Of course, Lily had to trek across the damn continent to make it happen.

Of course, this completely sucked.

Lily squinted out the windshield. Creatures could be tracking her as she drove by. A deer could shoot out into the road and demolish the Jeep in a heartbeat. She could run into a patch of ice, spin out, and careen down Stannard Mountain. The Jeep could malfunction, leaving her to freeze to death in the driver's seat.

"Knock it off, Hinsdale."

She shoved a handful of jellybeans from the bag in the cup holder into her mouth. She'd been doing so since she landed at the airport, got her suitcase, and rented the Jeep. She was three-fourths of the way through this bag—her second bag. Fortunately, she'd packed ten.

She focused on the noise her chewing made. The radio was of no use with none of the stations coming in clearly this deep into the woods. Why hadn't she brought one of her treasured movie soundtracks?

Lily picked up her cell phone, but didn't know who to call. Most of her friends in California would be unreachable with the time difference. Another rainbow mix of jellybeans made its way to her lips. If she kept this going, she'd be up all night on a sugar rush. Probably didn't matter anyway. She'd be up all night listening for sounds of large beasts prowling outside her grandmother's cabin.

Fingering the cell phone again, her last link to the real world, Lily considered calling her boss, Drew Ashburn. Knowing her distaste for the woods, he'd felt bad about sending her to Vermont, but his job was also on the line. If Lily failed in her attempt to make this rustic resort work on this property, Drew would be in trouble too. Part of what made her and Drew so successful as a professional team was they always came through. She'd always proposed ingenious designs, he'd always orchestrated the carryout of those designs, and the higher-ups had always been more than pleased. The surveys guests filled out consistently mentioned how well the themes had been constructed in the resorts. Underwater themes, safari themes, rock-and-roll themes, even vampire and Martian themes.

This won't be any different, Lily assured herself. *You can make this work as you've made all the others work. Rita wants natural, rustic. She's going to get natural, rustic.*

Tree branches scraped against the side of the Jeep as Lily passed, and she let out a yelp.

"Stop being such a fool."

After another ten minutes of riding through her personal nightmare, the glow of a streetlight illuminated the gated entrance to Grandma Gail's property. The driveway was covered in more than two inches of snow because it hadn't been plowed.

"Wonderful." Lily turned on the Jeep's 4 x 4 and said a silent prayer as she pressed her foot on the gas pedal. The absence of snow was another thing on Lily's enormous list of Things to Love About California.

The Jeep handled the snowy inclines and declines, the slick twists and turns, with ease, and Lily was glad she had taken the car rental lady's advice to get this vehicle. An unfortunate putrid cream color—not at all sexy like the black amethyst pearl paint on her Lexus back home—the machine laughed in the face of the challenging driveway. Maybe it would keep her safe from *all* the dangers of Vermont.

A massive form came into view at the top of the driveway. Another streetlight revealed the cabin and the dagger-like icicles hanging from the porch roof. Lily had once seen a movie where the villain died from an icicle spearing into his head. His crimson blood had been vivid against the white snow as it seeped from the fatal wound.

"Quick, think of a comedy." Lily scoured her mental database of memorized and treasured movies, but nothing came to mind.

Pulling to a stop in front of the garage, she shut off the engine. She rummaged around in the envelope her father had given her containing the documents about the property and the right of first refusal agreement with the neighbor.

"Neighbor?" Lily peered out the windows. No indications existed that anyone lived close by. The blackness was endless in every direction.

Shivering, her fingers closed around the key to the cabin. Holding it in one hand, Lily gripped the steering wheel with her other hand. She had reached the moment she dreaded most—getting out of the car and walking to the cabin's front door. It wasn't a long walk, but anything could happen in that distance, as she well knew.

She shifted in her seat, letting her clothes rub against the scars on her back. Silly to be this afraid. She ran along Pearl Cove back home almost every morning. Certainly she was in good enough shape to zip from the Jeep to the house. And she was aware now. Not like when she was a kid staying with Grandma Gail at this cabin. She'd thought she was invincible then. She was better prepared, better armed now.

Why didn't you pack a rifle? Lily sifted out a long breath. "Because you're not a gun-toting lunatic, that's why."

After stealing two more jellybeans for good measure, she grabbed her purse, her laptop case, and her suitcase. She was only going to make this run in the dark once tonight. Counting to three, she threw open the driver side door, juggled all her paraphernalia as she got out of the car, and proceeded to drop each item at least once. Swearing, she looped her purse strap across her body, slung the laptop case strap over her shoulder, and picked up the suitcase.

Something in the shadows could be putting a damn napkin across its lap and deciding what part to eat first, Hinsdale.

On that thought, she swung the door shut and bolted for the cabin. She slipped twice, but never fell to the ground, before jamming the key into the lock. She tore into the cabin, slammed the door shut behind her, and disarmed the house alarm. She leaned against the door as if bracing for something terrible to come crashing inside.

Lily's heartbeat filled her ears along with the huffing breaths she took to calm herself. She flipped on the closest light switch and the huge chandelier in the foyer screamed to life.

Light. Light was good.

"Now if only Grandma Gail would come down the stairs, you'd be all set." Lily threw a glance to the top of the stairs, but of course, Grandma Gail was corked in an urn and sitting on one of the shelves in her father's living room in California. Her personal hero's laughter would never again fill this cabin or this world.

Lily set her suitcase, laptop, and purse down in the foyer and walked through the house holding an umbrella she'd found by the door like a sword. She turned on every light in the cabin. Every light until the place was as lit as a California beach in the middle of the afternoon.

She went to the sunken great room with its floor to vaulted ceiling fireplace and pressed a button on the end table by the huge leather sectional. Two enormous, wooden doors on the wall perpendicular to the fireplace slid open to reveal a flat screen TV almost the size of a garage door.

Hitting another button, Lily opened the drawer below the TV containing the DVD player.

She jogged back to her suitcase and pulled out the bag of movies she'd brought. She didn't plan on staying in Vermont for long—just long enough to meet with this neighbor guy and draw up some designs for the new resort—but she'd brought items from California to help keep her mind off being so isolated in the woods. Jellybeans, movies, a stuffed tiger she'd had since she was twelve.

She popped in *While You Were Sleeping* with Sandra Bullock and Bill Pullman and let the characters' voices fill the cavernous house. Lily liked space in a house, but Grandma Gail had gone overboard here. Though she'd spared no expense furnishing it, the place was cold and unwelcoming. Much too big for one person.

Why did you like it here, Grandma Gail? Sure, the house was beautiful and architecturally brilliant with its log walls, stone accents, and metal work, but it made Lily feel so small.

Vulnerable.

She locked the front door and walked through the rest of the first floor, making sure every door and window was secured in the great room, kitchen, dining room, library, gym, bathrooms, and laundry room before setting the house alarm again. She grabbed her suitcase and climbed the stairs to the second floor where the master bedroom, two guest bedrooms, and two bathrooms waited in silence. Everything was just as she remembered it as a kid.

Would that hot tub out back still be there? Lily shook off the chill running through her body at the thought of the hot tub.

She stood at the doorway of the master bedroom and decided to sleep there. No way was she staying in the guest room she'd used when she was ten. Out of the question. Besides, the master bathroom had an oversized tub, and a bath sounded like just the thing to settle the jellybean buzz currently inflicting Lily's system.

She set her suitcase on the bed and decided against unpacking. *Not staying long enough.* Instead she moved the suitcase to the cushioned chaise by the sliding glass doors. The black abyss beyond the doors raised the hairs on the back of Lily's neck. She yanked on the cord for the blinds, sending them shushing along the track. With a quick flick of her wrist, Lily closed them, keeping the sinister darkness outside hidden.

She went back downstairs and watched the movie for a little while before deciding to take it upstairs. In the bedroom, she slipped the DVD into the TV hanging on the wall and turned the volume up so she would be able to hear it in the bathroom next door. After grabbing her toiletry kit, she entered the bathroom and paused at her grandmother's bathrobe hanging on the back of the door, as if she'd planned on slipping into it the next time she came to the cabin. Lily buried her face in the velvety fabric and breathed in Grandma Gail's scent—a cross between lilacs and baby powder.

She slid to the marble floor, pulling the robe down into her lap, and she cried. Cried over the frustration of being somewhere she didn't want to be, over blurting things out in meetings without thinking of the consequences, over not having anyone to comfort her right now, over never seeing Grandma Gail again.

Over what might be in store for her when she went outside tomorrow.

Lily tried to shake off the gloom, but it had a tight grip tonight. "Pull yourself together."

She never felt this pathetic in California. She was alive there and important. She was in the center of things back west. Here, she was just a scared child again.

"You'll never convince this maple syrup guy to let you sell this land to Utopia if you show up in this state." Lily reached to the sink and pulled herself to standing. She gazed at her reflection in the mirror. Her mascara had run down her cheeks in two black rivers, but her eyes were still the usual vibrant blue-green. Her tan rocked in the lights around the mirror. Her hair was a little wild after the plane ride, but the red-gold curls that fell to her shoulders were still ready for a night on the town.

"No action here, girls." Lily ran her fingers through her hair, separating the curls and fluffing the entire hairdo in the process. Sighing, she pulled off her calf-high leather boots, jeans, corduroy blazer, and the white blouse she'd worn underneath. Folding the clothes neatly, she set them on the chaise beside her suitcase and pulled out underwear and fuzzy fleece pajamas.

She read the card Drew had included with the pajamas. *If I can't keep you warm at night, maybe these will.*

That should have melted her, but all she heard behind the words was desperation. Drew was great to work with, but why didn't he understand they couldn't continue an intimate relationship? They'd had some fun, but it wasn't going anywhere. He had to see that too. They made a better professional match than a personal one.

Alas, she didn't have any warm pajamas to bring to Vermont. Her California sleepwear consisted of a silk camisole and matching shorts. She'd freeze her tits off in that get-up here.

Lily filled the tub with hot water and eased herself in while Sandra and Bill fell in love on the TV. The suds soothed her tensed muscles, and she burrowed deeper into their citrus kiss. Why was falling in love always so simple in the movies? How did those characters know they were made for each other? If those movies had another thirty minutes to them, couldn't someone more perfect for the main character come along and sweep her off her feet? Couldn't she be happier with the next guy?

Is that why I won't settle for Drew? Was she holding out for someone better? Lily closed her eyes and pictured Drew next to her in bed as he'd been on several occasions. What was it about him that kept her from saying he was The One? He loved her. In some form. She could see it in the way he looked at her as if the world weren't crawling with hundreds of other women willing to be with him. In the way he kissed her when she let him. In the comfortable way he touched her.

Why isn't that enough?

She opened her eyes and remembered Grandma Gail's description of her grandfather. When Lily was fifteen and finally noticing boys, she had asked Grandma Gail why she picked Grandpa Henry to marry. She'd said, "He's the only man to ever make me really mad and really happy. And he has a spectacular ass."

Lily had been excited to find that kind of love. Fresh out of college, she took an entry level job at Utopia Resorts where she'd tried out several possibilities from coworkers to guests to captains of cruise ships docking at the resorts. By the time she'd become Senior Hotel Designer, she had caught Drew's eye. He was the only one she'd gone out with formally more than five times. The only one she'd had sex with on a regular basis, but they'd both kept it loose and open. They'd seen other people in between their romps. Only lately had Drew been pressing for something more definite.

Maybe she'd watched too many romantic movies. Was she being unrealistic? Perhaps when she got back to California in a few days, she would tell Drew they could give it a try. Lily didn't think he'd fire her if it all went into the shitter. He was more professional than that, and she was good at her job. He'd only be hurting himself if he canned her.

Lily stayed in the tub until her fingers resembled raisins, and the water had become a lukewarm tea. She toweled off, slipped on the fuzzy pajamas, and flopped onto the king-sized bed in time to see Bill drop the engagement ring in Sandra's tray at the train terminal. Drew probably had an elaborate plan for such an occasion. He liked to do things big, expensively, and with drama.

As the end credits scrolled by, Lily picked up her cell phone sitting on the bedside table. She could call Drew right now and tell him the decision she'd made. He'd be delighted to hear it.

But would she?

Chapter Three

Rick reclined on the couch with *The DaVinci Code* open in his lap, but he had reread the same sentence at least ten times. It still wasn't making any sense, because his mind was not on the story. Instead, all the jobs he was supposed to be doing today flipped through his mind like a rapid-fire slideshow. Installing more taps on his land and the neighbor's. Giving the pans in the evaporator a final rinse. Chopping firewood for the sugarhouse furnace.

The syrup bottles he'd ordered had to be sanitized, but maybe he could do that later today. Pull up a chair to the big sink in the sugarhouse. He felt a little better at having thought of that notion, though he doubted he'd be able to make it all the way to the sugarhouse. God, he needed to be doing *something*. Sitting on the couch was going to drive him insane. It had before.

"Rick?" Hope called.

"In the living room," he yelled back.

Hope and Sage appeared each wearing a snowsuit. Hope's was pink and Sage's was purple. Their boots were white and trimmed in glittery fur, and under their fuzzy white hats, two fat, blond braids snaked down each of their backs. They resembled Swedish ski team applicants. Rick would have laughed if he weren't so damn mad at himself for tripping like a fool.

"We're going to head out to finish plugging the trees." Sage lowered into one of the corduroy-covered recliners facing the couch.

"Make sure you use the 7/16 bit on the auger to drill the holes," Rick said.

"Yes, sir." Hope sat in the rocking chair facing the fireplace and saluted him.

"Drill at an upward slant of about ten degrees." Rick pantomimed drilling with his hands. "So water doesn't get in. And be certain the spiles are secure. If they come loose—"

Rick stopped when Sage stood and marched over to the couch. She put her hands on her hips and glowered down at him. If she didn't weigh only slightly more than a hundred pounds, he would have been scared of the look on her face.

"Drilling holes in trees and hammering in a couple spouts isn't rocket science, Rick," she said. "I think between the two of us we have brainpower almost equal to yours, Great Tree Whisperer. We can handle this."

"I really hope we don't break a nail." Hope studied her fingers and smirked as she rocked in her chair.

"Yeah." Sage took a step back from the couch. "Or ruin our hairdos."

"What if we come back looking like him?" Hope teased.

"Then we shouldn't come back," Sage said. "We'll have to resign ourselves to living in the forest, away from civilization." She gestured to Poe sitting beside the couch. "We'll be forced to live amongst the coyotes."

Hope and Sage enjoyed a hearty round of laughter, while Rick threw a pillow from the couch at each of them. "Nice to taunt a guy when he's down. Real nice."

"You know we love you, Ricky." Sage bent down and moved his tea out of reach on the coffee table chest and winked.

"Don't call me Ricky." He reached for Sage, but she sidestepped his grasp.

"Nothing you can do about it, invalid." Hope grinned and got up from her seat. "C'mon, Sage. We better get a move on if we're going to finish putting those black thingies in the trees."

"Right. Forty-five degree downward angle." Sage followed her sister out of the living room.

"Ten degree, upward angle," Rick hollered though he knew his cousins were busting his balls again.

"Maple trees are the ones with the white bark, right?" Hope asked around a laugh.

"No," Sage said. "Maples have the pinecones."

"You know which ones are the maples!" Rick shouted. Shaking his head, he started on his book but looked up when Hope came back into the living room. She picked up the two pillows he'd thrown and stuffed them behind him, fluffing them a bit. She also moved his tea back where he could reach it. Dropping a light kiss on his cheek, she said, "See ya, Rick."

He hadn't had to ask his cousins to finish the taps. They took one look at him last night when Aunt Joy brought him dinner, and they'd volunteered. The two of them could be doing a ton of other things today, but they were helping him out.

Rick glared down the length of the couch at his casted ankle and rolled his eyes up to the ceiling. *How fucking stupid.*

At least he had finally warmed up at some point during the night. He'd opted to stay on the couch. Just as comfortable as his bed, and it saved Aunt Joy the trouble of trying to help him to his bedroom, which she would have insisted on doing. She'd brought him extra blankets and a pillow from his bed. Rick half expected her to read him a bedtime story and tuck him in as she had during most of his childhood. Aunt Joy was a fantastic storyteller, and truthfully, he wouldn't have minded a story last night to get his mind off the day's events.

Now hours stretched ahead of him. An entire day of being stuck on the couch with an ache throbbing in his ankle. He'd taken the wonder drugs, but they weren't masking all the pain. Then again, Rick was more aware today than he had been yesterday. He'd had a full night to reflect on the idiocy of his actions and the resulting embarrassing consequences of running after a sled in snowshoes. With any luck, Hope and Sage wouldn't bring this faux pas up at every turn.

He closed the book and set it on the chest. After listening for a moment, he determined that Hope and Sage had collected the necessary equipment from the garage and were gone. He pulled off the blankets and eased his legs off the couch. He tapped his right foot against the hardwood floor, contemplating. Yes, the doctor said to stay off his ankle for the week, but surely that was a general statement. It didn't apply to everyone who had a severely sprained ankle. Certainly some people needed less time than that. He'd made it to the bathroom a couple of times so far, albeit awkwardly and stubbing the big toe on his right foot. Twice. What harm could a trip to the kitchen cause?

Rick gripped the end of the couch with one hand and reached for the cane leaning against the end table with his other hand. Summoning what little strength he could find, he rose to his feet, letting his weight rest mostly on his right leg. He gripped the cane in his left hand and prepared to step away from the couch.

"Richard Michael Stannard, you get your ass back on that couch this instant!" Aunt Joy stormed into the living room as if she planned to tackle him if necessary.

Rick's head snapped up and he lost his balance. He fell between the couch and the chest, banging his elbow on the corner of the chest along the way. The floor smacked against his tailbone.

Damn, hickory is a hard wood.

Poe darted to him, pushing her nose into his face.

"Shit," he spat. "Poe, get out of here." He shoved her, and she whimpered.

"Oh, dear!" Aunt Joy rushed over and hooked her arms under his. She hoisted with all her might, but couldn't budge Rick. "Sugar, even though you don't look like it, you weigh more than a barn full of cows. Why do you have to be such a giant?" She sat on the edge of the couch as Rick lifted himself onto the cushion beside her.

"Why do you have to plow in and scare the piss out of me?" He rubbed his elbow and used his right leg to keep Poe back.

Aunt Joy clucked her tongue, and Poe trotted over to her. She gave the coyote a rubbing between the ears then coaxed her into the kitchen. She fussed with Poe's food and water bowls—something Rick would have done first thing this morning if he had been able. When Aunt Joy came back to the living room, she repositioned his legs on the couch and propped his ankle on some pillows. "You're not supposed to be walking around."

"I wasn't 'walking around.' Maybe I was going to the bathroom."

"Were you going to the bathroom?" Aunt Joy gave him the Stannard Stare—a look that said she'd know if he were lying.

Rick shook his head.

"Well, no use in making matters worse by gallivanting around the house, sugar. That ankle is good and busted, and if you don't follow doctor's orders, you'll only pay for it later. You know that." Aunt Joy stared at him for a long, solemn moment. He hated when she looked at him that way. As if she were picturing what a disaster he'd been after New York.

"Stop it," he said, his voice full of warning.

"Well, get that pitiful look out of those blue eyes, kid. You're made of tougher stuff than this."

Aunt Joy left the living room, but returned a few moments later carrying a canvas bag. "I brought you some books. Ones you haven't read a million times, some word searches, and a deck of cards." She tossed the cards onto his lap. "Play Solitaire. You're good at games that don't involve interaction with the rest of us humans. I'm going to make you some breakfast then head to the store."

She placed the bag beside the couch and left for the kitchen. Rick listened as she clanged silverware and bowls. He counted the blades on the ceiling fan hanging above him then picked up the deck of cards and threw it across the living room. The box exploded in a shower of spades, clubs, diamonds, and hearts. Poe scampered in to investigate the mess and bark at Rick.

"Aw, shut up." There had to be a way to be productive today. He couldn't feel this useless all day. Not going to happen.

He peeked in the bag at the books Aunt Joy had brought. A couple James Pattersons, a David McCauley, a *Men's Health* magazine. Holy Hell. This was what he had been reduced to. A helpless pity case.

Just like after New York. His heart pumped a little faster in his chest and he tried to rub away the feeling. This wasn't going to happen again.

"The oatmeal's a little watery, but it'll do." Aunt Joy bustled in toting a tray, which she placed over Rick's lap. She was right. The oatmeal was runny, but she'd arranged a strawberry, two blueberries, and a melon wedge to create a smiley face on the toast. He was about to smile at her attempt, but she grabbed him by the chin and wrenched his head so he had to look at her.

"What's wrong?" She focused on his eyes as if she were trying to read his mind.

"Nothing." He tried to shake his head free, but her grip was steel.

"You're vampire pale, Rick, and I don't mean in that sexy, paranormal, undead way, like in those books Hope and Sage are always reading." She pressed two fingers to his neck. "Jesus, sugar, your pulse is racing. What happened?"

"Nothing," he repeated.

"You were thinking about New York, weren't you? Would you go back if—"

"You know I wouldn't. I belong here. Vermont is my home." He hoped saying it aloud would calm him. All he needed was the serenity of the woods and the simple life he'd carved out for himself here. Aside from his ankle, he'd been healthy as a horse—a strapping stallion—since his move back to Vermont. He planned on keeping it that way.

Rick balled some of the blanket covering his legs into his fist. "I don't like the city for many reasons. My… experience… was the universe's way of letting me know this is where I should be."

"Seems a cosmic sticky note would have done the job easier: 'Rick, stay with trees. Love, The Universe.' Right?"

He surprised himself by laughing. Only Aunt Joy could turn his mood around with her silly ways of looking at things.

"Now that's a sound I like to hear." Aunt Joy ruffled Rick's blond hair. "I want to hear more of it, sugar."

"I'll try." And he would, for Aunt Joy. Not going to be easy. Not with a wrecked ankle and loads of time to sit and stew about nothing and everything.

Chapter Four

Rick opened his eyes to find Poe sprawled atop his arm, her head resting on his shoulder in bed. His hand had gone numb from the coyote's weight, as if it were separate from his body. His ankle felt a little like that as well. As if it belonged to some other imbecile who didn't know that running in snowshoes was a dumb idea.

He'd stopped taking the pain medication two days ago, because he absolutely hated to add any new pills to his daily regimen. His ankle throbbed a bit, but sometimes feeling the pain was a good thing. Made him feel alive.

"C'mon, Poe." He reached over and nudged the mass of fur beside him. "Wake up, girl." He poked her again, and she raised her furry head. Her golden eyes blinked sleepily, and her jaw opened in a huge coyote yawn. "Morning." Rick rubbed her cheeks, and she let out little noises of approval.

He sat up in bed and rested against the headboard. He hadn't bothered to pull down the shades last night and now the sun streamed in through the bedroom windows. He closed the book still open on the other side of the bed and dropped it on the pile on his nightstand.

"Why don't we spend the morning in the store organizing the books, Poe?" That was a good sit-down activity. One his aunt wouldn't yell at him for doing.

Poe ruffed once and jumped off the bed. Her nails made soft scratchy taps on the floor as she trotted out of the bedroom and down the hall.

Rick sat on the edge of the bed for a few moments, feeling the weight of the air cast on his leg. He stretched out his arms then rubbed at his tailbone, still bruised from his fall in the woods. Grabbing the cane he'd left hooked on the headboard, he shuffled to his closet and selected a pair of blue work jeans, a black thermal shirt, and a gray hooded sweatshirt. After letting his pajama pants drop to his ankles, he sat on the end of the bed and wrestled his jeans on over the air cast. The pant leg of his jeans bunched up above the cast and he considered cutting the denim. He didn't own a ton of clothes, however, and couldn't justify destroying a pair of jeans that still had many years left in them.

He pulled on the thermal shirt over the white T-shirt he'd worn to bed. He had a fleeting memory of a long ago summertime when he used to wear only boxer shorts to bed.

Not anymore. There were things that needed covering now.

After cleaning up in the bathroom, Rick made his way to the kitchen where he had a quick bowl of cereal and a glass of orange juice. When he unlocked the store and walked inside, he was amazed at how much work his aunt and cousins had already done. The bakery case was gleaming, fresh paper doilies in place waiting for the confections Aunt Joy, Hope, and Sage would make. The barnwood floor had been swept and washed so, although scarred and dinged, it still appeared freshened. Rick even liked the new arrangement Hope had used on the few tables in the store now that he studied it. The shelves for the maple syrup had been repainted in a green that matched the wording on the new labels Hope had made. The words "Stannard Mountain Pure Vermont Maple Syrup" in green made a circle around an orangey-red maple leaf. A faint shadow of a purplish-blue mountain range ran behind the words and leaf.

His aunt and cousins had worked twice as hard to make up for what he wasn't able to do. He'd begged them to do something fun for themselves today before things picked up and the season got underway, which was right around the corner. He could tell by the air as he'd hobbled from his cabin to the store. The winter bite was gone. Soon the daytime temperatures would be warmer while the nights were still freezing. The sap would start flowing any day now.

Rick pulled up a chair to the boxes of books Hope and Sage had left in the store by the display shelves. Poe took up residence on the floor beside him and sniffed all the corners of the closest box. He began loading the books on the shelves, turning some of the covers outward so customers could get a good look at them. He didn't spend a lot of time in the store when customers were in there. He preferred a more behind the scenes involvement in the business and that was part of what had made him not so successful in New York. He liked dealing with the equipment, the actual trees, the land as well as the financial side. Running the business from the city had only allowed him to crunch the numbers and collect the profits. Maybe some folks liked that hands-off approach, but not Rick. He wanted to smell the melting winter, the blooming spring, and the boiling sap.

As he continued stacking books, Poe padded to the door and woofed once at it.

"No customers today, Poe. Not yet."

She barked again at the door and as she sat by it, a soft knock echoed in the store. Rick put down the books he had in his lap and limped to the nearest window. A Jeep he didn't recognize was in front of the store along with footprints in the remaining patch of snow. The knock came again, but he couldn't see who was at the door. He contemplated not answering as he often did when the phone rang, but figured it wouldn't waste much time to explain the store wasn't open yet.

He ambled to the door, resting his hand on the tables as he passed by without the cane. As he neared the door, another knock sounded.

"Okay, okay," he said. "I'm coming." He cursed his slowness and hoped he'd be rid of the cast soon. Not likely, judging by the ache, but a man could hope.

He reached the door and pulled it open. What was standing on the other side of it made him forget his own name.

A woman. Not much shorter than him with reddish-blond hair that brushed her shoulders and curled about a face meant for makeup commercials. Her skin had a wonderful glow he'd never seen on any native Vermonter, and her eyes were blue-green jewels. Slim, black jeans spanned down two long, shapely legs and disappeared into brown, knee-high leather boots that belonged on a runway not on his partly muddy, partly snowy doorstep. The rust-colored dress coat that hung to her thighs also seemed out of place in this setting, but not out of place on her. The woman was perfection in that coat, and the cream-colored scarf she had looped around her neck fascinated Rick.

Poe barked and the woman jumped. "Is that a coyote?" Her voice, soft yet assertive, matched her delicate mouth and intense eyes, but she looked as if she were ready to run for her vehicle.

"Yeah, but she won't hurt you. She's been raised to think she's a big hamster." *What is this woman doing here?* Then the pieces fell into place in his mind. "You're one of Hope or Sage's friends, right?" That had to be it, but he didn't remember ever seeing this one. He didn't think he could forget her if he had seen her. God, she was tall.

"No," she said. "I don't know Hope or Sage. I'm looking for whoever signed this." She pulled an envelope out of her shoulder bag and rifled through it. While keeping a wary eye on Poe, she handed Rick one of the documents, and he scanned it quickly.

"You're looking for me then." Why did that make something in his stomach tighten?

"You're the neighbor? You knew Gail Hinsdale?" A section of snow slid off the roof and landed in a pile about a foot away from the woman. She stumbled back and threw a glance all around her, almost dropping the envelope in the process.

"Come in," Rick said, though he hadn't remembered consciously deciding to invite her inside.

"Thank you." She knocked the mud and snow off her boots and squeezed past him into the store. She smelled like grapefruit and coconut and sunshine. Like something far too exotic to be here with him. "Could you…" She motioned to Poe and made a shooing gesture with her gloved hand.

"Sure. C'mon, Poe." Rick smacked his thigh and shuffled toward the kitchen behind the pastry case. He pushed open the door and guided Poe in. She whimpered on the other side when she realized he'd locked the door.

Poor girl. Rick felt like a big, fat meany.

"I appreciate that. Wild animals unsettle me." The woman pulled off her leather gloves to reveal long, slim fingers with nails polished a deep crimson.

"She's not wild," Rick said.

"Right. Tell that to her teeth." The woman dropped the envelope on one of the tables and unlooped the scarf to expose a slender neck. She turned in a tight circle to survey the store. What was she thinking? She obviously came from a place where the stores didn't look like his.

"You knew Gail Hinsdale?" She leveled her gaze on Rick, then flicked a glance down to his ankle. "Do you want to sit down?"

"I think I'm supposed to ask you that." He indicated the chair across from the one he currently had a death grip on.

She slid the chair out and sat on it, but just on the edge, not like she meant to stay for any length of time. This saddened Rick, because for the first time in his life, he didn't have the urge to get rid of company.

He eased onto the opposite chair, and the muscles in his entire body relaxed as the pressure was taken off his ankle. The woman noticed.

"What happened there?" She peeked under the table.

"Snowshoeing incident." He shrugged, determined not to explain any further though the woman waited a moment as if he might. "How is Gail? I haven't seen her in a little while."

The woman's lips twisted down at the corners, and Rick had this ridiculous urge to scoot over to her side of the table and… and do something.

"Gail died." Those piercing blue-green eyes grew watery. "My grandmother is gone."

"I'm so sorry," Rick said. "She was real generous with allowing me to tap her trees. Nearly doubled my productivity." He had reaped nothing but benefits from his arrangement with Gail Hinsdale. One of the smartest, healthiest business moves he'd ever made.

"She left me the property." The woman extended her hand. "I'm Lily Hinsdale."

Taking her hand in his and noting how cold her fingers were, he said, "Rick Stannard." He looked at the envelope again. "Are you thinking of moving to the property?"

At this, Lily let out a loud laugh. "Moving to Vermont? Are you serious? I don't want to be here right now, never mind *live* here." She brushed her hair out of her face with a shaky finger.

"What's wrong with Vermont?" Rick asked. It was the perfect place as far as he was concerned.

"Umm, everything." Lily stretched her magnificent legs out to the side of the table and peered down at her boots. Cringing, she knocked her heels together letting caked mud drop to the floor. "Vermont is no California."

California, of course. That explained the tan and the fashion. And the disgust for mud.

"Vermont has a lot to offer." Why did he feel the need to defend his fair state? Why did he want this woman to like Vermont?

"I'm sure, but I'm… high maintenance. Don't have any real love for flannel or fleece. And don't get me started about the woods." She peeled off her coat revealing a fluffy brown sweater that ruffled at the collar and the wrists. Rick had never seen a sweater that fancy.

"The woods are the best part of Vermont," he said.

"The woods are Hell."

"I'll bet I could change your mind about that." Had he stepped out of his body? Who was this guy, talking to this woman, and actually picturing himself leading her on a hike in the thawing woods?

Lily regarded him for a silent moment, and for once, he didn't like the quiet. What was she thinking? *Probably that I'm the exact opposite of every guy she knows in California.*

"No. I'm certain the woods and I don't mix. Anyway, I'm here about the property, not to discuss the nonexistent finer points of this forgotten realm known as Vermont." She brushed at her hair again, and the trembling in her hand was still there. Why was she so nervous? "I have a proposition for you."

"Yes, I'll buy the land from you." He'd wanted to do that before Gail had constructed her fortress on the property, but he hadn't had the money then. He had it now thanks to her letting him lease her maple trees and his barn-building business.

"Oh, umm, no. I don't want to sell the property to you," Lily said. "I want to sell it to another buyer and buy yours."

A horrible ringing grew in volume in Rick's ears. "What?"

"Your land. I want it. Well, actually, I don't want it personally." She dug around in her shoulder bag and produced a business card. "I work for Utopia Resorts. You've heard of us, right?"

Rick stared at the card on the table and shook his head.

"Utopia Resorts. You know, 'Escape Everything,' as our commercials say." Lily waved her hands as if she were convinced it would only take Rick a moment to say, "Oh, yeah. *That* Utopia Resorts."

He didn't travel. How would he know about some resort?

"Okay." Lily huffed out a breath. "What are you, a hermit or something?"

"Sort of. Yeah."

"How not interesting." Lily extracted another set of documents from the envelope and a pen. "Anyway. We want to take my grandmother's property and your adjoining land to create a rustic resort. My grandmother's property is not large enough by itself, but with yours it'll be the perfect size. I'm aware of the deal you had with my grandmother. With your consent to sell her land to

Utopia, I can offer you generous compensation for yours. After a couple sound investments, you'd be set for life off this deal. You wouldn't need to run this little syrup and store business anymore."

Little syrup and store business? The blood was roaring in Rick's veins. Had he known this vision of loveliness was the Grim Reaper and Miss No Manners all rolled into one, he never would have let her into his store or onto his land. He certainly wouldn't have allowed himself to picture tasting those lips of hers.

The syrup business is mine. Mine. The word kept cycling around his mind, faster and faster until he could hear it in his breathing, in his pulse.

"Calm down." Rick clamped his hand on the edge of the table.

"I am calm," Lily said.

"Wasn't talking to you." He awkwardly got to his feet and limped away toward the bookshelves. He opened the kitchen door and let Poe scamper out.

Eat the bad lady, Poe. Go ahead.

"Look, Mr. Stannard, Utopia Resorts brings a great deal of jobs to an area. You'd be doing the state of Vermont a huge favor by accepting my offer."

Lily tracked Poe's every movement. Again, she appeared ready to flee from the store if necessary. *Good. Flee. Flee now.*

"Miss Hinsdale, I'm afraid I can't help you." He ran a hand over his face. "This area is not right for one of your resorts. Think of all the trees you'll have to clear in order to build. The woods won't be the woods anymore." He had shambled back to the table. He noticed the faint smile on Lily's face as if destroying the woods had been a pleasant notion to her.

"C'mon now," she said. "You can't honestly say you enjoy living in the middle of nowhere, next to no one."

"I do enjoy it, and I plan on enjoying it until I croak running my 'little syrup and store business,' if you don't mind. Find another spot. In fact, find another state. What's the matter? Is your precious California running out of space?"

Lily stood and slid her arms into the sleeves of her coat. "I can see you're a little upset, Mr. Stannard. Perhaps I'll leave these documents with you to look over either alone or with your lawyer." She paused in buttoning her coat. "You do have a lawyer, don't you?"

Rick grunted in response as Poe circled around Lily like a fur-covered shark.

"Think about what a wonderful opportunity this is for you and… do you have a family?"

"Of course I have a family." He knew she meant a wife and kids, but Aunt Joy and his cousins depended on this place as much as he did, and they were his family, dammit.

"Well, accepting our offer could mean a whole new life for all of you. A better life." She coiled her scarf around her neck, and Rick recalled the steps involved in tying a noose knot.

"We like our old life and if you leave those papers, they're going to end up in my fireplace tonight."

"Don't be like that, Mr. Stannard." She walked over to him, her gaze still targeting Poe. She pointed to the used books. "These could all be brand new books in a brand new house in a brand new location."

"I don't like brand new. I like broken in and comfortable."

"That's what people who don't know any better say." Lily hoisted her purse to her shoulder and headed for the door. "I'll be back tomorrow." She opened the door and left.

Rick stood like a statue for a good five minutes before Poe pushed her nose into his knees. He lowered into the chair beside him. Poe put her head in his lap, but for once, the coyote's presence offered him no comfort.

"I should have known when she didn't like you that she was trouble." Everyone loved Poe.

Rick stared at the envelope Lily had left on the table. "Why wait?" he said to Poe. He got up from the chair, his head aching more than his ankle at this point, and picked up the cane. "If Miss California thinks she can waltz into *my* store and bust *my* balls, she's mistaken. It'll take something bigger and badder than her to push us out."

Poe barked her agreement and followed Rick into the kitchen. He rustled up a match and lit one edge of the envelope. It didn't take long for the documents to be reduced to a pile of smoldering ash in the sink.

"We're not going anywhere, Poe."

Chapter Five

Lily sat on the couch in her grandmother's great room, sipping coffee. Plain, regular coffee. She'd driven thirty minutes after her encounter with the neighbor only to find not a single café in the area. The best she could do was a small convenience store/gas station pit that sold coffee. Grounds. In a can. She had to actually brew it herself back at the cabin. The muddy results were barely consumable. She missed Tam, her assistant, bringing her a nonfat Supreme Choco Meltie like she did every morning at work.

"I've got to get out of here," she said to the sketchpad in her lap. At least the complete lack of commerce and entertainment had allowed her to organize the ideas she had dumped out when Rita had put her on the spot back at Utopia. And fortunately, the designs weren't total shit. She had filled seven pages in her pad with exterior and interior layouts, landscaping plans, and a few promotional ideas.

She opened the design program on her laptop. Lily spent another two hours working on more detailed plans and emailed what she had accomplished to Drew. He would love them. The question was, would that neighbor muck up the works with his refusal to sell his property? Her grandmother's property alone wasn't large enough for a Utopia Resort.

Lily hadn't expected Rick Stannard. She'd gotten up that morning thinking she'd head next door—once she found where next door was—and meet this simple, backwoods guy. She'd dazzle him with her dollar signs and talk of a better life. He'd snatch up the chance to be able to afford a real haircut, clothes that didn't involve suspenders, and dental work to fix undoubtedly crooked or missing teeth.

Rick, however, had lovely, dark golden hair—lots of it—cut into a floppy, haphazard style. His hint of beard and mustache framed a set of lips Lily had inspected a little too closely. His jeans and sweatshirt were clean and covered a well-built body with what she was sure her grandmother would have labeled "a spectacular ass." As soon as he'd opened the door she'd noted a body several inches taller than hers. She hadn't felt the need to slouch in his presence. Even with the slight heels on her boots—her almost ruined by mud boots—she still had to look up to see Rick's face.

A nice surprise.

His eyes were a pale blue that reminded Lily of a hazy California morning. They were full of more intelligence than she had thought possible for someone who considered it a good idea to live this far out in the woods. With a coyote, no less. She was certain that animal would rip her to bits if given the chance. Did Rick let that thing into his house? How did he sleep at night?

Shaking her head, she closed her design program and opened her email. She clicked on one from Grandma Gail dated just two weeks ago.

Hey, Clone. Meet for lunch on Wednesday?

Lily sniffed and looked out the window. She'd attended her grandmother's funeral on Wednesday instead.

How could you be gone, Grandma Gail?

Gail Hinsdale was the liveliest person Lily had ever known. She always referred to Lily as "The Clone." They had the same blue-green eyes, shoulder-length, strawberry-blond curls, tall, lanky build. Grandma Gail was the only person to truly understand the downsides to being a human telephone pole.

Recently retired from her legendary talk show host career, Gail had met every star from Harrison Ford to Will Smith. She knew positively everyone in Hollywood, no exceptions. No one ever refused an interview. Gail had launched many acting careers in her time and was famed for her ability to bring the stars "into your living room."

A world without Gail Hinsdale was a world off its axis.

Lily wiped at the tear slowly cutting a path down her cheek. This was not the time to fall to pieces. She'd kept it together through the funeral, through her father tossing the Vermont property at her, through Rita and the "let's build a Utopia Resort in the wild" campaign, and even through the constant presence of Drew, who would apparently use Lily's grieving as a way to rekindle their personal relationship.

She regretted getting involved with her boss on a personal level, and it wasn't easy trying to undo that. The man was always right there, working on something with her, and lately, making more outward advances—advances Lily worried others in the office were noticing. It was one thing to fool around after hours, scratch an itch, and all that, but trying to hold her hand or kiss her in the middle of a meeting was not acceptable.

Drew was a successful businessman, a fair boss, and a fabulous dancer. He lived in an enormous house right on the water a few streets away from Gems Utopia where Lily had a penthouse. He drove a car almost as nice as hers.

Almost.

He also understood how ridiculously focused she was on her job, her designs, her new ideas. She wasn't sure another man would tolerate the way she obsessed over a design until perfection was achieved. Drew fed that obsession, encouraged it, demanded it.

And yet, he wasn't The One. It was why she hadn't called him the other night to say they could give it a try.

Lily wanted her own Tom Hanks like in *You've Got Mail*. That movie was one of her favorites. One of Grandma Gail's favorites too. They'd watched it a million times together, and Grandma Gail said she'd had a Tom Hanks in Lily's grandfather, who had died years ago. Lily didn't think she'd ever find one. Not with Drew on her ass around the clock.

He insisted upon escorting her to every Utopia event, mainly the resort chain's killer galas—one of which Lily was missing by going on this trek to Vermont. Every month the company threw enormous bashes meant to make the guests feel like celebrities. This month Gems Utopia was the host. Made of a layer of thick Plexiglass pressed over zillions of sparkling, but fake gemstones, the entire lobby floor of this resort glittered like a fine jewelry store case. During the day, when the sun dripped in from enormous skylights overhead, the floor was dazzling. The effect was one Lily had worked long hours to design.

The elevators were painted white with gold trim made to look like giant gift boxes, and the railing on the main staircase resembled a string of pearls. Each floor was named after a gemstone. Ruby, sapphire, emerald, amethyst, onyx, and opal. A diamond ring-shaped pool glittered on the first floor along with a restaurant named Ruby's and a theater called The Velvet Box.

Lily tried not to imagine which famous person she would have been eating with if she had been able to go to the gala. It would have been easier to list who she *wouldn't* have eaten with.

Is it petty to lament missing a party after losing Grandma Gail?

Lily shook her head. Grandma Gail, wherever she was now, was probably pretty pissed about missing the party too. They'd always had a ball at the Utopia galas, trying to out-dress, out-eat, and out-dance each other. Lily had bought a killer dress for this party too. An electric blue number with rhinestone shoulder straps and a high, empire waist. She would have turned heads in that thing.

Maybe even a head worth turning this time.

A dress of that caliber would be useless in Vermont, so Lily had left it—reluctantly—in her bedroom closet at home. Maybe she'd debut it at next month's bash. Good thing another gala was always around the corner. Merry-making was important.

Noise was important.

Quiet, on the other hand, was deafening and, damn, these woods were quiet.

Lily closed her laptop and brought her coffee mug to the kitchen. She dumped the remaining sludge into the sink, deposited the mug into the dishwasher, and did a double take at the kitchen window.

In the circle of light from the telephone pole near the driveway, an enormous moose stood stoically right next to the Jeep. His head supported a massive set of antlers and the underside of his hide was matted with mud. He angled his head as if listening to something then swung to face Lily watching from the window. The moose let out a low grunt, and a female joined him.

Lily gripped the granite countertop while she held her breath. Did moose charge houses? Could they see her? Smell her? How many teeth did moose have? Those hooves appeared capable of crushing bones.

With another grunt, the male moose turned around and headed into the woods. The female followed and within moments, Lily could see no trace of them. The only evidence of their existence was a set of tracks in the muddy, snow-patched driveway and the thudding heartbeat of one petrified human.

"Calm down," Lily told herself and thought of Rick telling himself the same thing after she'd made her proposition. He'd looked as if he were going to explode. His fists had curled tightly by his sides. Despite his injured ankle, he had managed to put a little stomp into his walk as he left her at the table, giving her a view of said spectacular ass. Then he'd gotten downright nasty with his threat to burn the sale documents.

"Immature."

Her cell phone rang and she jumped out of her skin. The sound was so loud in the quiet of the cabin, and her mind was still on mammoth beasts outside and attractive, though stubborn, neighbors.

After stopping to turn on the TV in the living room for some background noise, Lily retrieved her phone and said, "Hi, Drew."

"Hi. How's it going, honey?"

"Aside from the moose stalking me outside the house you mean?" She sat on the couch and stretched her neck down and back, left to right, trying to relieve the tightened muscles. She needed a massage. Maybe she'd have Tam schedule one for when she got back to California. Hopefully that would be soon.

"Poor baby," Drew said. "I wish Rita would have let me come with you."

The words "me too" would have said what Lily had decided about Drew last night, but she couldn't get them to come out of her mouth. Instead she said, "Did you get my designs?"

"Yes. That's why I'm calling," he said. "They're fantastic as always. You're absolutely brilliant. Did you meet with the neighbor?"

"Yes," Lily said, "and that did not go as brilliantly."

"What happened?"

"He doesn't want to sell. Mr. Stannard seemed offended that I asked. Even if he agrees to let me sell my grandmother's land, it's not big enough for a resort." Lily grabbed the remote control and scanned through the TV menu. She found *Dirty Dancing* and selected it. She'd crave a Utopia Resorts gala even more after watching Patrick Swayze and Jennifer Grey dance, but oh well. She'd be home for the next gala.

"He's easily taken care of," Drew said. "Everyone has a price and we can afford to pay a high one. We went in with a low offer, but you have leeway to add to that. Work your magic, Lily."

"I don't know if my magic is going to work on him," she said as Patrick taught Jennifer the cha-cha.

"Why not? Is he blind?" Drew laughed.

"So my magic has to do with my appearance?" Lily asked. "Not my expertise, my professionalism, my intellect?"

"Whoa," Drew said. "I didn't say that. I'm sorry. I was just making a joke. A bad one apparently. You're wound up tight."

She rubbed her temples and pulled her legs up onto the couch. She yanked down the quilt folded over the back of the couch and covered herself with it. "I didn't mean to jump down your throat, Drew."

What is my problem? She pictured Rick saying he liked his old life. That he preferred broken in. Nobody preferred that. Not in Lily's world.

"It's okay. You're under a little stress here."

"A little? I'm stuck in the woods with growling beasts and a curmudgeonly neighbor. California is a whole freaking continent away. If we don't make this new resort idea work, Rita will not be pleased. How is that a *little* stress?" She wasn't fond of the whining in her voice, but it saturated every word.

"Okay. Take it easy. It'll all work out. You want me to give this Stannard guy a call myself?"

"No." She blew out a long breath and rested her head on the armrest of the couch. She stared up at the vaulted ceiling so incredibly far away. Four gigantic skylights let in the darkening night. Lily could see a few bright stars. For a moment, she felt insignificant.

"Lily?"

"Yeah."

"Are you all right?" Drew said.

"I will be as soon as my feet touch down in Cali."

"Give me Stannard's number. I'll call him tomorrow and try to get things rolling."

"Let me have another go at it," she said. "Maybe he needs the night to think it over and look through the documents. I'll bring some of the designs with me. Try to convince him of how nice the resort will be."

"Okay. Call me after you meet with him again."

"Roger that."

"Good night, Lily. I miss you."

She checked the clock on the fireplace mantle. 6:30 p.m. In California, it was much earlier, and the sun would still be shining. Drew was still at work, his tie still secured around his collar, his hair still perfectly in place. He probably had fun plans to go to the theater or have drinks with friends after work.

What does Rick do for fun? Lily had noticed his hands while they sat at the table in his store.

They weren't like Drew's at all. Not manicured and smooth. Not short and slender. They were calloused and scarred. Long and solid. *What would they feel like on her skin?*

"Good night, Drew. I'll be in touch." She hung up and dropped her phone in her lap. "Why are you comparing Rick to Drew, moron? They're not even the same species."

She pulled the quilt over her head as Patrick and Jennifer made love in Patrick's studio. She let out a frustrated grumble and peeled the quilt off. Good thing Drew wasn't here. She would have given in to his flirting no doubt and ended up in bed with him because he was available.

Does that make me a horrible person?

It didn't in California. Many of her friends had causal sex partners. Folks that hooked up now and then during a dry season. Here in the woods, though, it seemed as if "hooking up" wouldn't be enough. A gal would need someone who was going to stick around and protect her from the wild. Someone who would hold her during the long, cold night.

After watching more of the movie, Lily wrapped the quilt around her shoulders and got up. She was on her way to the kitchen when a loud clang outside froze her in the hallway. She shot a look to the huge windows flanking the fireplace, but couldn't see past the drawn curtains.

Another clang sounded, but it didn't sound as if it were coming from outside the living room.

Sounded closer to the kitchen. Outside the garage maybe? Lily battled with staying where she was or heading toward the sound.

"Please don't hurt me. Please don't hurt me." She inched closer to the switch for the garage floodlights. Her breathing was dangerously close to the hyperventilation phase. She felt a little woozy. She flicked on the lights and screamed when eyes reflected back to her.

The sudden burst of light made the creature hiss and jump from the stone wall bordering a garden beside the garage. A raccoon. He'd knocked over some metal flowerpots Lily's grandmother had on the wall. His striped tail swished as he vanished into the darkness.

"Overgrown rodent," Lily mumbled as she shut off the light and double-checked the doors and windows. Another glance at the clock revealed disappointing news. Only 7:00 p.m. In California 7:00 p.m. meant more than enough time to meet a group for dinner at Ruby's. More than enough time to catch live music and have drinks at Fuega's two blocks over from Gems. More than enough time to dance at The Jam Circus in San Diego.

In Vermont, 7:00 p.m. meant reciting lines to movies until she got sleepy. *If* she got sleepy.

****

Rick hardly slept though he had been tired from all the hobbling around he'd done during the day—his first full day on his feet. Lazing in bed had been what his body wanted, but not his mind. His brain kept analyzing and dissecting his interaction with Lily Hinsdale.

"Who does she think she is?" he asked Poe as he globbed shaving cream onto his hand.

The coyote sat in the hallway by the bathroom door and used her hind leg to scratch at her neck. Rick watched her then shaved around his slight beard and mustache to keep everything neat.

"Imagine her thinking you'd hurt her. You wouldn't hurt anything." He rinsed, dried his face with a towel, and put his razor back in its drawer. He turned to Poe and waved her over. She obediently entered the bathroom and stood on all fours right in front of him. "Sit."

Poe dropped her rump until she was seated on the small, fluffy rug in front of the vanity. She looked up at Rick with big, yellow eyes and let out a short ruff.

"You're right, Poe. No more talking about that mean Miss Hinsdale. On to other, more productive things. Come."

He stopped in his bedroom and grabbed the cane. He found he didn't need it so much schlepping around the house, but if he were to head to the store, he'd take it. Between the little bit of snow, the patches of mud, and the general rough terrain, walking from his cabin to the store was an exercise in caution with two good ankles, never mind only one.

He ate a quick breakfast, longing for some pancakes instead of the oatmeal he shoveled down instead, and put his insulated flannel coat on over his sweatshirt and jeans. He slid his right foot into a black work boot then made sure the Velcro straps on the air cast were tight on his left foot. The tighter it was, the less pain he felt with each step. The less pain, the less he was reminded of how he should have let the damn sled go instead of running after it.

When he and Poe emerged from the garage, Rick was surprised at how warm it was outside. Probably close to 50°F. The melting snow dripped from the trees and mud squished under his feet… and onto his sock peeking from the air cast. His toes were instantly wet. Eyeing the muddy path to the store, Rick decided it didn't make sense to change the sock now. Fortunately, he had extra socks in the sugarhouse for when he went out in the woods and got wet. He'd put on a new one once he got there.

With a stop to check a few taps, he confirmed the sap wasn't running yet, but it would be. He could feel it in the air. The woods were beginning to smell like the woods again after being asleep under the snow for months. This was truly his favorite time of the year. This in-between time, when one season surrendered to the next. When the trees shared their natural goodness with him so he could make a living on the land he loved.

When… an ugly cream-colored Jeep was parked in front of his store.

"Oh, I don't think so." He shuffled as fast as he could with Poe jogging along beside him.

He swung open the door and marched in to find Aunt Joy, Hope, and Sage sitting at a table. With *her*. Their laughter filled the empty store and burrowed right underneath his skin.

"What are you doing?" he roared.

All four women jumped in their seats, and Rick had to contain his satisfaction. He hooked the cane on the nearest chair and limped over to them. Pointing a finger at Lily, he said, "You. Get out. Now."

"Rick," Aunt Joy said. "Where have your manners gone?"

"*My* manners? Are you kidding me?" He lasered a glare at Lily. "I don't know what you think you're doing, but you're not welcome here."

"That's it," Sage said to Hope. "He's finally lost all of his social skills."

"Shut up, Sage."

Sage shrank back in her seat, and Rick clamped his mouth shut. He didn't usually snap at his cousins like that. This… this outsider was turning him into a monster.

"Did she tell you what she's doing here?" He gestured to Lily. *Why does she have to be wearing a low-cut, black sweater that hugs her amazing body?* He shook his head and looked back to Sage.

"She's staying at Gail's house," Hope said. "Gail passed away. She was Lily's grandmother." Hope rested a hand on Lily's and gave her a compassionate look.

"So maybe you could try to act like a human, Rick," Sage said, "and be nice to the girl who just lost her grandmother, huh?" She shook her feathery blond hair out of her face.

"I'm not going to be nice to her," he said. "She's leaving." He slid Lily's purse off the back of the chair and made a move to grab her by the bicep.

"Rick, you will not lay a hand on our guest." Aunt Joy's tone froze his hand just shy of Lily.

"It's okay, Joy," Lily said.

Joy? First name basis. So nice we're all chums here.

Rick tossed Lily's purse onto the table where it landed like a bag of rocks. It upended the saucer Lily's teacup rested on and sent the tea into her lap. She popped up from her seat as did Aunt Joy, Hope, and Sage.

"Rick!" his aunt and cousins said together.

He tried to feel triumphant over the dark, wet stain on Lily's light blue jeans, but he couldn't get past the way the denim molded to her thighs and tapered down her legs. Amazingly long legs. She was so much taller than his aunt and his cousins. They were mere dolls next to her.

"Get some towels, Hope," Aunt Joy said as she handed Lily some napkins in the meantime. "I'm sorry about my nephew." She turned to Rick. "What's your problem? This is Robert Hinsdale's daughter. Robert Hinsdale, the actor. The one I *adore*," she said through clenched teeth. "I know you don't do people very well, but I've never seen you be this rude."

"Tell them." Rick stared at Lily, and she swallowed as if she had trouble doing so. He'd interrupted her game, her attempt to win over his family then dive in for the kill.

"Tell us what?" Sage asked.

"This is not Miss Hinsdale's first trip in here, is it?" He pulled another chair over and sat. He would have loved to remain standing to appear more imposing, but his ankle was screaming from walking so fast to the store. Plus, his foot was soaked with mud.

"I stopped in yesterday." Lily took a towel from Hope and dabbed at the stain on her jeans. "To make a deal with Mr. Stannard."

"What kind of a deal?" Aunt Joy sounded suspicious now. *Good.*

"Well, I was getting around to telling you before the Abominable Snowman came in." She shot Rick a glare. "I work for Utopia Resorts and—"

"Those fancy hotels with the themes?" Sage asked.

"So not everyone is a recluse up here, I see." Lily nodded at Sage. "Yes, I design those resorts."

"Oh, my God," Hope said. "Sage and I have been saving a little money every year with the wild notion of visiting one of those resorts sometime."

"You have?" Lily and Rick said at the same time. Lily with encouragement, Rick with disdain.

"Well, sure," Sage said. "They're beautiful hotels and who wouldn't want to escape *this*." She threw her hands out indicating everything around her. "I mean, I love it here and all, but it is a bit monotonous."

"And quiet," Hope added. "So quiet."

"I've noticed the quiet." Lily folded the towel and placed it on the table. "California is not like this at all."

"No, it isn't," Rick said. "And I'm not going to let you turn Vermont into another California. One is all we need."

"I never said I wanted to recreate California here," Lily said, a laughing edge to her voice that irritated Rick. "If you'd let me finish my discussion yesterday, you would have seen that Utopia wants to keep this resort natural, outdoorsy."

"And get rid of my home, my business, my woods." Rick shook his head. "Not going to happen. I don't want to live next door to a fancy resort either. No one around here does."

"I'm sorry about your grandmother," Aunt Joy finally said, "but I have to agree with my nephew. This is no place for a mega-resort."

Finally. Someone is making some sense. Rick nodded at Aunt Joy, and she patted his hand.

Lily reached into her bag and pulled out a small laptop. "Let me show you some of the designs I've drawn up."

"We're not interested, Miss Hinsdale," Rick said. But why was he interested in the way her strawberry curls fell around her neck? In the small freckle below her right eye?

He focused on Poe trotting in the door he'd left open and tried to erase his stupid thoughts about Lily pushing through his sensible annoyance. The coyote sniffed the air and turned her head toward Rick. He dropped a hand in a subtle sign to call her over, and she obeyed like always.

Lily skittered behind Hope and Sage. "Mr. Stannard, please," she said. "That animal frightens me."

"This animal is welcome here," he said. "You, on the other hand, are not."

"Okay, Rick," Sage said. "None of us wants to hand this land over, but maybe we could at least try to be civil to Lily. She's come all this way. She's lost her grandmother." Sage threw a glance back to Lily still cowering behind them. "She obviously has an issue with coyotes."

"Not just coyotes," Lily said. "All animals."

"Did you have some childhood trauma or something?" Hope asked.

"I'm not here to discuss that." Lily straightened to her full height, which made hiding behind Hope and Sage look ridiculous, but Rick could still see the fear in her big blue-green eyes.

"Lily," Aunt Joy began, "Poe won't hurt you. She's no predator. Too accustomed to getting her food from a can to know how to attack anything."

Lily didn't look convinced. In fact, she appeared to be shifting into a deeper stage of anxiety. Rick recognized the pale skin, the trembling hands, the thin sheen of sweat on her brow. He'd experienced all those symptoms and more. He hated them.

"Poe, lie down." Rick pointed to the small wood stove Aunt Joy had fired up for the day. The coyote nuzzled his knee and pranced to the stove. She circled a few times in front of it then settled down on the floor.

Lily returned to a color characteristic of the living. A faint blush played on her cheeks, and a heat crawled over Rick's skin.

Clearing his throat, he said, "Look, I'm sure your designs are lovely." He motioned to her laptop still open on the table. "I'll even agree to selling your grandmother's land to someone who will let me continue to lease the maple trees if you don't want to sell it to me. I'm not going to sell you my land, however. Besides, tourists that do come to Vermont, don't come to stay in huge hotels. They stay in log cabins, or campers, or tents in the unspoiled woods."

A shudder worked its way down Lily's body. *What in the hell happened to her to make her so afraid of the woods?* Rick bit down on his lower lip to keep from asking. He didn't care. All he cared about was keeping his property.

"That's because there are no resorts for people to stay in around here." Lily tossed a wary glance toward Poe then slowly maneuvered out from behind Sage and Hope. She tapped a few keys on her laptop and spun it around to face Rick. "If Utopia builds this, the tourists will be lining up to visit. Guaranteed."

Aunt Joy, Hope, and Sage formed a semi-circle behind Rick so they could see the screen.

"Wow," Hope said.

"Unbelievable," Sage added.

"Is that a waterwheel?" Aunt Joy asked.

"It's amazing," Rick said, "but it doesn't belong here." He shut the laptop and pushed it toward Lily.

"You're talented though," Aunt Joy said. "No denying that."

"Thank you." Lily put the laptop back in her bag and extracted an envelope that looked remarkably like the one she had left with Rick yesterday. "I don't know if you perused the documents—"

"I burned them, as promised," Rick interrupted.

"I see."

If she sees, why is she pulling out new documents? He ground his teeth together, certain that growling was next. If Lily didn't like wild animals, she certainly wasn't going to like him in about five minutes.

"Well, I have authorization to up the offer on your land, Mr. Stannard." Lily flipped through the papers, put one on the table, turned it right side up to Rick, and slid it toward him.

Without dropping his gaze for a glance at the figure, he said, "I'm not selling."

Sage reached her arm over Rick's shoulder and picked up the document. "Holy shit! Rick, are you sure? They're prepared to pay you—"

She stopped when he held up a hand. "There is no amount of money that would make me leave. This is my home. My only home. There is nowhere else."

Aunt Joy's hand rested on his shoulder. She gave him a little squeeze. He took the gesture to be part "I'm on your side" and part "Stay calm, sugar."

"I'm afraid we can't help you, Lily," Aunt Joy said. "Pretty as those designs are, this land keeps us fed, sheltered, and healthy." She gestured to Rick's ankle. "Most of the time, that is."

He shifted under Aunt Joy's hold. This land kept him from ending up a big pile of shot nerves. He needed to be here, but something in the expression on Lily's face, the downward pull of her full lips, made him want to help her.

"Can't you let me buy Gail's property?" he asked. "You've made it clear that you don't want it, so why take a total loss? You can't make any money for your company, but you could walk away with a nice sum for yourself and be rid of Vermont. We would both be happy."

"As happy as Rick gets anyway," Sage said.

"Zip it." He leveled his gaze back on Lily.

"It's not that easy," she said. "Utopia is set on this theme, this area."

"Well, don't the current residents have a say?" Rick smacked his hand onto the table, causing the teacups and saucers to jangle. Hope cleared them away, and Sage helped. The two of them gave Lily a nod then disappeared into the kitchen. Aunt Joy slid her hand off Rick's shoulder.

"Surely you've run into other locations that you couldn't acquire," she said to Lily.

"Never." Lily tilted her head up a little victoriously. "Every proposed resort design has come to fruition in its originally intended location."

"Hate to break your record," Rick said.

"No, you don't, Mr. Stannard." She stuffed the papers back into the envelope. "I think you rather enjoy breaking my record."

"I'm not trying to be a jerk here."

"Well, you're succeeding as if you were born to be one." Lily jammed the envelope back into her purse as Aunt Joy quietly slipped into the kitchen.

He silently cursed the abandonment of his family as he battled this… this demon. He stood and said, "Look, how would you like it if I marched over to California, went to whatever lair you call your home, and told you I wanted to knock it down and put up a monster hotel in its place? What would you say to that?"

"I live in a hotel, so I'd say hurray to progress and offer my design services." She smiled at him. A poisonous spider smile.

He paced away from her, his stomach all knotted up and a fire blazing in his ankle. He couldn't take a deep breath either and that concerned him. He counted to ten.

Turning to face Lily again, he said, "You need to leave, okay? Please."

He expected her to protest, but instead she slipped on her coat—a short, black leather one today—and hiked her purse up onto her shoulder. She took a step closer to Rick, and he smelled that grapefruit-coconut-sunshine scent again. Nothing in Vermont smelled like her.

"I'll go, Mr. Stannard," she said, "but I will be back. When I have a deal to make, I make it."

She was close enough for him to reach out and kiss her. *Why am I thinking of doing that?*

He took a step back and cursed when his stance wobbled a bit. The hint of a smile at the corners of Lily's mouth told him she had achieved her goal of making him uncomfortable. *Is it her goal to arouse me as well?*

"I'll see you." She headed for the door, but stopped in her tracks when Poe rose to her feet and blocked the exit.

Lily rolled her shoulders, seeming to talk herself into walking past the coyote. Rick could have called Poe off, but why should he? Lily Hinsdale was trying to prove she was a tough businesswoman, and he was prepared to go ahead and let her.

Her fingers drummed on the sides of her thighs as she moved in slow motion toward the door. She didn't make a sound as she turned the knob, never removing her gaze from the coyote. Rick wanted to laugh, but something about the scene made him sad.

What had happened to her? No one should have to be that afraid. He knew about being afraid. It sucked.

Chapter Six

Lily stared at the laptop in front of her as the soundtrack for *The Lord of the Rings* played through its speakers. The sale documents were up on the screen. Sage had been impressed by the amount of money being offered for Rick's land. Maybe with a slight increase, Lily could get Rick's attention. She couldn't shake the feeling that she had his attention on matters not involving his land. He'd watched her when she spoke, as if he were studying the way her lips moved instead of listening to her words. He'd obviously heard what she'd said. He just didn't *want* to hear any of it. That had her blood boiling. She wasn't used to being disregarded.

"How do I make him hear it?" Tapping her index finger on the J key, Lily examined the top sum Utopia was willing to offer Rick. Not time to throw that figure out. No emergency yet, but close. She'd talked with him twice and gotten nowhere, and she wasn't keen on the idea of staying in the woods much longer. Her California tan was fading under cloudy Vermont skies, and the list of animals she'd encountered already gnawed at her. Coyote, moose, raccoon.

How much longer before there's an... incident? Lily rubbed her hands together in an attempt to warm herself. A fire blazed in the library's fireplace, but the chill was deep inside her. Down where a ten-year old girl still hid.

Her cell phone rang, and she lowered the volume on the music to answer it.

"Lily Hinsdale."

"Hello, Lily. It's Rita."

Oh, boy. "Hello, Rita. How's everything in California?" *Small talk will save me.* In the past, Lily had avoided whole conversations she didn't want to have with a little small talk diversionary tactic. It had to work right now, because she didn't have good news for the vice president of Utopia Resorts. Not yet.

"You know California. Everything here is always wonderful." Rita laughed, and Lily let out a small sigh of relief that the woman was in a jovial mood. "We're planning for the Gems Utopia gala at the end of the month. The Gems ones are always my favorites."

"Mine too. So glamorous."

"Gives me an excuse to buy something glitzy, and I do love to shop."

"No better pastime if you ask me." Lily hoped Rita didn't pick up on the nervous flutter in her voice.

"I'm calling because we want to do a short presentation about the new Vermont Utopia at the Gems gala. Figure we can entice our guests to check it out once it's completed. No reason our rich customers can't vacation with the blue-collar folk. There should be something for everyone at the new location. We thought you could put something together for the Vermont project. You know, take some pictures of the area while you're there." Rita paused and all Lily could hear was her own heart hammering against her ribs. "You have secured the property, correct?"

"Almost." Lily barely got the word out. "Just fine tuning some of the details." *Liar!* She rolled her shoulders. "I've had two meetings with the owner of the property adjacent to my grandmother's. It's..." She paused to check her notes. "It's over three hundred acres."

"Wonderful. Combined with Gail Hinsdale's land we should be able to build another spectacular resort. Drew shared some of your designs with me yesterday. I forwarded them to the president."

Lily sunk down until her forehead rested on the desk. She rocked her head back and forth trying to talk herself out of vomiting.

"Webster absolutely loved the sketches. They're so unique. Unlike anything we've tried before." Rita sounded giddy, and Lily so wanted to trade places with her.

"Great," she managed. *No turning back now that Utopia's president has seen the designs.* Lily stared at the ornate pattern on the Oriental rug under the desk. *Why didn't I propose another resort for China?* "I'm going to see the neighbor again and hope to close the deal."

"The sooner, the better, Lily," Rita said. "We need your genius back here. Take care, and we'll schedule a meeting when you get back. Bye."

"Bye," Lily whispered though Rita was gone. Staring at her phone, she contemplated venturing downstairs to the wine cellar. She hadn't wanted to go down there, fearing mice or snakes or other vicious monsters, but a glass of wine might do something to settle her nerves.

"If you don't close this deal, you're screwed, Hinsdale." She straightened in her seat and focused on the sale documents. There had to be a way to convince this Rick character to hand over his land. Nothing had stood in her way before. Nothing was going to stand in her way now. Certainly not an irritating northern redneck. A tall, pale-eyed, northern redneck who made flannel look appealing.

Lily shook her head. *Flannel is not appealing and neither is Mr. Stannard.* With that decided, she got up and went to the kitchen for a glass of something. She just couldn't make the trip downstairs. She wasn't that desperate yet.

As she reached for a glass in the cabinet beside the sink, she caught sight of two women walking up the front steps of the cabin. One of them held a basket with a checkered cloth over it and the other was holding… *a bottle of wine?* Lily threw a glance up to the ceiling. *There is a God.*

The doorbell rang as soon as she had made her way to the foyer. She opened the door, and Hope and Sage stood there smiling.

“Hi,” Sage said. “We’ve come to make up for our cousin’s completely Neanderthal behavior.”

“Oh, Sage.” Hope tapped the basket into her sister’s elbow. “Rick can’t help it. That’s the way he is.”

“And I *am* trying to steal his land,” Lily offered.

“There is that,” Sage said, “but Hope and I weren’t going to let that get in our way of seeing the inside of this house and the fabulous clothes you have in your suitcase.”

“We don’t get out much,” Hope confessed with a shrug. “You’re the first interesting person that’s happened by in… in…”

“Forever,” Sage finished. “Nothing exciting ever happens here.”

“Not that we don’t love it here,” Hope said.

“Right,” Sage agreed. “We do. We don’t want a huge resort here either, though it could bring hundreds of single, attractive men our way.”

“Hadn’t considered that,” Hope said as she chewed on her bottom lip.

“Utopia Resorts does have a habit of employing single, attractive men. It pleases the guests.” If she could get these two on her side and maybe the aunt, she’d have a female force to pounce on Rick. Lily never underestimated female forces. “Come in, ladies.”

Hope and Sage knocked the mud off their boots and handed Lily the basket and wine while they sat on the iron bench in the foyer.

"Homemade bread's in the basket," Hope said as she removed her boots. "We always do a trial run in the store's kitchen to make sure all the equipment is still working."

"And we figured you needed some wine after dealing with Rick." Sage stood after placing her boots on the little rug by the front door.

Lily caught a glimpse of their feet and laughed. Hope had a neon green sock on her right foot and a bright blue sock on her left. Sage had the reverse.

Hope wiggled her toes. "We try to be trendy, but no one appreciates it here."

"No one even looks at us here." Sage took the wine bottle back from Lily and wandered farther into the house.

"I'm sure that's not true," Lily said. They were both beautiful young women with their slim figures and long, light blonde hair.

"Okay," Sage said as she meandered into the kitchen. "The men that look at us here are old enough to be our grandfathers."

"Or young enough to be our sons." Hope lowered her brows as she rested her elbows on the back of one of the bar stools at the kitchen island.

"There have to be men your age too," Lily said. Hope and Sage couldn't be that much younger than her.

"Not ones we haven't already tried on for size." Sage opened cabinets until she found the wine glasses. She pulled down three and brought them to the island where she'd left the wine.

"None of them were a perfect fit," Hope said.

"Perfect fit? None of them were an okay-this-will-do fit." Sage poured wine for all three of them.

Lily found herself wondering what kind of a fit Rick would be then quickly picked up her wine glass and took a gulp as if to erase the thought. She didn't care how he would or wouldn't fit. He was so in another world from hers. A world Lily didn't want to have anything to do with. She understood how Hope and Sage felt though. Men were around, but never the right ones.

"You want to see the rest of the place?" Lily asked.

"Yes, please," Sage and Hope answered together.

All three women took their wine on a tour of the cabin. Hope and Sage ogled every room, touched every piece of furniture, and asked questions about absolutely everything. Lily enjoyed their chatter and for a little while forgot she was stranded in the woods. The sounds of other people filled the shadowy crevasses and made the threat of waiting animals a distant concern. She ended up on the couch between Hope and Sage watching *How to Lose a Guy in 10 Days.* She told tales about

Matthew McConaughey and Kate Hudson, both of whom she'd met with Grandma Gail. She shared her jellybeans and laughed until her stomach hurt.

Sage leaned her head on Lily's shoulder. "Too bad we're supposed to hate you," she said. "You're really cool."

"Yeah," Hope said. "Can't you find another spot for the hotel, Lily? We'd like to be friends, but our allegiance has to be to Rick."

"The miserable grump," Sage muttered.

"Why is he miserable?" Lily asked. "It's more than me wanting his land, isn't it?"

"Shit, yeah," Sage said. "He's been miserable ever since he—"

A furious pounding on the front door of the cabin cut off her words. Lily popped up from the couch, certain a wild beast was ramming the door down to stampede into the house and gorge her with its antlers. The doorbell rang in several long blasts.

Do animals ring doorbells? Lily set her winc glass down on the coffee table.

Hope peeked out the living room window facing the front of the house. "Oops. Sage, we're caught in enemy territory."

"Rick's out there?" Sage ran to Hope and peeked out. "Shit. Hit the lights. We need an escape plan." The sisters gripped each other.

"Don't be silly," Lily said as she made her way to the door. "We're all adults here. You can visit me if you want to."

"That's a nice theory," Hope said.

"But it's total bullshit," Sage said.

The two women stood beside the window using the drapes to conceal themselves. Shaking her head, Lily fluffed her hair then hoped Sage and Hope hadn't seen her do so.

Squaring her shoulders, she opened the front door. Rick's body filled the threshold. Filled it well. His hips were slightly offset as he kept the weight off his injured leg, but the rest of him was… appetizing. He still wore the jeans and flannel coat he'd had on this morning, but a few stains dotted the jeans now as if he'd been working with grease or something. One of his hands leaned against the doorframe while the other gripped the cane.

Lily was about to say something—what, she wasn't sure—when Rick asked, "Where are they?"

"Where are who?"

"Don't play games with me. I know they're here." Rick narrowed his eyes and searched over her shoulder then down to the rug by the door. "Those are so not your boots. Hope? Sage? Get your asses out here."

"They don't have to leave," Lily said. *Who does this guy think he is?*

"Yes, yes they do. They don't belong in here. With *you.*" He dropped the hand on the doorframe and shifted his weight. Some of the fury in his eyes morphed into a look of pain instead.

"Why don't you come in, Mr. Stannard, and sit down?" Lily moved to the side to make room for Rick to walk in, but he shook his head.

"I don't want to come in. I want my cousins to come out." He raised his voice at the end. "Right now."

Hope and Sage appeared in the foyer. "It's the Big Bad Wolf," Sage said as she sat to put on her boots. Hope lowered next to her and did the same.

"I can't believe you two are actually over here." He paced away from the front door to the edge of the porch.

Lily let her gaze travel the length of him, hovering a few extra seconds at the curve of his butt in his jeans. Spectacular, for sure.

"How did you know we were here?" Hope asked.

Rick pointed the cane at the meandering trail of footprints in the muddy driveway. "You don't need to be a detective. You two have no sense."

"Cut them a break," Lily said. "They were just being nice. Maybe you should try the same. You might like it."

Hope and Sage froze in their tying of bootlaces and stared up at Lily as if she had done something truly insane.

"I am nice." Rick turned around to face her. "When people are nice to me. My nice is in short supply, however, and I don't waste it on people who want to make me homeless."

"I don't want to make you homeless," Lily shot back. "I want to give you enough money to afford a bigger home on a bigger piece of land."

"That home and that land," he pointed to the woods in the direction of his place, "are perfect for me. Perfect. Nothing else will be right."

"How do you know if you don't try somewhere else?" Lily asked.

"Oh, man," Sage said.

"We have to get out of here," Hope whispered. "Lily, it's been lovely. Thank you." They both stepped onto the porch.

"Yes, we sincerely hope he doesn't kill you. He's moving a lot slower with that ankle, so you'll probably be all right," Sage said as Rick made a move to go after her.

"Probably," Hope added. "Run if you have to. No shame in running."

They edged by Rick who half-growled at them, and Lily watched their huddling forms disappear down the driveway. Rick stood for a long, silent moment at the edge of the porch. Lily's mind scrambled around for a way to get him to come inside. If she could just convince him to sell…

"I did live somewhere else." His voice was a controlled whisper as if it took him great effort to utter the words.

"Where?" Lily stepped out onto the porch and threw a glance to the left and right. Surely no animals would approach with Rick standing there like a fuming human barricade.

"New York City."

Lily wasn't sure she'd heard him correctly. *New York City?* She couldn't picture him in a tiny city like Providence, Rhode Island, never mind New York City. "What happened?"

"It didn't take. I belong here. I will stay here."

"Well, I don't want to buy *all* of Vermont for Utopia." She stood next to him and leaned against the porch railing. The wind stirred up and something smoky, woodsy, reached out to her. It took her a few moments to realize the scent came from Rick.

"No, you just want the one piece that means everything to me." He gestured to the trees in front of them. "The two pieces."

"I can't sell you this property, Rick." Lily clamped her lips closed at the use of his first name. It had slipped out, but her ears rather liked the sound of it.

He narrowed his pale blue eyes. "Can't or won't?"

"Can't. I really can't. My orders are to secure these two properties for Utopia Resorts."

"What happens if you don't?"

"I'm going to piss off a lot of people with salaries bigger than mine. The president of Utopia Resorts saw my designs and approved them for this location." Lily shivered a little at the breeze gnawing through her sweater.

"Do you like your job?" Rick shifted again, and Lily so wanted him to come inside. To sit. That was all. Nothing more.

"I love my job," she said.

"So do I."

****

He wanted to hate her. He really did. Rick wanted to let his wrath loose on Lily so she'd pack up her sexy outfits and head on back to California. So she'd leave him the hell alone, and he could continue his quiet little existence hidden away from the world. Vermont was as much a prescription for him as any pill ever was.

"If I did find another spot in Vermont," Lily began, "not that I have the time to do so, but if I did, would you be okay with that?"

Well, this is unexpected. She seemed like the type to get one plan into her pretty little head and stick with it. What was making her consider folding on taking his land?

"No, I wouldn't be okay with that," he said. "A super hotel doesn't belong anywhere in Vermont. It doesn't go with the way of life up here."

"And by 'life,' you mean no life." Lily threw up her hands and let them flop down against her hips. "This is the most boring place I've ever been. There is absolutely nothing to do here."

Rick shuffled back and sat on the wooden bench on the porch. He knew he'd pushed his limits walking over from his place, but he'd been so mad at Hope and Sage he hadn't been thinking practically. Now he was paying. His ankle throbbed, sending flashes of pain up his entire leg.

"There are things to do here," he said.

"Besides making maple syrup?" she asked. "Like what?" She stayed where she was leaning against the porch railing, but Rick imagined her sitting next to him on the bench.

Don't do that, man.

"Snowmobiling, skiing, hiking, canoeing, bicycling, snowshoeing, though I'd be careful with that one." He indicated his left leg stretched out in front of him. "Mountain climbing, fishing, hunting…" Rick glanced up at Lily to see if he'd named enough activities to convince her.

"Those are all outside things." Her arms were folded across her chest as if she were cold in that black sweater offering a hint of the breasts it covered.

"Well, there's a lot of outdoors to explore here."

"I prefer exploring the insides of stores, restaurants, bars, dance clubs…"

An image of her tight body dancing to some bass-heavy club music had Rick's hand curling around the cane resting against his knee.

"I mean, I couldn't even get a cup of coffee anywhere around here," she said.

"That's because you don't know where to go," he said. "In about a week or so, the best coffee will be right next door. Aunt Joy makes six different kinds with maple syrup in them, but for now, decent coffee is at Black Wolf Tavern two streets over that way." He pointed to the west.

"Two real streets or these snowy and muddy one-lane jobs?" Lily waved a hand at the driveway.

"Snowy and muddy one-lanes, but it's worth it for good coffee, no?"

"I'd murder for good coffee," she said. "What if I want dinner, alcohol, or live music?"

"Also Black Wolf Tavern. Jake Peters, the owner, has it all over there. It's where the locals gather."

She took a few steps away from the railing closer to Rick. "Do *you* gather there?"

"Me?" He shook his head. "I'm not so much of a gatherer, but Hope and Sage hang out there. I'm sure they'd love to take you, the traitors."

"They weren't trying to piss you off." Lily sat on the edge of the bench and hooked some of her hair behind her ear. Rick was fascinated by the way the curls bunched up and sat on her shoulder.

"Trying? No, they don't have to try. It comes naturally to those two."

"I'm not trying to piss you off either, Rick. It's not my intent. It all looked good on paper, you know? I wanted to get rid of this place. Your place is right next door. Together the properties are the perfect size for Utopia."

He looked around. "Why do you want to get rid of this place? It's a coveted spot among the locals. I'm not the only one who wants to buy it,

Lily." Her name rolled off his tongue, and something warm stirred in his chest.

Her skin went pale, her California goldenness high-tailing it right off her face. "I don't want anything to do with this place."

She rocked in her seat for a moment as if consoling herself. Rick had the urge to slide his arm around her shoulders and pull her close. He sat on his hand to keep from doing so.

"When I was a little girl," she started, "I visited my grandmother here. I was in the hot tub around back and—"

A phone ringing inside interrupted Lily. The sound of it pulled her out of her story, and she filed it back where she kept it locked apparently.

"I'd better get that." She stood and Rick hauled himself to his feet. "Did you walk here?"

He nodded. "It didn't seem like a bad idea at the time, but now…"

She walked toward the front door then paused. "Don't go anywhere. I'll give you a ride back. Just let me answer that."

"You don't have to. I'm okay." Rick started for the stairs, but his left leg buckled beneath him when he took a step. He had time to grab the railing so he didn't crash to the ground. When Lily's hand touched his back, he stopped breathing for a moment.

"Come in and wait. Please." She jogged inside and he could hear her answering the phone.

He made his way to the door and stood there. He felt as if he were throwing away all his arguments against Lily if he crossed the threshold. He could call his aunt or cousins. They'd come and get him. Hope and Sage owed him now, but something about the inside of that eccentric and pretentious house called to him. Some force he couldn't see pulled at his body.

When Lily appeared around the corner, phone to her ear, and waved him in, Rick couldn't stop his feet from stepping inside. She led him to the great room and pointed to the couch. He craned his head up to take in the huge expanse of the room and turned in a wobbly circle to view it all. A purply-blue sky was framed in each of the skylights above, and Rick knew if he didn't go now, there wouldn't be enough light for him to walk home if he wanted to. A quick glance toward Lily, however, had him lowering to the couch.

If I hang around, maybe I can convince her to pick another state for her ridiculous hotel. Sounded doable, logical. A perfectly good reason to be sitting on her couch.

The leather creaked and moaned against his jeans as he repositioned himself. Too noisy, too fancy. This wasn't a couch. More like a piece of art meant for a museum, not a home.

Lily paced by and turned on the TV. She flicked on the overhead lights in the great room and the hall lights. The kitchen ones too. Squinting in the brightness, Rick watched her as she walked away, spun on her heel, and walked back toward him. The hand not holding the phone flapped around as she spoke. He could only hear her side of the conversation, but it didn't sound as if it were going well.

"Not yet," she said.

A pause as she listened.

"No."

Another pause and a stop to the pacing. She eyed Rick and shook her head at whatever the caller was saying.

"I said it's not necessary. Look, I have a guest, so I should—"

Pause. Her head went back as she studied the ceiling. Rick wanted to run his fingers down the length of her throat. The skin there looked amazingly smooth. He cleared his throat trying to rid himself of the thought.

"It doesn't matter who my guest is. I have one and that's that. I'm working."

Lily threw herself into the matching leather recliner near the couch. A muscle twitched in her jaw as she listened to what must have been a tirade.

"Don't come here. I mean it. I'm all right, and Rita wants you there. I'll be back soon. Don't worry. Bye."

Lily hung up and let her phone fall onto the cushion beneath her. Her chest heaved up and down as she stared at the coffee table between them.

"Husband?" Rick asked before he could stop himself.

"No."

"Boyfriend?"

"Boss." Lily finally looked over at Rick. He'd thought he'd seen her bad mood already when she'd come to the store, but her eyes shot fire right now.

"Oh." He wasn't sure what else to say. He wasn't any good at this talking stuff, and all the lights blaring down on him made him feel so exposed.

"Didn't sound like I was speaking to my boss, did it?" Lily leaned forward, resting her elbows on her knees.

"Not really. No. But that's none of my business."

"Normally, I would agree with you, but actually Drew Ashburn *is* your business. More specifically, your problem. If I don't get you to sell your land to Utopia, he'll try."

"So let him." Rick shrugged.

"Think you're invincible?"

He let out a short laugh. "Not at all, but on this, I am a mountain. I won't be moved."

"Okay, because we're throwing metaphors around, Drew is dynamite. If he wants a mountain moved, he's going to move it." She stood and started, pacing again across the great room. "It's what makes him good at his job, but annoying to have a relationship with."

"I see." Boss and boyfriend. That was the way they played it in California.

"No." Lily sat beside him on the couch, closer than was safe for either of them. "It's not like that. Well, it was. For a little while. But I've been trying to break it off for months now. He just won't hear it. He keeps wanting more and..." She peeked over at Rick. "I don't know why I'm telling you this. Forget it." She stood again. "I need some time to think of a plan."

"A plan to steal my land?" He wanted off this Ferris wheel with her.

"No. A new plan. Drew might come here, though I told him not to. He knows I'm freaked about being in Vermont, and he thinks he can make me feel better. He also thinks he'll be able to change your mind. He wants to close the deal."

Rick wanted to ask why she was freaked. She had almost told him before the phone call, but it didn't seem right to ask her now. She was pretty frazzled. And which deal did this Drew guy want to close? The hotel deal or the Lily deal? Probably both, and though Rick didn't know him, he didn't want Drew to succeed at either.

"Don't you have to get approval from the state to build a huge hotel?" Red tape. That could work for his case.

"Yes, but Utopia has a powerful legal team that handles all that. It's in the works according to Drew."

Rick found that hard to believe. Certainly other Vermonters didn't want this resort any more than he did. It clashed with everything the state stood for.

As if reading his thoughts, Lily said, "Most people respond to dollars and cents, Rick. It didn't work on you, but in these economic times, people are doing things they wouldn't ordinarily do. Why not accept a perfectly legal offer from a success-guaranteed company now instead of resorting to some other means of survival later?"

"You have a point."

"I do? Good. Now sell me your land." Lily reached for that damn envelope on the coffee table next to her laptop.

"Nice try, but not a chance." He grinned when he said this and noted the defeat in Lily's eyes barely masked the amusement present on her lips.

"C'mon, you'd be helping a girl out if you signed these and agreed to the sale." She wiggled a pen in front of him.

"Helping a girl out isn't a bad idea." Rick took the pen.

"It isn't?" Lily's eyebrows arched hopefully as she slid the sale documents onto his lap.

"I'm not signing these, Lily."

"I know." She let out a breath and leaned back against the couch.

"But, what if we could show Utopia Resorts that this isn't the right location?" He pushed to the edge of the couch and angled to face Lily. "You have a camera with you?"

"I brought a digital one and I've got my phone."

"Good. Come over tomorrow. We'll make a little production that shows my business, the woods and all her beauty, the small town mentality around here. Your company will see this is literally the middle of nowhere. People won't come here to stay in a resort no matter how natural its theme. It's not the right place. We'll show them."

Lily's brows drew together as she pulled on her lower lip. "Do you think it'll work?"

"No idea, but it's all we have."

When did Lily and I become a we? Rick shifted the cane from his left hand to his right and back to his left. He wasn't sure what he was doing, but he would do whatever it took to keep his property, his life, his quiet.

"I guess it's worth a try. We'll have to do it all tomorrow, so I can email it to Drew before he hops on the next plane here."

"Let him come. Seeing it firsthand would probably be better."

"You don't want Drew here," Lily said. "Trust me. We want to avoid that. I've seen him in action. He can get pretty… passionate about achieving a goal. We need to handle this ourselves."

"And we will." Rick stretched out his left leg and let out a groan.

"Let me get you back to your place." Lily reached for her car keys in a leaf-shaped bowl on the coffee table. “Don’t you have some drugs for that?”

“I stopped taking them a week after I sprained my ankle.”

She stood, but turned around as he got to his feet, relying heavily on the cane. “Why would you stop taking them? You look as if you’re hurting right now.”

“I overdid it walking here, but I don’t need more pills.” He followed her, moving at the embarrassing speed of an old geezer.

“You need something.” She held the front door open as she grabbed her coat.

Rick motioned for her to go first and stepped onto the porch after her. He enjoyed the sway of her hips as she walked toward the Jeep.

Lily was right. He did need something, but not for his ankle.

Chapter Seven

Lily sat in the Jeep in Rick's driveway watching him limp to his front door. She probably should have gotten out and helped him, but a little voice in her head said getting that close to him would be dangerous. She'd have to scoot up beside him, circle an arm around his waist, and let him lean on her.

No. She couldn't have that. Besides, he didn't seem like someone who wanted help. A-man's-got-to-take-care-of-himself type for sure.

When Rick reached the door of his cabin, he gave her a small wave, and the stupid desire to run inside with him nearly overwhelmed her.

Run inside and do what, moron? He's making my life complicated by not selling. I despise him.

Lily gripped the steering wheel, managed an aloof wave back, and put the Jeep in reverse. As Rick disappeared into his cabin, that coyote of his came skulking out of the woods beside the driveway. It paused as it saw the Jeep, licked its chops, and released a quick bark, its German Shepherd-like ears twitching. The front door of the cabin opened again, but the coyote didn't race into the house. Instead, its golden eyes got caught in the headlights and focused on Lily. Images of it jumping to the hood of the Jeep and pounding its muzzle into the windshield until it shattered into a million pieces flashed in Lily's mind.

"Poe, get in here." Rick's voice floated on the breeze and pulled the coyote from its scrutiny of Lily. With another bark and a swish of its bushy tail, it slipped into the cabin, and Rick shut the door.

Lily hit the gas and turned the Jeep around. Mud and slushy snow splashed up onto the windows as she gunned it down Rick's driveway wanting to get out of there before anything else considered her prey. In three minutes she was rolling to a stop in front of her grandmother's cabin. Almost fully dark now, she faced the task of getting from the Jeep to the cabin again while secret things behind the trees watched her every move. She hadn't thought much about what lurked outside when Rick was sitting on her couch earlier, but now she couldn't think of anything else.

"Suck it up and do it, Hinsdale."

She pulled the key out of the ignition and zipped up her coat. Why hadn't she left a floodlight on? Too busy worrying about the ankle of a complete stranger who was making this entire trip a bigger ordeal than it already was. She could have been back in California right now if Rick had only signed the papers agreeing to sell his land. It should have been so simple. Instead, she was still in

Vermont, still huddled in the Jeep, still wondering exactly how many animals lived in the nearby woods and how hungry they might be.

She put a hand to her chest, willing her heart to calm the hell down. "Pull yourself together and get inside."

She opened the Jeep door and ran for the house. After tripping on the front steps, Lily managed to make it inside with just a small scrape on her palm where she'd stopped her fall. A little trickle of blood welled up in her hand, and her mind magnified it to traumatic proportions. Running to the closest bathroom, Lily thrust her hand under the faucet and washed the insignificant slice. She grabbed tissues and blotted at the injury. It only took a few moments for the cut to stop bleeding, but her hands were shaking.

"You're such a mess."

She threw away the tissues and spent a moment looking at herself in the mirror. Her grandmother's eyes stared back at her.

"How could you like it here, Grandma Gail? I don't get it."

Lily and her grandmother had been alike in so many ways, but this Vermont business made them seem like complete opposites. How could her grandmother like both the liveliness of California and the solitude of Vermont? The two states were like separate universes.

After a quick shower—something about being naked and vulnerable made a long shower impossible tonight—Lily took her laptop into the great room. The TV was still on and now *X-Men* was playing. Some Hugh Jackman before bed was always a good idea.

Letting Wolverine's sarcasm follow her into the kitchen, she put together a salad from the few groceries she'd bought while hunting for coffee this morning. She buttered a slice of the bread Hope and Sage had brought over. She took a bite and closed her eyes.

"Wow. Those two know what they're doing in the baking department." Garlic and rosemary were infused right into the loaf, and the toasted crust was a golden delight. Bread fit for a goddess. She had two more slices without butter, and they were just as good.

Saving some for toast in the morning, Lily retired to the great room with the intent of drawing up new designs for a hotel in another location. Maybe if she came up with a theme so unbelievable, corporate would go for building it somewhere far from Vermont.

In truth, if she did succeed in acquiring Rick's property and Utopia Resorts went forward with the construction, it would mean more visits to Vermont for her. More trips to the woods to oversee building, troubleshoot, promote. Spending time in Greece and France and Italy was one thing. Being stuck in Vermont, completely devoid of culture, cuisine, and company was another situation entirely.

Lily did have fun this afternoon with Hope and Sage. She had to admit that. They were hysterical, and the way they teased Rick was a hoot. She could picture herself being friends with them. Good friends.

And Rick. He'd surprised her again. Here she was trying to yank his land out from under his feet, and he offered to help her convince corporate to find another place. Who does that? He should be furious with her. He was. Why did he change his mind?

Or is he acting?

Lily tapped a finger to her lips as she considered that unpleasant notion. Maybe he was trying to get on her good side. Trying to charm her with his willingness to "help" solve her current dilemma. A dilemma he created. He probably didn't give a rat's ass if she lost her job. He only wanted to protect his home and emerge victorious from this battle they were having. Lily didn't like being played. Not one bit.

The house phone rang, and she stared at it on the end table by the couch. Who would call that number? Anyone who knew she was there knew to call her cell. She waited until her grandmother's voice sounded from the answering machine.

"Hello. You've reached Gail Hinsdale, but I'm only taking emergency calls right now, and it's not an emergency, is it?" A slight pause. *"I didn't think so. I'll be happy to talk to you when I'm back*

in California. Bye." For a minute, Lily felt as if her grandmother was in the room with her.

"Lily?" A man's voice. Not Drew's. Not her father's. "Lily, I know you're in there. I can see every light from my cabin. Your house is glowing through the trees."

Rick? Lily shut off the lamp closest to the couch and picked up the phone.

"Hello?" she said.

"What's with all the lights anyway? Afraid of the dark?"

"No." *Afraid of what's hiding in the dark.* "I need to be able to see."

"Even in the rooms you're not in right now? It's a waste of energy."

"What do you care? You're not paying for the electricity."

"No, but conservation of resources is a group effort."

"Call me selfish," Lily said.

"Selfish." The teasing edge in Rick's voice was sexy. Very sexy. Too sexy.

"Is there a point to this call?" Lily wanted to be annoyed, but somehow she was amused instead. She shut off the TV.

"I was wondering if you brought any boots that aren't so California. The two pairs I've seen you in so far will not be good for hiking."

He's noticed my boots. What else has he noticed?

"I'm sorry, did you say hiking?" she asked. "You aren't in any condition to hike with that ankle." And there was no way she was going hiking.

"No, unfortunately, I'm not, but Hope and Sage agreed to take you out into the woods to get some footage."

"The woods?" Lily suddenly couldn't swallow.

"Yeah, the woods. That's the main reason a resort wouldn't work around here. The woods are full of animals that make their homes there. A resort would truly upset their habitats, upset the natural balance."

Full of animals. Lily knew the woods were full of animals, of course, but hearing Rick say it out loud made her scars tingle. She shifted her shoulders back and forth on the couch hoping to quiet the memories.

"Look, we don't have time to trample through the woods. Maybe Hope and Sage could use my camera and take pictures, video, whatever, while you and I work on another aspect." That sounded sensible.

"Lily," Rick said, "why are you afraid of the woods?"

"I'm not afraid of the woods." *I'm petrified by them.*

"Everybody's afraid of something," he whispered.

"What are you afraid of, Rick?"

He laughed, a quick, raspy sound that made Lily close her eyes and lean her head back. “Maybe sometime, when we’re both in an honest mood or very drunk, we can trade stories,” Rick said.

“Not tonight.” Lily was both relieved and saddened.

“No, not tonight.” He was quiet for a moment. “Okay, we’ll send Hope and Sage out on assignment and see what they come up with. We’ll focus on my business and take it from there.”

“Sounds good. I’ll see you in the morning.”

“Come to the sugarhouse. It’s the building behind the store.”

“Okay.” Lily got up and peeked through the dining room window. “How come I don’t see any lights from your place through the trees?”

“I’ve only got one light on by the bed where I am right now. My bedroom is on the other side of the house, not facing your property.”

Lily pictured Rick’s bedroom and found herself getting sweaty as she did so. Suddenly a light appeared in the distance.

“Is that you?” she asked.

“Yep, in the kitchen now. All this talking is making me thirsty.”

“That’s right. Hermits don’t chit-chat, do they?”

“This isn’t chit-chat. We’re making plans. Important ones. I wouldn’t have called otherwise. I never use the phone.”

Lily heard something being poured, then a bark.

"Poe says hello," Rick said.

"Sounded more like 'feed me.' How do you sleep at night with that beast in your house?"

"Ouch. Poe is willing to let the beast comment slide, but that was uncalled for," Rick said. "I told you and my aunt told you that Poe isn't wild. I've had her since she was a pup. She doesn't know any life but the domestic one she's been living."

"Right, until she tears your face off in your sleep."

"She wouldn't do that." He sounded so sure.

"How do you know?"

Rick didn't answer right away. What was he doing? What was he thinking? What was he wearing? What *wasn't* he wearing?

"Poe knows she's lucky to have me. She'd probably be dead if I hadn't taken her in. Her mother had abandoned her, and she was starving when I found her. I fed her. I cared for her. I…" He stopped and drew in a breath.

"You loved her."

"Yeah. Corny, right?"

The light went out between the trees, and Lily knew Rick was headed back to his bedroom. That coyote was probably on his heels and ready to snuggle up to him under the covers.

Was it stupid to be jealous of a mutt?

****

Rick stood in front of his closet and surveyed the miniscule selection of clothes. T-shirts, thermal shirts, flannel shirts, sweatshirts, sweaters, jeans. All pretty plain, all pretty worn.

"So what?" he said to Poe who was stretched out on his bed, her head resting on her front paws as she watched him. "It's a regular workday. Why should my clothes matter?"

Poe woofed and wagged her tail.

"Lily is not a guest. In fact, she's the enemy. We have to remember that, Poe. We wouldn't need to collect reasons why a resort is no good here if it weren't for her."

Rick yanked down a blue thermal shirt and a blue-and-black-checkered flannel shirt. They were Aunt Joy's favorites. She always said blue made his eyes pop, and he told himself he was wearing them for her.

He rushed through breakfast, actually considered taking the pain pills for his ankle so it wouldn't be a problem today, but decided against it. He'd have to remember to sit here and there. It didn't hurt as bad as he expected it to after all the time he'd spent on it yesterday. He closed his fingers around the cane, but decided against that too. Feeling like a senior citizen at his age sucked.

When he and Poe arrived at the store, Hope was standing on a chair rewriting the menu on the enormous chalkboard hanging on the wall behind the pastry case. Sage stood below her reading items off a sheet of paper. They both turned around when bells chimed and Poe howled.

"What are those?" Rick pointed to three golf ball sized bells hanging above the store's door.

"Jeez, Rick," Sage said. "I know you don't get out much, but you should know bells when you see them."

"And hear them," Hope added.

"Don't you two ever get tired of being smart asses?" Rick limped in and straightened a few books on the shelves. Poe sat by the door still eyeing the bells.

"No, never," Sage said.

"We're just so good at it," Hope said.

"What are we good at?" Aunt Joy came out of the kitchen. She had her hair covered with a bandana and a towel in her hand. That meant only one thing—she was doing some serious cleaning of the refrigerator in the back. She had a thing about that refrigerator being spotless when the season started. As if she couldn't work unless she was certain absolutely every corner of that appliance had been wiped, sanitized, and dried.

"We're good at annoying Ricky," Sage said.

"Gifted," Rick said.

"That's my girls." Aunt Joy gave Sage a hug as she passed by and dropped the towel she carried onto the pastry case.

"Don't encourage them, Aunt Joy. And don't call me Ricky." He nudged Poe and coaxed her to follow him. He headed toward the kitchen so he could cut through to the sugarhouse.

"Aren't you going to wait for Lily out here?" Sage called.

"Lily?" Aunt Joy hooked her hand on Rick's arm before he could vanish into the kitchen. He knew getting Smart Ass One and Two involved was a mistake. "Why is Lily coming here? I thought she was the villain trying to steal your sanctuary."

"Rick decided to date her instead," Sage said.

"I did not." A sudden heat crept up Rick's face. He wanted all three of these women to clear out.

"Easy there, Big Fella." Hope turned around on the chair where she was still standing and patted Rick on the shoulder. "You know, we could take your touchiness to mean it actually *is* a date you're having with Lily today."

Aunt Joy stepped between them before Rick had the chance to say or do anything. He would never hurt his cousins though their taunting was incessant. Sometimes he wanted to knock their heads together and be done with it.

"Why is Lily coming here, Rick?" Aunt Joy looked him in the eye from a foot below him.

"I think I've convinced her a resort wouldn't work here." He gently freed himself from Aunt Joy's grip.

"Our Ricky has got some charm after all," Sage said.

"Keep it up, Sage. Go ahead." He leaned against the kitchen threshold to take the weight off his ankle. "Don't call me Ricky."

Sage stuck her tongue out at him. "Too bad you only use that charm on strangers."

"Beautiful strangers," Hope added, which sent her and Sage into a round of chuckles. Even Aunt Joy had a grin on her face.

Rick reached to the pastry case and grabbed the towel. He balled it up and threw it at the chalkboard. At least a third of what Hope had written in her perfect handwriting smudged.

"Rick!" Hope hopped off the chair and gave him a push. "You're a jerk."

"I'm a jerk? Me?" Rick angled his hands at himself. "You two have been nonstop on my back since I came in here."

"Then don't come in here." Sage climbed onto the chair and handed the paper to Hope. She took the towel and wiped the entire chalkboard clean.

"I'll come in here whenever I damn well please," Rick said.

The bells above the door jangled and everybody froze. Lily stood in the front doorway, and Rick forgot everything else for a moment. She wore a long red sweater that belted around her tiny waist. A cream-colored shirt peeked from beneath the sweater, its ruffled collar framing the smooth skin at Lily's neck. The blue jeans covering her lower half made Rick wish he were those jeans.

Brown suede boots snaked to her knees. Her strawberry curls appeared redder today, and those blue-green eyes made Rick think of exotic places he'd never visited.

"I know you said to go to the sugarhouse around back, but I heard you in here." Lily stepped farther into the store. "You guys all right?"

"Super," Sage said.

"Fantastic," Hope agreed. "Mom?"

"I'm a little confused, but otherwise wonderful." Aunt Joy shook her head. "I'm going back to my cleaning." She gave Lily a wave and stopped in front of Rick. "Boy, you look so nice in blue." She patted his cheek and went into the kitchen.

"He does look nice in blue," Hope said. "Don't you think so, Lily?"

Lily smiled, and the temperature in the store skyrocketed. Rick rolled up his sleeves and shot a death glare at Hope.

"Did you bring your camera?" Rick asked Lily. Best to get down to business and stop wasting time. Also best to get rid of Hope and Sage before they embarrassed him on a large scale. Cracking his nuts when it was the three of them was one thing, but he couldn't have them doing so with Lily here.

Lily dug around in her purse and held up a digital camera.

Rick walked around the pastry case and got a whiff of that grapefruit-coconut-sunshine smell as he neared Lily. The scent didn't belong in the store, but he took a second to inhale deeply anyway. He took the camera, his fingers brushing against Lily's for the briefest of moments. That quick touch did something to his body. Something he couldn't explain. Something he didn't want to acknowledge.

Clearing his throat, he said, "Dumb and Dumber, take this camera and get lost."

"We're in the middle of something." Sage rested a hand on her hip.

"Sage, obey me." Rick couldn't contain the twitch in his lips as he fought not to laugh. He knew how to get on his cousins' nerves just as well as they got on his. They'd been playing this game for years, and truthfully he'd miss it if it stopped.

"Obey you? I don't think so." Sage got off the chair and marched over to Rick who shuffled behind Lily before his cousin could get to him. "Nice, Rick. Use the guest as your shield. Real gentlemanly."

"I'm not sure I want to get involved in this." Lily threw a glance over her shoulder at Rick, but her lips were turned up in a Hollywood-worthy grin. She would have melted an audience with that smile.

Sage regarded Lily for a silent moment then flicked her gaze to Rick. He braced himself for some comment meant to truly humiliate him, but instead Sage held out her hand for the camera.

"As you wish, master." She took the camera, winked at Rick, and turned around. "C'mon, Hope. Let's play Wild Kingdom."

Sage pulled Hope through the kitchen, leaving only Lily and Rick in the storefront. Neither of them moved, but Rick said, "What just happened?"

"I think you won." She turned around, and he realized how close they were standing. He took a few limps back and tried to breathe.

"Interesting," he said. "I never win."

"Well, congratulations," Lily said. "I missed out on all this fun. Only child and so are my parents. No siblings, no cousins."

"But you had a famous grandmother," Rick said. "That had to be fun."

"Definitely." She let her purse slip off her shoulder and dropped it onto the nearest table. "My father is an actor too. Robert Hinsdale."

"Oh, right. Aunt Joy loves his movies. You don't look anything like him."

"Good. I don't want to look like a sixty-something-year-old actor."

"You do, however, look like Gail."

"I'll take that as a compliment."

"As it was meant." That heat washed over Rick again. Concerning. *Am I coming down with something?* He didn't feel sick aside from the feverish episode happening right now. "You may be as nice as Gail too."

"May? You haven't decided yet?" Lily pulled her laptop out of her purse and powered it up.

"When I first met you the other day," Rick began, "you know, when you were all 'let's make a deal' about taking my land, I thought you were evil. Not at all like Gail who had been so generous with allowing me to increase my productivity by leasing her trees."

Lily's shoulders sagged a little. "Maybe I am evil. I came in here, guns blazing, just thinking about myself. I didn't give a shit that this was your home and that you might actually like living here."

"And now?"

He slid out a chair and sat, letting out a small sigh. Lily lowered into the chair opposite him then pulled out the one next to her. She patted the seat and pointed to his foot. He maneuvered his leg onto the chair, and his ankle thanked him by not throbbing so much.

"And now I'm not sure." Lily hooked some of her hair behind her ear, and Rick couldn't take his eyes off the red-gold curls. "I mean, I could never live here, but that doesn't mean you can't love it. I can see that you do."

"I have everything I need here," Rick said.

Almost everything.

Chapter Eight

"These are some new designs I came up with last night." Lily turned the laptop around so Rick could see the screen. "Figured if I wowed corporate with another idea, they'd abandoned this Vermont one."

She couldn't rely on a few pictures of trees to change their minds. Utopia was an enormous corporation that did whatever it wanted, whenever it wanted. She had witnessed it being ruthless firsthand. They squashed whatever got in their way like bugs, and generally speaking, Lily liked that about the company. That kind of power was godly. She shared some of that power and enjoyed wielding it.

Usually.

Rick leaned forward and scrolled through the designs. An Arctic theme. Glaciers Utopia. All ice and snow and caves. One sketch showed the front doors of the resort. Two huge polar bears standing on their hind legs formed an archway, and a typed note next to the sketch said, "Mirrored doors with painted snowflakes."

"Well, I'm wowed," Rick said. "These are incredible. I don't see how your company wouldn't go for this idea." He looked truly impressed, and Lily shoved aside the wave of bashfulness lapping at her shores.

"Would you visit this resort?"

His blue eyes stopped scanning her designs. "I don't travel." He said it as if it were a firm truth. Something carved in stone.

"Ever?"

"Nope. I told you, everything I need is here."

"You're not curious about what else is out there?" Lily gestured to the front door.

"That's what the Internet is for," he said. "I don't actually have to leave my house to see the world."

Lily shook her head. "Not the same."

"Close enough for me." Rick rubbed a hand at the center of his chest, caught himself doing so, and dropped his hand to his lap. "You travel a lot?"

"All the time. Mostly for work." She couldn't remember the last time she'd actually had a true vacation. Whenever she traveled for Utopia, she managed to squeeze in a little sight-seeing, usually with Drew crawling up her ass while she tried to enjoy wherever they were. She'd never gone to any of those places alone.

Except this time. To a place she hadn't wanted to visit.

"Where have you been?" Rick rested his hand on the thigh of his elevated leg. He massaged the muscles there, and that had Lily wondering at the muscles in other places. Like under that flannel and beneath that blue thermal shirt, which for the record, Rick did look very nice in.

Maybe more than very nice.

"France, Greece, Italy, Japan, China, Russia, Canada, Mexico, and all over the United States." Reciting the list made her tired. Had she really been to all those places? Why did it all seem like a dream? Why did the memories not seem like her own?

"What's the matter?" Rick asked.

"Nothing, why?"

"You look sad."

"I was thinking I don't travel for me. I go for work. Because someone told me I had to go in order to get a paycheck. My memories of those places are all about the resorts mainly. I mean, I went to the Eiffel Tower and it was great, but I don't remember what I ate there or what had to be a fantastic view of Paris. I don't have any photos that don't involve hotel construction. I remember Versailles Utopia and making rooms themed after famous painters." Lily exhaled a long breath. "None of those trips were vacations. None of them were personal."

Lily looked up to find Rick studying her. His pupils were huge, barely a ring of ocean blue surrounding them. She was caught in the depths of those pools. Suddenly *everything* felt personal.

Rick shook his head as if waking from a trance. He pulled his leg off the chair beside Lily, and a crease formed between his golden eyebrows. He tapped the laptop and said, “These are good. C’mon back to the sugarhouse, and I’ll show you how everything works.”

He used the table to stand, steadied himself, then hobbled toward the front door. “We’ll go out this way. If I know Aunt Joy, it smells like bleach back there.” He gestured to the door behind the pastry case.

“When does the store open?” She grabbed her laptop and purse and followed him. He held the door for her, and she had to pass him to get out. Being that close to him in the doorway felt… good. She may have lingered an extra moment, taking in that woodsy smell of him, trying to rustle up why she hated Vermont.

Poe squeezed between their legs, the coyote’s body brushing up against Lily. She squeaked and jumped outside. *Oh, right.* Reason number one to hate Vermont—ferocious creatures.

“She won’t hurt you.” Rick’s voice was low and right by her ear. “I promise.”

She nodded as the coyote pawed at something in the dirt. Then Poe got to her hind legs to sniff inside empty barrels at either side of the store’s front door. Lily had to admit the animal didn’t look like much more than an oversized dog.

Not that Lily was fond of dogs either, but when the coyote circled back and pushed her nose into Rick's outstretched hand, she did seem harmless.

"Come here, Lily." Rick pushed on Poe's rump until the coyote sat beside him.

Lily dropped her gaze, noticing she'd backed away from Rick and the coyote without consciously meaning to do so.

Keep my distance from that beast. And the man.

She shook her head. "I'm fine right here. Shouldn't we get going? We don't have a lot of time." She glanced at her watch.

"I think you need an intervention."

"An intervention? For what?"

In California, the folks she knew that needed interventions were usually addicted to drugs or alcohol or sex. Or all of the above. She never did drugs, only drank alcohol at galas, and sex… well, she was taking a break from that. Hard to remember why she was taking a break from sex as she watched Rick scratch that coyote's neck as if he knew his fingers were capable of bringing great pleasure.

"You've got an animal phobia, and while some animals are dangerous and caution should be used around them, my coyote does not fall into that category. I think you should start with her." He kneeled down beside Poe, wincing a bit as he adjusted his weight, and smoothed the fur around the coyote's cheeks. Poe's eyes closed, and she lowered her head to Rick's knee. "Come pet her."

A subtle pleading snuck into his eyes. Why did he care if she was scared of animals or not? It mattered to him. Lily could tell in the way he stared at her, in the way he held the coyote still.

She twisted the straps of her purse as she took a few steps forward. Her heart hammered in her chest, but her feet kept taking her closer to this man who insisted she touch his coyote. Now she hadn't heard a pick-up line like that before.

Hey, sweetheart, wanna touch my coyote?

Poe lifted her head from Rick's knee at the sound of gravel crunching beneath Lily's boots. Lily threw a glance around wondering how quickly she could make it to her Jeep should the coyote wish to eat her.

"Don't be nervous," Rick said. "Poe is gentle."

"Why is she named after a lunatic then?" Lily paused a few feet away.

"Edgar Allen Poe was a genius who I happened to be reading at the time I found her." Rick pushed Poe's bottom to the ground again. "Sit and wait for Lily to come to you, girl." He glanced up at Lily again. "C'mon. You said we don't have time to waste. Let's go."

"Insisting I make friends with her *is* wasting time. Why don't we hurry along to the sugarhut and get on with it?"

"Sugarhouse. And making friends with Poe is not wasting time. It's a first step." He didn't move from his position beside the coyote. No escaping this situation. She'd have to touch the mangy mutt.

"Fine." Lily clenched and unclenched her fists by her sides. She pushed her hair behind her left ear and closed the distance between her and Rick. She would have much rather have petted him, but that was not the invitation he had extended.

Taking in a breath and holding it, Lily walked around to the side of the coyote and extended a hand. Without making a sound, she let her fingers drop onto Poe's back then retreated a few feet.

Poe turned her head to watch Lily, but made no move to pounce on her. Didn't even make a noise or anything. Just blinked big, golden eyes. Beautiful eyes.

"See?" Rick said. "No growling, no bared teeth, no vicious attack on your person."

"Not right now anyway. It's still possible." Lily wiped her hand on her thigh.

"As long as you don't hurt Poe, she won't hurt you." He ran his hand along the coyote's back, and she lowered to her belly.

"I knew there was a catch." Lily increased the distance between her and the animal. Enough intervention for today.

"It's true of most animals," Rick said. "Even the wild ones. If they don't see you as a threat, they'll leave you alone. Animals don't go looking for trouble."

"Some of them do," Lily mumbled under her breath.

"What?" Rick asked.

"Nothing. Let's get to work." She jiggled her purse where she'd stowed her laptop.

"Okay." He let Poe lick his face while Lily watched, horrified. The coyote's teeth were practically grazing Rick's chin. Nothing but blond beard hairs to protect him from having a chunk of his handsome face taken out, but he didn't seem the least bit concerned. Lily didn't think she would ever understand that level of trust in an animal. She barely trusted the humans she knew that much.

Rick leaned his hand on the coyote as he tried to push to standing, but Poe kept moving in a small circle. Lily watched for a few moments wondering what her role was in this situation. Did Rick want help? Did he want it from her? Did she want to help him?

Yes. She did. *Shit.*

Lily crossed the small distance between them and gently nudged the coyote out of the way with her leg. Poe didn't put up a fight. Instead she licked Lily's fingers before running around the corner of the store toward the sugarhouse.

"Gross." Fresh slobber glistened on Lily's hand.

"It means she likes you." Rick accepted the other hand Lily extended to him.

"Wonderful. She better not expect a lick from me any time soon." Lily put her hand on Rick's elbow as he stood. She didn't let go until she was sure he was steady. Maybe she held on a few more moments, for precaution. Not because touching him made the sleeping dragon inside her uncoil from its slumber. Not because she could feel the toned muscles in his arm as she held it. Not at all.

"Thanks." Rick brushed some dirt off the knees of his jeans and rubbed his elbow.

Had her touch done something to him as well? He looked daydreamy for an instant before swooping his arm out in the direction of where Poe had gone. Lily headed that way and was aware of Rick shuffling closely behind her, one of his hands holding onto the buildings as they passed.

She focused on the plastic tubing spiderwebbing through the trees, connecting them.

"Is the sap running now?" She figured a work-centered question might get her back on track, because her body couldn't even find the track right now.

"Let's see." He diverted off the gravel pathway to the sugarhouse and went to the nearest tree with a tap in it.

Lily stayed on the path, holding onto her purse as if it were a parachute.

Rick studied her over his shoulder. "You won't be able to see from there, Lily. Come here."

Why does he keep asking me to come here? Especially when *here* meant next to animals or into the woods? *Better yet, why am I listening to him?*

Obediently, she came to stand beside Rick as he pointed to one of the plastic tubes. Clear fluid trickled inside and flowed to a larger tube.

"Guess that answers my question."

"The flow will get stronger soon. The temperatures for day and night are almost perfect." His eyes held an excitement as if he were watching magic or something. "The sap follows these tubes," he continued, "and gets dumped into storage tanks."

Rick led Lily to the sugarhouse. He unlocked the door and again allowed her to pass inside before him. Drew always went in first wherever they went. He liked to drag Lily along behind him as if she were his personal groupie. He complimented her often and wasn't afraid to spend loads of money on her, but the little things, like opening a car door and walking side by side, said a lot about how two people felt about one another.

Inside the sugarhouse, Rick turned on the lights, and Lily was impressed with the set up. Everything was sparkling clean yet still smelled like maple syrup.

"From the storage tanks," Rick pointed out the window where the tanks were located, "the sap goes to the evaporator, which is this." He pulled two large pans out of a machine to show Lily. "One is the flue pan, where the sap flows first. The bottom has flues to provide a greater heating surface. The second pan is the syrup pan."

"How do you know when the sap is syrup?" Lily pulled out her cell phone and began texting notes of what Rick was saying.

"We use a hydrometer to check the density," Rick said. "You have to be careful, because if the sap is cooked too thick, it'll crystallize. If it's cooked too thin, it'll ferment."

"What happens when the density is just right?" Lily peeked into a tank next to the evaporator.

"The syrup is drawn from the syrup pan and filtered here to remove sugar sand which develops during the boiling process." He tapped the tank beside Lily.

"Where does the heat come from?"

"I use a wood furnace, because I've got tons of wood here to burn. One cord of wood produces about twenty-five gallons of syrup. Other folks use oil, electricity, or natural gas, but wood has always worked for me."

That explained why the man smelled of freshly cut forest. Lily allowed herself a moment to picture Rick wielding an ax to split logs. For some reason he wasn't wearing a shirt while doing the chore. A lovely image.

He pointed to the ceiling of the sugarhouse where huge vents were evenly spaced out. "I've got a fan system that channels the steam outside. It gets pretty hot in here when the evaporator's running."

It's pretty hot in here now. The shirtless lumberjack vision refused to make an exit from Lily's mind.

"What do you add to the syrup?" Good. Some of her logical brain was still in charge. Lily got ready to type a list of ingredients she would no doubt have to ask Rick to spell.

"I don't add anything. Once the sap is boiled, it's syrup."

"That's it?" She looked up from her phone.

"That's it. Completely natural and the pancake's best friend."

"Oh, pancakes are my absolute favorite," Lily said, sighing a little. "I could eat them for breakfast, lunch, and dinner." She pressed her palm to her stomach, the mere thought of pancakes making her mouth water.

"I feel exactly the same way about pancakes," Rick said.

They had a moment of just looking at one another before Lily said, "In California, my grandmother and I went to Sasha's Bistro at least once a month. They have the best blueberry pancakes on the planet."

"But do they have Stannard Mountain Pure Vermont Maple Syrup to douse said best blueberry pancakes?" He leaned against the counter behind him.

"Sadly, no."

"Well, it's decided then. Lunch today is blueberry pancakes with *my* syrup. You won't be able to have any other syrup once you've tried it." He looked pretty sure of himself, and that confidence made Lily's inner dragon's eyes pop open. She was afraid if that dragon came all the way awake, there'd be no getting her back to sleep.

Rick reached behind him and pulled down a wooden rack with small bottles of syrup in them. "This shows the grades of syrup that can be made."

Lily set her purse down on the counter and stood in front of Rick. She leaned closer to get a better look at the syrup samples. "They're different colors."

Rick nodded. "These are Grade A." He pointed to the first four bottles in the rack. "They allow more light to pass than Grade B. We have Grade A Light Amber, which has a mild flavor. Grade A Medium Amber is fuller and darker. Grade A Dark Amber has a strong flavor. The strongest, Extra Dark, is used for cooking, and this last bottle shows Grade B."

"And your aunt and cousins use the syrup in things they make for the store?"

"Yep, they make maple sugar and maple cream, maple candies, cookies, cakes, breads. You name it, they'll try to cram some maple syrup into it somehow. The coffee is what keeps a steady stream of regulars coming in though."

"You sell books too?"

"Swap them. People bring in books and take books. That started out as my own obsession." Rick scanned the sugarhouse. "I think I've told you everything about how this place runs. Come to my cabin. I'll show you how unhealthy my love of books is. Hope and Sage should be finishing up with the pictures, and we can work on whatever it is we're going to come up with at my house."

The dragon's head was up now. A wing stretched out as Lily followed Rick to the door. Knowing she was about to see the inside of his home made her feel as if she'd passed a test. He didn't strike her as the type of guy who invited many people, let alone women, into his private quarters. What had she done to warrant such an invitation?

Tried to swipe his land. That's what she'd done. None of this made sense. Did Rick not truly believe that Utopia Resorts didn't take no for an answer? Was he that sure his home was safe?

Lily wasn't.

****

Rick couldn't understand why he had invited Lily to his cabin. Other than Hope, Sage, and Aunt Joy, who pretty much barged in whenever they felt like it, he never had guests. Guests tended to interrupt the quiet he loved so much. Guests required polite small talk and beverages and other social skills he lacked.

But there was Lily. Walking right beside him. Her fragrance made the woods smell like a drink that would be fun to consume, but leave you with one hell of a headache in the morning. Showing Lily around the sugarhouse had made talking to her easy. His throat was actually a little scratchy from explaining how everything worked. He never talked this much. He glanced at his watch and was amazed he'd managed a full month's worth of conversation before 10:00 a.m. A new record since being out of the city for sure.

He opened his front door and stood to the side to let Lily enter. He liked how she hesitated a moment every time he let her go ahead of him. As if she wasn't used to the simple courtesy. Didn't Californian men have manners?

He stepped into the house after Lily, and her cell phone rang in her purse. She let out a grumble as she rummaged around and extracted the phone.

After looking at the little blue screen, she said, "Not now," and tossed the phone back into her purse. A semi-scowl marched onto her face. "Drew. I talked to him this morning. Twice. I told him I was working on new designs. That I didn't think the deal was going to happen here. That a resort would ruin the landscape." She puffed out a breath and wandered a little deeper into the house. "He's not happy. Called me an environmentalist." She shrugged as she dumped her purse on the couch and sat next to it.

Rick liked the look of her in his living room. She made it appear cozy. "That's not a bad thing. Being an environmentalist." He sat in the recliner next to the couch.

"It is in the world I live in." She flopped back, letting her head rest on the back of the couch.

A week ago, Rick had considered that couch a prison while he had to stay off his ankle. Now he wanted nothing more than to sidle up next to Lily with one of his favorite books. He wanted her feet in his lap as he read her poetry by a blazing fire.

He wanted things he shouldn't.

She was so not in his league. No woman was. He'd chosen a life of uncomplicated solitude for a reason. That life had been working for him so far.

Lily's phone rang again in her purse. "I'm really pissing Drew off."

Rick was held captive by the slight smile on her lips. "Why do you look as if that pleases you?"

She gave him an innocent look he didn't buy for a second. "Maybe he deserves this treatment. He's always got everything under his control. I'm like this big wildcard right now." She waved her hands over her head. "We've done every project together. Now, I'm over here without him, suggesting a change in plans, and it's making him nervous. He should trust my professional judgment by now."

Lily leaned forward and rested her elbows on her knees. The movement caused the ruffled shirt under the red sweater to hang away from her chest. A tantalizing bit of cleavage exposed itself, and Rick had to quickly think of something else.

Of course, nothing else would come to mind but the tops of what had to be amazing breasts under that shirt.

Maybe they're fake. Californians were always making enhancements, weren't they?

Nothing else about Lily looked fake though. Her hair fell in natural curls about a face not hidden by tons of makeup. Her clothes were fashionable and probably expensive, but not flamboyant. No, Lily wasn't enhanced. She was simply the product of some marvelous DNA.

Her phone rang again, and Rick wanted to drop the damn thing into the pond on his property. How did people live with cell phones that constantly rang? His own was usually stuffed in a coat pocket but never on. Who would call him?

"I'm so going to get fired," Lily said.

"No," he said. "We're not going to let that happen, but just in case it does, what else are you good at?" *Driving men wild, perhaps?*

"Not much. I design hotels and watch movies. Lots of them. I suppose I could be a professional movie watcher." She sat back and took the magnificent view with her. "Do you do something else in the off season? Besides read." She got up to peruse the shelves. "Holy shit, there are a lot of books in here."

"When I'm not reading, I build barns." He limped to the shelves and pulled a photo album out. He handed it to Lily and deliberately sat on the couch instead of the recliner. He put his foot up on the chest in front of the couch and waited to see where Lily would sit to look at the album.

She opened it while standing at the bookshelves, and his experiment was foiled.

"Oh, my. These are gorgeous." Lily meandered back to the couch and sat so her back leaned against the armrest. She bent her left leg up onto the cushion that separated her from Rick and rested the album on that leg.

Interesting. She'd chosen the couch, but had put up a barrier between them. How hard would it be to remove that barrier? *And why the hell do I want to?*

"Did you study architecture?" Lily asked as she paged through the album. She ran slender fingers over the photos, and Rick loved the way she tapped a fingertip on certain aspects of some of the barns. The doors on one. The windows on another.

"Not formally," Rick said. "I took a few courses on building and design, but never went any further."

"You've got a real talent. These are amazing." She leaned over one picture—a barn he'd done in New Hampshire. The doors and windows had elaborate ironwork detailing around them. He'd enjoyed welding that design, and the customer had been thrilled with the finished look. "Maybe you want to give me your land and work for Utopia Resorts? They'd take one look at these and offer you a job on the spot."

"I just do barns. That's it." The mere thought of having to pump out hotels, assembly-line style, made Rick's hands sweat. He could take his time on the barns he built in the off-seasons and could say no to jobs if he felt like it. That eliminated a great deal of the stress. He also could work by himself, which allowed him to do things the way he wanted to.

"You have to make this difficult, don't you?" Lily said with a grin.

"You wouldn't respect me if I caved now." Rick returned the grin. He liked exchanging quips with her in his living room. Though they were still talking about taking his land away, the conversation had another layer now. Something he couldn't quite put a finger on simmered beneath their words.

"I would respect you. I promise." Lily held up her palm as if taking an oath then used that hand to turn the page of the album. Her blue-green eyes widened at the series of photos she found there. "Oh, this one is my favorite."

Rick slid a little closer, his thigh touching her knee on the cushion between them. He angled his head so he could see which barn she was viewing.

"That one is on Gail's property," he said.

"My grandmother's land has a barn?" Lily's brows furrowed above those dazzling eyes.

"Haven't you explored at all over there?" Why wouldn't she want to know all there is to know about that piece of paradise her grandmother had owned?

"No. I came here on a mission. A mission I'm failing at miserably."

But you're succeeding in other areas. Rick studied his hands, trying to ignore the tightening of… things… in his body as he sat this close to Lily.

"Where is the barn?" She studied the photos again, turning the album this way and that to see the barn from all angles.

"You know the path to the left of the house as you drive up?" Rick asked.

"Okay." Lily shook her head and shrugged.

"Jeez, Lily. Phase Two of your intervention. I'll show you the barn—and the path apparently—later."

"It has to be still light out. I'm not traipsing around outside in the dark." Lily's cheeks paled a bit, and her gaze cut into Rick. Man, she was so terrified of something out there.

"You ready to tell me why you don't like the woods or animals?" Rick couldn't explain this crazy need to help her get over her fears whatever the reason for them.

"You ready to tell me why you don't ever leave this place? Why you don't travel?" Lily asked.

"Guess we're still at an impasse," he said. "Okay, shall we strategize then?" He took the album from Lily's lap, closed it, and set it on the chest.

Some of the color had returned to Lily's cheeks as she dug out her laptop and her phone. "Can I ask you some business-related questions? I want to paint a picture of how much this land means to your livelihood."

He nodded. This land meant everything to his livelihood and not just in the financial sense.

"How long have you owned this land?" Lily's fingers sat poised over her laptop keyboard.

"It's been in the Stannard family for generations, but it's only been used for sugaring for the past ten years."

"That's it?"

"What were you expecting?"

"I don't know. That you came from a long line of maple syrup makers."

"No." Rick shifted away from Lily. He couldn't think clearly sitting that close. "My father was a mason, and my mother was a florist. They both died when I was eleven, so I didn't get a good look at either of those careers."

"Wow, eleven is young to lose both your parents. I'm sorry." Lily looked up from her laptop, an expression on her face as if she were picturing a parentless eleven-year old boy.

"Thanks. Plane crash. Took my uncle too. My father's brother, who was Aunt Joy's husband."

"Did Joy raise you?" Lily abandoned her laptop now, and her leg slid off the couch cushion. Her hand rested on that cushion instead, and dammit, Rick wanted to reach for it.

"Raised me right alongside Hope and Sage. Don't know where I'd be without Aunt Joy."

Probably in a psychiatric ward or six feet under the ground. He bristled at those thoughts.

"You're lucky to have her. I can tell she still looks out for you."

"Maybe too much sometimes." He gestured to his ankle. "She was all over me about staying off this for the first week. I was ready to kill her."

Lily laughed, and Rick wanted to hear that sound again and again. "What about your family? What's it like growing up around famous people?"

"It's a blast," she said. "My parents divorced when I was ten. My mom lives in Rhode Island, my dad in California. I opted to stay with him."

"Because Hollywood life suited you."

"That and because my mom didn't want me." Lily studied a chunky sapphire ring on the middle finger of her left hand. She wiggled it one way then twisted it back.

Rick imagined that rejection was almost worse than losing a parent to death. Knowing your mother *preferred* a life without you had to sting.

"Her loss," Rick said.

"Thanks." Lily drummed her fingers on the cushion. "Anyway, I stayed with my dad, and after about three years of him deciding being divorced wasn't the end of the world, he started seeing the actress Jeri Kappen."

"Also one of Aunt Joy's favorites. She stars in a lot of stuff with your father, right?" Good thing Aunt Joy loved Robert Hinsdale movies or else

Rick wouldn't be able to hold up his end of the conversation. He never watched TV or movies. He'd rather get lost in one of his books.

"They met while filming *Forever Rose* and have been together ever since. They're not married though. Dad says he's afraid it'll turn Jeri crazy and she'll leave him, but he knows she's around for good. They're a perfect match."

"And you spent time with Gail no doubt? I'll bet she adored you if she left you that masterpiece over there." Rick motioned out his living room window in the direction of Gail's property.

"I spent a ton of time with Grandma Gail, especially when Dad and Jeri were filming. She had her regular show, but that usually taped in the mornings. In the summer when I wasn't in school, I'd watch her tape, get to meet all the celebs, have lunch with them sometimes, then Grandma and I would 'do Hollywood' as she termed it."

Lily untied the belt at her waist and took off her red sweater. Rick fell instantly in love with the soft shirt she had on underneath. The ruffles around the neckline made him think of the past, very *Pride and Prejudice*.

"We'd shop on Rodeo Drive, meet friends for dinner, go to movie premieres. We had a ball."

She fell quiet for a moment, and when the first tear hit her jeans, Lily rubbed at it absently. When the others followed, Rick found himself putting an arm around her shoulders. She shook with crying, but didn't make any noise. Neither did he. This was the closest he'd been to a woman in forever. He'd never told any woman he'd dated in New York about his parents' death, and he'd certainly never asked a woman about her family.

But he wanted to know Lily. He wanted to comfort her.

She leaned into him as the tears continued to fall. "I'm sorry." Her voice was barely a whisper.

"Don't be." Rick brought a hand up and brushed her hair aside so he could see her face. "You're allowed to miss her, Lily."

"She used to call me Clone."

"I can see why." He let his thumb slide across her smooth cheek. "Though…"

Lily's eyes were bluer behind the unshed tears. "Though what?"

"You're prettier." Rick let his hand fall from her face, and her curls bounced back into position to rest at her cheek. "Yes, definitely prettier."

She sniffled and before Rick had time to realize it, he was leaning forward. Pressing his lips to Lily's. She didn't try to stop him. Didn't run away. Instead, she slid her hand up to his shoulder and pulled him closer. The heat of her lips reached every molecule of Rick's body. Chaste pecks turned to a deeper sampling of one another until he wasn't conscious of anything else but Lily.

Her other hand rested on his thigh and tightened as they continued to kiss. A small part of his brain cautioned that this could all be a tactic. A smooth ploy to get him to give up his land, but wasn't he the one who initiated the kiss? He admitted he didn't know Lily well, but something in the way she kissed him told him this wasn't a game.

But if it wasn't a game, what the hell was it?

Chapter Nine

Lily had no idea what she was doing, but damn, it felt right. Rick's kiss was gentle, but a silent demand played under the surface. She wanted to supply that demand. Give more. Take more.

Her hand slid up into his hair, and Rick pressed his lips against hers a little harder, more possessively. When his hand ran up her arm and rested in the curve of her neck, his skin all hot against her own, she caught his bottom lip between her teeth and tugged. This sent them both into another round of deep kissing. So deep. Lips, tongues, hands, all moving to a choreographed rhythm Lily didn't have to think about. Natural, instinctual. Magical.

Rick lowered her so her head was cradled by the couch's armrest. He pulled her legs into his lap with a quick sweep of his hands. After putting his arms to either side of her body, he rested his palms beside her shoulders on the cushion below her and looked at her for a moment. Instead of saying something as Lily thought he was going to, he bent his elbows and leaned over her. His lips grazed her jaw, and he paused between tentative nibbles to look her in the eye, to gauge her reaction. When she wrapped her arms around him, pressed him closer, he forged a more confident path from her chin down her throat.

Lily arched her body so more of it touched Rick's. She snaked her hands under his flannel shirt and traced her fingers along the muscles of his back, wanting the thermal shirt he wore to disintegrate so she could touch bare skin. Feel him. Know him.

Rick made a noise deep in his throat, and Lily's inner dragon spiraled into the sky, fully awake and hungry. So hungry. It had never been this way with anyone. Certainly not Drew. He was a great kisser. Skilled. Creative. But Rick's kiss lit a fire inside her. Wild and sizzling.

She angled her head to the side when Rick went exploring around the rim of her ear. Her eyes were closed, and when she opened them, two golden eyes encased in fur stared back at her. Poe's nose was mere inches from Lily's as the coyote sniffed the air between them. A short bark had Lily jumping and Rick pulling away.

"Jealous, Poe?" He pushed the coyote back, and Lily was able to breathe again. The coyote looked as if it were mere seconds away from deciding she didn't like what Rick was doing. Lily's mind wasted no time sketching in the gruesome details of the animal's retaliation to this offense.

Rick sat up and ran a hand through his tousled hair as he held Poe back with his leg. He peered down at Lily who wasn't quite sure if she should sit up or stay still. Which wouldn't unleash the coyote's fury?

"She's just curious," he said. "It's not every day Poe walks into the living room to find me kissing a beautiful woman."

"She looks like she wants me to leave." Lily gripped the back of the couch and slowly pushed to sitting, trying to move as little as possible, always keeping her gaze on the coyote.

"No, she doesn't want you to leave," Rick said. "Neither do I." He pointed to the rug in front of the fireplace and gave Poe a nudge. "Down."

Poe licked Rick's hand, evaluated Lily again then trotted to the rug. She lowered to the floor, sinking her head onto her paws. Golden eyes disappeared into a face of fur.

"I'm sorry if she startled you." Rick rubbed his hands down his thighs as he chewed on his bottom lip. "I forgot everything else but kissing you."

"Me too." Lily relaxed now that the coyote wasn't staring her down. "That ever happen to you before?"

"No. I don't ever let go enough to forget. You?" He swept his gaze over her face and settled on her lips. Did he want another taste? Lily sure as hell did.

"No one's ever been able to make me forget. I'm always thinking of a hundred other things, but just now there was only… only you."

Rick smiled. “Only us.” He pulled on one of Lily’s curls until it uncoiled and sprung back into place. “Why don’t we get those pancakes going? I’m suddenly ravenous.”

He stood, and Lily watched a flicker of pain scurry across his face as he took a step.

“Forgot how much that hurt too?” Lily got up and stood beside him.

“Yeah, so maybe you’ll kiss me some more later? For health reasons.” He arched a hopeful brow.

“Depends on how good the maple syrup is.” She passed him and headed for the kitchen. “You sit. I’ll make the pancakes. Tell me where everything is.”

Soon the small cabin smelled like hot coffee, warm blueberries, and maple syrup. Lily sat across from Rick at his kitchen table while he poured syrup on her pancakes.

“It’s important to get good coverage,” he said. “You don’t want to miss any spots.”

Rick had missed a couple spots when they had kissed. Maybe he could catch them in round two. God, would there be a round two? Should there be? Lily’s head swam with wild possibilities.

As she used her fork to cut into a pancake, her cell phone sounded from the living room. Again.

“You did say your boss was persistent.” Rick took a bite of his drenched pancake then sipped his coffee.

"Have I also said he can be annoying? Out loud, I mean. I know I've said it in my head on countless occasions." She popped the pancake bite into her mouth. The syrup transformed the pancake from mere breakfast food into a profound, life-changing experience. Was that true of everything in this little cabin?

"I guess my syrup meets your approval?" Rick said.

"More than. How did you know?" She wiped her mouth on the napkin she'd thrown across her lap. Fine dining habit.

"The sigh, followed by other yummy noises, clued me in." Rick paused in his eating to look at Lily.

"My God. Did I really do that? I didn't realize. Shit, this must be good syrup." She picked up the Mason jar that contained the amber delight. "Great label."

"Hope designed it. She made new ones for this year's batch. Similar style, but bolder colors."

"Where does this stuff get sold?" Lily took another bite and kept the approval quiet this time.

"All over New England."

"You ever think of branching out with this business?"

Rick put down his fork and slowly ran his napkin across his lips. He put his hands flat on the table, seeming to collect himself.

"I did branch out for a little while."

"In New York?" She knew she was inching onto dangerous ground—personal ground—but after kissing him she had this urgent need to know more about him.

He nodded. "I managed the business from there, while employees ran things here. We were churning out the goods and selling them over half the country. It went well for a little while, but the city didn't agree with me." He smoothed the front of his thermal shirt with his palm.

He was careful not to look at her while he talked. Lily took that to mean he'd said all he was going to on the matter. If Rick's feelings for the city were anything like her feelings for the woods, she understood. She so understood.

He refilled his coffee mug and angled the pot toward hers. "More?"

She slid her mug over to him and he poured. They ate in companionable silence until forks scraped against empty plates.

"A shame," Lily said, eyeing the blueberry-stained spots on her dish.

"But knowing more could be made another time is some consolation," Rick said. "You make a good pancake, Lily."

"You make a good syrup, Rick." Her gaze targeted his lips. *How good would that syrup taste off those puppies?* She looked away before she climbed across the table to find out. "Actually pancakes are the *only* thing I know how to make. Grandma Gail too. She taught me how." She didn't tell Rick that Grandma Gail also said a good pancake was better than sex.

"You don't cook anything else?" Rick asked.

"Not really. I go out to eat a lot for my job, and the hotel I live in has a restaurant on the first floor."

"And there's always room service, I guess." Rick's eyebrows crinkled together as if the thought of living the way Lily did made no sense to him.

"You're telling me you cook every night for just you?" Lily pictured him eating alone at this kitchen table and the image left her feeling cold.

"Not every night, but most I do. Sometimes Aunt Joy and my cousins are sniffing around, so I'll cook for all four of us. Or they bring me something. Or I go to their house."

Lily felt better hearing that he had his family. Had he ever had a woman who he cooked for or who cooked for him? He must have. There had to be a long line of women who wanted into his life. Where were they?

"Help me clean up?" Rick gathered the plates. "I think I have it in me to stand at the sink and wash, if you'll dry."

"I can do that." Lily grabbed the coffee pot and followed him to the sink.

He plugged the drain, turned on the hot water, and added soap. When the suds foamed, the words "bubble bath" flashed in neon colors in Lily's mind. Bubble bath with Rick, to be precise.

When he leaned against the counter and rolled up the sleeves of his flannel shirt, the movement captivated Lily. Like watching a striptease. As each inch of his forearm got uncovered, she wished for more.

What is wrong with me? She hadn't been this… this horny, ever. Sure, she hadn't had sex in a little while. She'd made a point not to lead Drew on anymore or use him. She'd said they were done being a couple and she'd meant it. Tried to stay true to it. She'd been okay with no sex too. Yes, Drew was good at it—skilled, in fact—but she didn't go into withdrawal or anything over not being with him anymore.

But right now? She wanted to tear into this quiet man who hated the city and considered wild animals pets. Rick was so incredibly wrong for her. He wasn't flashy, overconfident, worldly. But he was passionate. She had the sense that whatever he did, he gave it his all.

They fell into another easy rhythm as he washed and she dried. Once in a while, Lily's fingers touched Rick's as he handed her something. Each time they made contact, her stomach fluttered a little more. A mundane task like drying dishes should not have turned her on so much, but it did. Standing next to Rick in his homey kitchen, and not having to slouch to appear shorter, sent ripples of desire throughout her body.

Rick handed her the last mug and scooped up a handful of bubbles. He held them near her nose, and she went cross-eyed looking at them. “Anything else need washing?”

Before Lily could rip off her clothes and scream, “Yes! Me,” Sage and Hope spilled through the front door. Rick dropped his hand, leaving a few stray bubbles floating in the air.

“Hey, why does it smell like pancakes in here?” Sage paraded into the kitchen as she pulled off her gloves.

“We just finished lunch.” Rick let the water drain from the sink, but didn’t turn around.

“Oh, *we* did, did *we*?” Sage looked from Rick to Lily and narrowed her eyes.

She knows we kissed. Somehow Sage knew. Lily’s heart pumped overtime as she waited for Sage to say something else.

“We got some great pictures,” Hope said as she joined them in the kitchen. She was fiddling with Lily’s camera and oblivious to the tension in the room.

“And what did you two accomplish?” Sage smirked and studied Rick’s back.

“Lily’s got some new designs she’ll propose to her company,” he said, looking over his shoulder at Sage. “Why don’t you show them, Lily? I’ll be there in a minute. Just going to finish up in here.”

Lily got the distinct impression he didn’t want to move from the sink until his cousins were cleared out of the kitchen. Rick had an almost white-knuckled grip on the counter, and he was taking some deep breaths.

Sage hesitated then followed Hope who was headed for the living room. Lily leaned closer to Rick and whispered, “You okay?”

He watched Sage and Hope settle on the couch and huddle over Lily’s camera, reviewing the shots they’d taken. “Uh-huh. Just the thought of bubbles and you together may have overexcited me.” Rick swallowed and stared out the window over the sink. The corner of his mouth was turned up, but he wouldn’t look at Lily.

“You’re not alone in that department.”

She stretched out the dishtowel on the counter and retreated to the living room. Each step away from Rick quieted the stirrings inside her. With a little distance from him, she could think straight. Think about how they couldn’t actually be together. She had a life in California. A great life. One she’d spent a lot of years constructing, one design at a time. One resort at a time. One gala at a time.

She was having fun living that life. Exciting, rewarding, lucrative. She could buy whatever she wanted. Eat dinner in the fanciest of places. Hobnob with other successful people. She was busy. Didn’t have a lot of time to stop and think about what else she wanted.

Until now.

****

Rick listened to Hope and Sage talking with Lily in the living room while he counted to ten, twenty, thirty, forty.

Shit. He couldn't get the image of bubbles being the only thing Lily was wearing out of his head. He didn't use his tub often, but notions of having her naked body intertwined with his under hot, sudsy water made his penis feel like a rocket, ready to launch into unexplored territory.

"You can't stand here all day, dickhead," he mumbled.

He stared out the kitchen window and forced himself to think of the woods out there being cleared and a hotel being erected in its place. Rich tourists with their fancy cars zoomed by creating highway-like traffic where his simple dirt driveway now stood. Lounge chairs lined the pond at the front of his property, and empty wine glasses on tables glinted in the spotlights shining onto the water. Rick could hardly see the moon in this vision. The stars were muted too by the industrial brilliance the resort generated.

His woods were ruined.

Rick's jeans loosened once again. The need to defend his land and the wildlife it contained overpowered thoughts of Lily and sex. What had he been thinking anyway? Lily was not the woman for him. He couldn't provide the lifestyle she required. He had money, but none he wanted to blow on a relationship with Miss California.

Relationship? That was a joke too. Once she either abandoned the resort plans here in Vermont or—God, help him—managed to move forward, Lily would fly back to California where she belonged. She'd resume her fast-paced, high-stress life in the city, and he wouldn't be a part of that.

Couldn't be.

"Rick, get your ass in here," Sage called.

And get your head out of the clouds. He wiped down the kitchen counter and dropped the washcloth into the sink. He would have loved to walk confidently into the living room as if he hadn't kissed Lily in there. Kissed her and loved every minute of it, but the moment she looked up from hooking her camera to her laptop and smiled, his step wavered. It had less to do with his aching ankle and more to do with how that smile churned up waves of something in his chest. Good waves.

"Wait until you see, Rick." Hope got up from her seat next to Lily and motioned for Rick to take her spot. He fiddled with his pant leg, trying to get it to unbunch around the air cast and stalling over sitting beside Lily.

"These babies are National Geographic worthy," Sage said. "Come. Over. Here." She waved Rick over, and he was fresh out of evasive maneuvers.

Rick eased onto the couch and breathed in Lily's scent that now mingled with blueberries and syrup. He had a feeling she could roll around in moose shit, and he'd still like the smell of her.

He watched the screen as Lily pulled up the pictures and clicked through them. Patches of snow dotted the woods. Leafless maples mixed with needled pines stretched into the gray sky. Blue mountains, white-peaked and majestic, lined the horizon. He could almost smell the thawing land, the buds waiting to burst with life when spring came. His throat tightened at someone coming in and destroying even one pinecone of his haven.

"The next one is my fave," Hope said. She'd circled around to the back of the couch and leaned between Sage and Lily.

Lily clicked and shot to her feet at the photograph filling the screen. Her hands went to her chest, and her entire body trembled.

"I know," Sage said proudly. "Amazing, right?"

"That bear was just standing there by the water," Hope added. "Looked right at us, as if she were posing for a picture. She let us zoom in for a close-up. We should use this shot on our website, Rick. Beautiful, isn't she?"

"Lily?" Rick said.

She let out a little choking sound, and the next thing Rick knew, Lily was falling forward. He scrambled to the edge of the couch and grabbed her around the waist before she crashed down onto the chest. Rick pulled her onto his lap and cradled her head against his arm.

"Holy shit!" Sage slid the chest out of the way and kneeled in front of Rick.

"What happened?" Hope sat beside Rick and brushed Lily's hair out of her face. "God, Rick, she's as white as fresh snow."

"Lily?" He cupped her cheek, and her skin was clammy. She didn't stir at all in his lap. Totally out cold.

"I'll get a cold facecloth." Hope popped up and disappeared down the hall to the bathroom.

"Why did she pass out?" Sage grabbed Lily's wrist and felt for a pulse. "Jesus, her pulse is wild, Rick."

He felt for it too and agreed. He glanced back at the picture still on the laptop, his eyes connecting with the bear's. The creature was indeed beautiful, as Hope had said, but he could also see how it would be horrific.

For someone afraid of the woods.

Hope rounded the corner, toting a wet facecloth. She handed it to Rick, who slid back on the couch and positioned Lily more firmly in his lap. He knew he could easily press the facecloth to her brow if he slipped out from underneath her and laid her on the couch itself. But he didn't want to do that.

No, he wanted her close. He wanted her secure. He wanted her not to be afraid of anything. Of the woods. Of animals.

Of him.

"Lily." He folded the facecloth and rested it on her forehead. He moved it around to her cheeks, the back of her neck, and waited for her eyes to open.

"Should we call 911?" Sage asked.

"No," Rick said. "I think she just passed out."

"Because of a photograph?" Sage turned the computer so she could look at the bear.

Rick reached forward and slammed the laptop shut. Sage jumped a little at his movement. "Enough pictures for now."

"You told us to capture the magnificence of the woods, Rick." Sage stood. "It doesn't get more magnificent than that." She thrust her hand toward the computer.

Rick focused back on Lily in his lap. God, she was pale. Should he call 911? She wasn't hurt, but what if she…

He felt for her pulse again. It had slowed, but was that good or bad? His own pulse sped up.

"The pictures are great, Sage," he said. "I'm sorry. Thanks for taking them." He looked at Hope. "You too. Thanks."

Hope nodded, her cell phone in her hand and ready to call an ambulance.

"If she doesn't come to in the next few minutes, we'll call for help," Rick said.

His cousins lowered to their knees in front of him and watched Lily's chest rise and fall. Breathing. That was always a good sign.

"You think she's like you?" Sage asked.

"I sure as hell hope not." Rick continued moving the facecloth around Lily's face. "I wouldn't wish that on anyone."

Sage reached out and gave Rick's kneecap a squeeze. Their eyes met for a second, and Hope started to say something, but Lily's phone ringing in her purse stopped Hope.

Sage reached back to the chest and stuck her hand into Lily's purse.

"What are you doing?" Rick said.

"Whoever that is might know if Lily's got a condition we should know about." Sage flipped the phone on and said, "Hello, Lily Hinsdale's phone. Who's calling?"

Rick watched Sage, not sure if she was crazy or a genius, but almost certain Lily's boss was the caller.

"Well, Mr. Ashburn," Sage said, "Lily is indisposed at the moment. Tell me, does she pass out often?"

Rick rolled his eyes and held out his hand. "Give me that, will you?"

Sage shrugged and handed the phone to Rick. "I don't like this guy."

"Shhh." Rick took the phone and put it to his ear, not sure of what was going to come out of his own mouth. "Hello. Rick Stannard here. Lily is—"

"Where's Lily?" a deep male voice said. "Is she all right? What did you do to her?"

"We didn't do anything to her. Lily passed out after looking at some photographs," Rick said. "Why is she afraid of bears, Mr. Ashburn?"

A short laugh filtered through the phone. "Bears? What are you talking about? How long has Lily been out?"

"Not long." He shifted Lily in his lap and she mumbled something. "Actually, she's coming around right now, I think."

"Good. Tell her Drew called, and I'm calling back in fifteen minutes. Make sure she answers the damn phone. I've been trying to reach her all day." Drew paused. "Has Lily been with you all day, Mr. Stannard?"

"Rick. Yes, I showed her how my maple syrup business runs. You know, the business your company wants to destroy."

"I knew it," Drew said. "I knew Lily wasn't going against the proposed resort for Vermont on her own. She's never been against any of the resorts. Always completely on board. We've gotten along well together. For years. And not just at work." Drew stopped, and Rick assumed the guy was giving him time to get the not so subtle hint that Lily was his.

Funny, she didn't kiss as if she belonged to anyone.

"I thought maybe because part of it was going on her grandmother's property that she was having second thoughts, getting sentimental maybe," Drew continued. "But it's you, Mr. Stannard, isn't it?"

"If you're accusing me of fighting for my home, my land, and my business, then yes, it's me.

It's all me. You can't expect folks to give up their lifestyles for the benefit of your resorts." Rick had never met this Drew guy, but he didn't like him. Not one bit. He sounded like a real bastard.

"Tell Lily I called." Drew hung up before Rick could reply.

Rick handed the phone to Hope who dropped it back into Lily's purse. He gave the facecloth to Sage and pressed his hand to Lily's cheek, which wasn't so clammy anymore. Her cheeks were still pale, but her pulse felt normal.

"Lily, can you hear me?" he said.

She moaned and opened her eyes, blinking several times, before Rick thought she recognized him. Lily turned her head and looked at Sage and Hope who both waved at the same time, goofy smiles on their faces. She brought her hand up to her forehead and focused back on Rick.

"Did I pass out?" she asked.

"Dropped like a rock," Sage said.

Rick glared at Sage who bit down on her lower lip. "I caught you before you fell onto my coffee table. Do you feel okay?" Forgetting his cousins were right in front of him, he traced an index finger down Lily's cheek and her eyes closed again.

"I'm okay."

She opened her eyes and tried to sit up. Rick helped her, but if he were being honest, he would have been perfectly content to sit with her in his lap all night. Maybe longer.

She scooted off him and swung her feet down to the floor. Rubbing her temples, she said, "I do have a screaming headache though."

"I'll get you some aspirin." Hope got up and pulled Sage to her feet. "Come help me, Sage."

Rick picked up on Hope's unsaid message to her sister. She was trying to clear out so he could have a moment alone with Lily. Not that he needed one.

He didn't.

As soon as they were gone, Lily turned to face him. "I'm sorry about that. The photo caught me by surprise."

"The bear scared you." Rick rested his hands in his lap where warmth from Lily's body lingered. "Why?"

She pressed down on her closed laptop as if the bear might come tearing out of the machine. She moved away from the computer and huddled in the corner of the couch, her arms wrapped around her body.

"Lily, tell me what's wrong." Rick wanted to touch her, but got the sense if he did, she would pack up her stuff and run out of his house. That was the last thing he wanted.

She shook her head and ran her hands over her face. "Nothing's wrong. I'm okay now. Let's just forget it." Lily looked to the hallway. "Where are they with the aspirin? I need it like right now." She pressed two fingers to her temple and squeezed her eyes shut.

Sage and Hope tripped over each other as if they had been pressed against the wall in the hallway. Listening. The rats.

"Here's the aspirin." Hope handed Lily two white pills and a glass of water while Sage flopped into the recliner.

"An adult beverage would probably take the edge off better, Lily," Sage said. "Come out with Hope and me tonight. We're heading to Black Wolf Tavern. You can talk to some locals about the area."

"Yeah, come," Hope added. "We promise there won't be any b-e-a-r-s there."

Rick watched as Lily considered the invitation. When she glanced his way, he got a feeling in his stomach that teetered between excitement and dread.

"Will you come too?" Lily asked Rick.

Sage and Hope burst into laughter. "Now that's a good one," Sage said.

Rick ground his teeth together and thought seriously about throwing Sage out on her ass.

"Rick doesn't make regular appearances at Black Wolf Tavern," Hope said.

He wouldn't mind kicking Hope out too.

"He doesn't make a habit of mixing with the rest of the humans." Sage swung a leg over the armrest of the recliner and played with the end of her long blond braid.

"I'll go," Lily said, "if you go." She poked a finger into Rick's upper arm and electric shocks jolted through his body at the contact. "The way I figure it, I owe you a drink for not letting me crash land on your coffee table."

Rick was aware of Sage and Hope volleying their gazes between Lily and him as if they were witnessing something they'd never seen before. He supposed they were. How many women had asked him to go to a bar before Lily?

Zero.

How many invitations would he consider accepting?

One.

Chapter Ten

Lily stared at the ceiling as she lay on her grandmother's bed, willing her headache to go away. She kept seeing that photograph in all its terrifying detail. God, that bear looked as if it wanted to rip her to shreds. Teeth, claws, muscle. And to think Hope and Sage actually stood in front of the damn thing long enough to take pictures! A full body shudder rippled through her, and she pulled the quilts up to her neck.

"C'mon, just a couple hours of shut eye."

On the TV Nicholas Cage peered through a funky pair of bifocals to read the secrets on the back of the Declaration of Independence in *National Treasure.* "Just one hour. Enough to get rid of this headache and gear up for Black Wolf Tavern."

She couldn't believe Rick had agreed to meet her there. Part of her still thought he might not show up. He'd had such a deer-in-headlights look on his face when she'd ask him to join them. It made him extremely kissable, but Hope and Sage were playing audience and way too interested in what was unfolding for Lily to lean forward and taste his lips. Again.

But, shit, she wanted to.

Her mind jumped to being in Rick's lap. She may have pretended to be out cold a little longer than was necessary just to enjoy the feel of his thighs beneath her, his arm cradling her head, his hand on her cheek. A dirty trick while he was obviously concerned about her, but being in his lap was the closest to secure she'd ever felt. As if no wild animals could touch her. No silence could drown her.

No boss could threaten to fly to Vermont.

She'd answered her phone as she drove from Rick's over to Grandma Gail's place. Drew launched right into a jealous-infused wrath.

"What the hell is going on over there, Lily? You passed out?"

"A photograph caught me by surprise."

"You need to close this deal and come home. What's this Stannard guy doing to hold up the works?"

"He's trying to protect what belongs to him. Doesn't that make sense?"

"What? Are you on *his* team now? What happened to Utopia's team? My team?"

Lily had no trouble picturing Drew's expensive shoes pacing back and forth across his spacious office. "I'm still part of those teams, Drew, but Rick has a point, and I'm not feeling it over here. This isn't the right spot."

"It was the right spot a few days ago." Drew huffed. "You're not telling me everything."

"I'm telling you everything that concerns you, Drew." Lily didn't want to lie to him, but she wasn't going to offer up the fact that she'd shared a more than steamy round of kissing with Rick. Or the fact that she wanted more rounds.

"What's that supposed to mean? Did you fuck him?" Drew went absolutely silent on the other end. Lily couldn't hear any normal office background noise either. Nothing.

In that silence, her anger multiplied.

"Number one, how incredibly rude of you," she said. "Number two, you are my boss, Drew. Not my boyfriend, not my husband. We can both do whatever we want to do."

"That's not true," Drew said. "I can't do what I want to do. I want to do you, but you're over there screwing lumberjacks in the mother-fucking woods."

"I am not."

"I'm coming there."

"There's no need. I'll send you my new designs for an Arctic Utopia. I think Rita and Webster will love them, plus I'm working on a brief presentation about this area to showcase why it's not the right one for a resort. I'm going to wrap it up tonight and tomorrow and be back to Cali on Saturday. Sunday at the latest. It's all going to work out. Trust me."

Lily was impressed with her ability to sound so logical, when all she really wanted to do was hang up. How dare Drew accuse her of shacking up with Rick? She barely knew the man. Wasn't even sure why she had ended up kissing him today. Besides, sleeping with Rick would be a huge mistake. Huge.

"What about Gail's property?" Drew said.

"Rick wants to buy it. He's got lines in the trees over here to gather sap so unloading it to him makes sense."

"Whatever Rick wants, huh?" Drew sounded like a sulky child.

"I'm trying to do what's right for everyone. Mr. Stannard, me, Utopia, you."

"In that order too."

"Stop it." By this time, Lily had pulled in front of her grandmother's house. "I'll send you the designs. You'll like them. I promise. Got to run. I need to lie down. Got a banging headache from passing out."

"Where are you now?" Drew's way of asking if she was still with Rick.

"I'm running from the car to my grandmother's house." She scanned the woods nearby and caught sight of the path Rick had mentioned that led to the barn she'd seen in his album. Maybe tomorrow she'd go take a look. Convince Hope or Sage to go with her.

Not Rick. Time alone with Rick had proven to be risky.

"Be careful, Lily," Drew said. "Not just of the woods."

"Will do." She hung up as she unlocked the front door and went inside.

Now, she blinked over eyes gone dry from staring at the ceiling. How had things gotten so messy? This trip was supposed to be quick. Arrive, buy Rick's land, turn his property and Grandma Gail's over to Utopia, and finish designing the new resort. Boom, boom, boom. Simple. Like every other project had been. Why was this one so different? Why didn't she feel as if she were in control? How could she get control back?

Deciding she would attempt to get the upper hand this evening, Lily rolled to her side and closed her eyes, but it was no use. Sleep wasn't coming. Not now, but her headache did feel better. The aspirin was working and maybe being in the darkened bedroom had helped. A bubble bath might do the trick if she could manage not to picture Rick holding bubbles out to her as he had in his kitchen.

She slid out of the bed and padded to the master bathroom. She flicked on the lights, immediately squinting in their brightness. Too much. Her headache came pulsing back right behind her eyes. She shut off the lights and twisted open the blinds on the three huge windows in the bathroom. Personally, Lily didn't like windows in the bathroom. Her penthouse back in California had a mirrored wall in the bathroom instead, which she preferred, but the soft, late afternoon light that spilled into this bathroom was just right for her eyes.

She filled the tub with hot water and suds and removed her clothes. Lily gathered her hair up into a loose bun at the crown of her head and slid into the water. A sigh escaped from her throat as the bubbles covered her, all her muscles relaxing in the heat. She'd turned up the volume on the TV, and the actor's voices still reached her. Still provided her company and escape.

Lily closed her eyes and envisioned her penthouse tub, far away from the woods, the wild, and men who made Vermont seem habitable.

"Yeah, right. As if you could stand to live here, silly."

She burrowed deeper into the grapefruit-scented froth and tried not to think about the way Rick's lips had felt forging a trail down her neck. The way his short beard tickled her skin. The way his blue eyes said things his mouth wouldn't.

Lily tapped her fingers along the rim of the tub as she realized if Rick didn't come to Black Wolf Tavern tonight, she'd be disappointed.

Damn.

Forty-five minutes later, Lily ferreted around in her suitcase. Maybe she should have hung up her clothes. Things were getting wrinkled. She shook out a pair of dark blue jeans and slipped her pruned feet into them. The bath had done wonders for her, but a nervous something shook her stomach. She told herself seeing the bear had rattled her, but she knew that wasn't it. Not that kind of nervous. Not a bad nervous. More like an excitement, maybe. She refused to believe it had anything to do with possibly seeing Rick this evening at the tavern.

Still, she took some extra time picking out a fitted, powder blue, cashmere sweater with a deep V-neckline. One that made her breasts look perky and approachable.

Lily set her hair free from its bun and shook out the curls. A few finger-combs through and the strawberry blond coils fell into place. She touched up her makeup, not using much besides a little copper-brown eye shadow and black eyeliner. She stood back and inspected herself in the full-length mirror in the master bedroom. The overall look was well constructed, but something was missing.

Returning to her suitcase, Lily poked around in the accessories she'd brought along. All of it screamed California, so she wandered to her grandmother's walk-in closet and turned on the light. The room—yes, it was more a room than a closet—was stuffed to overflowing. Sweaters all neatly folded on shelves. Pants hanging on a rod between heavy coats and flannel.

"Grandma Gail, you actually owned flannel?" Lily fingered the sleeve of a green and gray checkered shirt and shook her head. Looking in the closet was like finding artifacts of an unknown species. After her "incident" in Vermont, Lily supposed she stopped acknowledging her grandmother owned this place and had clothing appropriate to the area. All of Lily's fond memories of Grandma Gail involved party dresses and fine fabrics and lots of people. This closet suggested her grandmother had a whole other life Lily had spent years ignoring.

How had Grandma Gail felt about that? Nothing was ever said to Lily about her phobia of the woods, but her grandmother wasn't one to push. That's what had made her so wonderful. Lily never had to feel uncomfortable around her. She could be Lily with all her neuroses, and Grandma Gail wouldn't try to change her, cure her.

She heaved in a deep breath and turned in a circle in the closet. Her gaze settled on a series of colorful scarves hanging on pegs on the back wall like a rainbow. She riffled through them until she found one swirled in shades of blue with shimmery silver specks. The material was crinkled cotton with a thready fringe along the ends. Lily slid it off its peg and looped it around her neck, inhaling a scent that didn't quite smell like the Grandma Gail she knew.

She went back to the mirror and studied her reflection again. Perfect. The scarf toned down the pomposity of the cashmere. Made Lily appear a little less flashing lights and Hollywood and a little more cow pastures and dirt roads. Lily wasn't sure why that pleased her. Maybe because it would have pissed Drew off.

After checking the time, she grabbed her purse and made sure her phone was inside. She had to remember that tonight was about observing and talking to the locals as much as about unwinding a little with Hope and Sage.

She wasn't going on a date. If Rick showed up, fine. She'd buy him that drink and that would be that. If he didn't come, no big deal. She'd still buy him a drink but consume it herself. In his honor.

Always good to have a plan. One that made sense and didn't fall apart with a few kisses.

****

"You really going to go?" Aunt Joy asked as she shoveled vegetable lasagna onto a plate and handed it to Rick. She'd invited him over for dinner and once she'd said lasagna was on the menu—even a healthy veggie one—he couldn't refuse.

Hearing the disbelief in his aunt's voice helped him make the decision he'd been wrestling with since Lily had left his house. "Probably not."

"But Lily's expecting you, isn't she?" Aunt Joy filled his glass with cranberry juice and sat across from him. She picked up her fork and cut into her lasagna.

"I suppose, but what do I care?" Rick shrugged. He didn't care. Lily wasn't anybody to him. In fact, she was causing him problems he wouldn't have had if she'd never shown up in Vermont. His land was in jeopardy and kissing her had been a brainless move. It didn't feel like it at the time, when her lips were soft against his, but now that he'd had a chance to step back and view the whole encounter, he knew it was pure foolishness.

"You don't care, huh?" Aunt Joy raised an eyebrow as she wiped the corners of her mouth with her napkin. "Could have fooled me, sugar. I think you see something you like about Miss Hinsdale." She arrowed her fork at him.

"I think you're a crazy old woman," he said. "You'd better be careful talking like that, or I'll be forced to send you to a facility."

Aunt Joy bunched up her napkin and threw it at Rick. He leaned to the left in time for the paper ball to sail past him.

"I'm not crazy, but you might be. You understand that a gal like Lily won't hang around here for long, right?" Aunt Joy said.

"No, she'll be on the quickest flight out as soon as she can. She's got a real phobia of the woods and wild animals. Think it's got something to do specifically with bears after her reaction to the photo Hope and Sage took."

"That's a great photo," Aunt Joy said. "Wonder what happened to make Lily so afraid?"

"Whatever happened made an impression. I never saw anyone pass out like she did." And he'd never been so compelled to help someone like he had been with Lily. Had to be because he loved the woods and animals and wanted everyone to feel the same. It had nothing to do with Lily in particular. Anyone with her reaction to wildlife needed to see there weren't any reasons to be so frightened. Sure, wild animals could be dangerous, but as he'd told Lily, mostly they wanted to be left alone.

Just as he did.

He had no desire to have a woman in his life who would be jabbering on all the time about stuff he didn't care about. Fashion, theater… God, he couldn't even imagine the things Lily probably liked to talk about. Rick liked doing what he wanted, when he wanted to. He didn't have to consider anyone else's needs but his own. And Poe's, but she was easy to take care of. Lily would not be. Rick could tell. If she did stay in Vermont, she'd be bored and complaining before he could blink an eye.

She needed to be boxed up and shipped back to California. Pronto.

"Maybe if you did go tonight," Aunt Joy started, "you could get Lily a little buzzed, and she'd tell you what happened between her and the bears."

"That would be sneaky and dishonest, Aunt Joy," he said, but the notion did have him wondering if Lily relaxed enough, would she spill her secrets? Would he spill his?

No way. He shook his head as he chewed his lasagna. He would not unload his tale of woe on Lily. She didn't need to know what he'd been through. It wasn't any of her business. She could be afraid of the woods. He could be afraid of the city. There'd be balance in the world.

Hope came into the kitchen and sniffed the air like a wolf. "Lasagna? I want some."

"C'mon over," Aunt Joy said. "I've set a place for you. Where's Sage?"

"She'll be around in a minute." Hope walked to the table, and Rick noted the sprucing up she'd done. Her blonde hair was brushed to shining and hanging straight down her back, angled bangs framing her face. She wore dark jeans and a black, corduroy blazer with a silver camisole underneath. Large, silver hoops gripped her earlobes, and a trio of silver bangles jingled on her wrist.

This was "stepping out for the night" Hope. The only hint left of his casual, pastry-baking, website-building cousin was the lime green socks she had on. Rick knew she'd slide boots on over those crazy socks, but he couldn't help smiling at that little bit of child-like fun she managed to hang onto when clearly she planned to "hunt" men tonight.

When Sage joined them, the predator image screamed loud and clear. Like Hope, Sage's hair had been straightened and fell like a blonde curtain about her face. Though there was a year between the sisters with Sage being the older, they looked like twins. They had the same triangular face with small noses and full lips. The big difference was in the eyes. Hope had deep brown eyes that showed how compassionate she was. Sage, on the other hand, had bright green eyes, like green fire, that suggested something electric about her.

Sage wore army green cargo pants that rode low on the waist. A black T-shirt hid beneath a short, denim jacket. A long string of pearls looped and knotted around her neck adding a touch of female to the otherwise military ensemble.

"Don't you girls look nice?" Aunt Joy got up to pour her daughters' drinks.

"Well, we don't get out much, Mom," Hope said.

"So when we do, we gotta make it count," Sage finished. "Besides, with Lily along we're sure to attract a crowd. The guys will be all interested in the new meat, but they'll stay to sniff around us." Sage gestured between her and her sister.

Rick tightened his grip on his fork. *New meat.* As in every guy in the tavern would be checking Lily out, flirting with her, trying to get their cow-manured paws on her.

Suddenly the lasagna didn't taste that great.

"I hope the guys are playing tonight," Hope said. She meant the local band, Shadow Hills, which called Black Wolf Tavern home most nights. Two of the five-piece band had gone to high school with Rick and if he were to be forced to call anyone in the vicinity friends, they'd be the ones. He'd had a few beers with them in the past, played a little guitar with them when they were practicing. For laughs. Nothing serious.

He'd been able to play the guitar since he first picked one up at the age of thirteen. No lessons. No reading music. Just strumming the strings in a way that sounded right to him. His middle school and high school music teachers had been amazed at the rare talent, encouraging Rick to pursue a career in music, but he hadn't had an interest in it more than fooling around. Performing was so… public.

"You want the guys to be there so you can get an eyeful of the drummer," Sage teased her sister.

Hope's cheeks shot to pink. "That is so untrue."

"That is fact, Hope. Don't deny it." Sage took a swig of her drink. "The way you ogle Sam Pearsson is embarrassing."

Hope looked down at her lasagna and shrugged. "I'm still thinking about how I feel about him."

Did she really have a thing for the drummer? Rick didn't know him, but the thought Hope might like him had Rick wanting to run an FBI check on the guy. Though his cousins annoyed the shit out of him most of the time, they were like sisters to him. He wouldn't want either of them to get involved with the wrong guy.

Maybe I need to go tonight. To protect Hope and Sage. Lord knew by the way they were dressed they'd cause a commotion at the tavern. They'd turn heads, and those same heads would be checking Lily out too.

Rick pushed his plate aside, all sense of appetite abandoning him.

"What's the matter, sugar?" Aunt Joy asked. "Something wrong with my cooking tonight?"

He shook his head and stood. He was getting better at steadying himself on the air cast and didn't have to wait so long before taking a step. "Full is all." He finished his cranberry juice and took his dish and glass to the sink. After scraping the remains of his dinner into the garbage, he settled the dish in the water Aunt Joy already had for washing and searched for the washcloth under the suds. Again a vision of Lily's body glistening with bubbles flashed in his mind and his man parts tightened.

"Leave those be, Rick," Aunt Joy said. "I'll get at them later."

"Yeah, Rick," Sage said. "Shouldn't you be running on home to get changed for your big night out amongst the living?"

"He hasn't decided if he's going yet," Aunt Joy said.

Rick turned around from the sink in time to see the smirk on his aunt's face. As if she didn't believe for one moment he wasn't going to go to the tavern. That twisted his boxers.

"I said probably not." He studied the mud stains on his exposed sock. God, he missed being able to wear two work boots. "I should stay off this for tonight. I've done too much walking today."

"You weren't walking when you had Lily in your lap," Sage noted.

Hope let out a quiet giggle then bit her lip to stop herself. Aunt Joy appeared to be suppressing a laugh too. He didn't need this crap.

"Thanks for the lasagna." He shuffled to his aunt, dropped a kiss on her cheek, and arrowed glares at Hope and Sage. "Stay out of trouble tonight."

"Who us?" Sage said.

"We don't get into trouble." Hope batted her eyes innocently.

"But we can't be responsible for what Lily will do. She told us about some of the galas her company has. Sounds as if she knows how to party," Sage said.

Hope held out a hand to Sage and they high-fived over the table. "We're finally going to have some fun." She clapped her own hands together in excitement.

"The question is," Sage began, "will Rick choose to have some fun?"

"He deserves to," Hope said.

He was getting irritated at the way they talked as if he weren't still standing there.

"Rick knows what's best for him," Aunt Joy said. "Leave him be." She stood and patted Rick's cheek. "Use your head, sugar."

"Always do." He kissed his aunt again and left through the front door. "What else would I use?" he asked as he climbed into his truck.

His head was always in charge. Always keeping him focused and calm. Healthy.

No, he couldn't get mixed up in complicated things, and Lily Hinsdale was guaranteed to be a complicated thing.

As he drove to his place, he purposely didn't look at the driveway leading to Gail's property. He tried to persuade himself that Hope and Sage knew how to take care of themselves in a bar full of testosterone.

He tried to convince himself he didn't want to see Lily tonight.

Chapter Eleven

Lily climbed out of Sage's car and immediately her boots sank into mud. The wet squelch of it made her long for the dry sidewalks of La Jolla. She'd taken the pretty patterns of red brick, pebbled concrete, and gray pavers for granted. A stroll past the bubbling fountains or the geranium pots hanging from the lampposts along the streets of her hometown would be a welcome activity right now.

She looked down at her soiled boots—her favorite black leather ones with the lace up backs that, lucky for her, had come in a flat heel. She'd probably never completely rid those boots of Vermont residue. Sigh.

Sage hooked her hand around Lily's elbow and steered her toward the wide wooden door of Black Wolf Tavern. Not much more than a rectangular barn painted hunter green and adorned with a carved sign announcing its name, the bar boasted a full parking lot. Lily wished her California friends could see her. They'd laugh their surgically-maintained asses off.

"I love this jacket, Lily." Hope fell into step on Lily's other side.

"Thanks." She had slipped her short, black leather coat over the sweater and scarf combo, transforming the look into something close to biker chick. Was it the right look? How would she know? She had no idea what to expect behind the doors of Black Wolf Tavern.

"I love the hair on both of you," Lily said. "I could never get mine that straight."

"Wouldn't bother going straight on you," Sage said. "Rick likes curly hair."

She was about to protest that it didn't matter to her what Rick liked, but as soon as Sage opened the door, music spilled out. Half country, half rock. An interesting sound. Hope let out a squeal then slapped her hand over her mouth.

"Told you!" Sage reached around Lily to grab onto Hope's arm. "You so want the drummer!"

"Okay, shut up." Hope grinned. "Sam is someone my age and he's so sexy beating those drums."

"Play your cards right, and maybe he'll beat *your* drums." Sage wiggled her eyebrows, and Lily laughed along with them as she scanned the inside of the bar. Wood-paneled walls lined the interior. A giant moose head hung on the far wall. Opposite that, a bar topped with a chunky half-log was lined with black stools. Behind the bar was a huge mirror with the silhouette of a wolf howling at the moon painted on it. A grisly sort of looking fellow also populated the area behind the bar and Lily figured he was the owner, Jake. Pool tables and dart boards were in the back corner. A spattering of booths and tables and a small stage where the band was set up finished off Black Wolf Tavern.

A place like this wouldn't stand a chance in La Jolla.

"Did Rick say if he was going to stop in?" Lily hoped she didn't sound too interested. When the girls had arrived at her grandmother's place sans Rick, her enthusiasm fizzled a bit.

"Funny how the phrase 'maybe he'll beat your drums' has Lily asking about Rick, isn't it, Hope?" Sage said over her shoulder as she led the way into the bar.

"Very funny," Hope agreed.

"I didn't mean… I just…" Lily sputtered.

"Right." Sage patted Lily's arm.

"Sure." Hope lifted to her toes and squeezed Lily around the shoulders.

Lily grumbled to herself as she followed Sage. Several hellos emerged from the crowd as the three of them weaved toward the bar. She felt eyes on her from every corner of the tavern.

The locals smell an outsider. Maybe animals weren't the only predators in these Vermont woods.

"First drinks are on me," Sage said. "What'll you have, Lily?"

"A soda to start." She rolled her shoulders and tried to relax. *There is nothing to be afraid of. There is nothing to be afraid of.* "I need to be sober to spark up some conversation with these people. I'm working, remember?" Yes, work. That was why she was here. The only reason she was here.

"Okay." Sage checked her watch. "You get thirty minutes to work." Her smile widened. "Then we play."

"Fair enough." Lily could compromise. Truthfully, she missed partying. This definitely wasn't going to be Hollywood-caliber merry-making, but it was something. She could have a good time and it was certainly better than spending the night in her grandmother's house wondering what bloodthirsty creatures stalked her from the woods.

Sage flagged down Jake and ordered wine for Hope, a beer for her, and Lily's soda. The three of them settled at a table in the middle of the bar where they had a good view of the band, and the drummer had a good view of Hope. Lily had spied the drummer, a well-muscled dude with shoulder length brown hair reminiscent of the 1980s, giving Hope the eye. A casual "Hey, there" mixed with a panicked "Oh, my God, you're here" glance. Cute, very cute.

Lily looked around, trying to target someone she should talk to. Her general strategy was to chit-chat, get a sense of the type of people who called Vermont home. She didn't want to ask them directly about a Utopia Resort in their backyards. If their reactions were anything like Rick's, she'd only create an uproar.

And where was Rick? He'd said he'd come, and now he'd backed out. Guess that deer-in-headlights look wasn't just a look. She'd driven right over him with her invitation. She shrugged. No big deal. The less she saw Rick, the better.

You're working. If she kept saying it, she could focus.

As Sage and Hope chatted with some friends of theirs, Lily sipped her soda and engaged in some people watching. An older couple sitting in a corner booth caught her attention. They looked as if they were permanent fixtures in the bar in their matching denim jackets. Comfortable regulars.

After Hope and Sage's friends left, Lily said, "Those two over there?" She pointed to the couple bent over beers and pretzels. "Would they be good to talk to?"

Hope craned her head to see between the other patrons. "Harry and Marsha Frideway?" She let out a little chuckle. "Yes, they'd be great to talk to."

"You'll need a signal though," Sage said as Hope nodded.

"A signal? For what?" Lily slid off her jacket and hung it on the back of her chair as Hope and Sage had already done. She dug her phone out of her purse.

"Once you sit with them, they will talk until the sun rises," Hope said.

"And sets, then rises again," Sage added. "Roll up the sleeves of your sweater when you want one of us to rescue you."

"Okay." Lily stood and maneuvered through the crowd. She was a full head taller than most of the patrons and had the urge to sit as soon as possible. Now that she thought about it some, why hadn't Hope and Sage remarked about her height? Surely, they had noticed when walking on either side of her. Maybe they were just being nice. That was a change. Most new people immediately reacted to her six-foot elevation above sea level. Lily decided she liked Hope and Sage a little more for keeping their comments to themselves.

As she approached the booth, Marsha looked up. The woman offered Lily a cherry of a smile and said, "You're new."

"I am. Would you mind if I asked you a couple questions about the area. I'm interested in Vermont." White lie, but for a good cause.

"Sure," Harry said. "Take a load off." He slid over making room for Lily on his side of the booth.

"Thank you. I'm Lily."

"Harry, and this is my beautiful wife, Marsha." Harry beamed sunshine as he looked Marsha's way. Lily's heart warmed at the affection apparent on his face.

"What do you want to know, sweetheart?" Marsha offered the basket of pretzels to Lily.

Lily popped one pretzel into her mouth to be polite, but soon regretted it because she was instantly thirsty. She yearned for her soda on the table so far away and decided to make this conversation as quick as possible.

"How long have you lived in Vermont?" she asked.

"All our lives," Harry said. "Ain't no better place to be."

"Have you traveled to other places?" *Or were all Vermonters hermits like Rick?*

"Of course," Marsha said. "We've been all over. Harry was in the army so we've been overseas. We've been places on vacation too. Hawaii, Bermuda, Alaska, the Caribbean, the Mediterranean."

"We love ourselves a cruise," Harry said. "Buffets around the clock. Living like the damn President for a week or two. It's fun feeling that important."

"But we always love coming home to Vermont the best." Marsha patted Harry's wrinkled hand on the table. He flipped his hand over and held Marsha's.

"You have family here as well?" Lily couldn't take her eyes off the couple's joined hands. How long had it been since she'd just held someone's hand?

Eons.

Harry ran his thumb over the thin skin on the back of Marsha's hand. "Four sons," he said proudly. "All military men as well. Two of them are out defending us right now. God bless them."

"The other two are at desks due to injury," Marsha said quietly.

"They're heroes, our boys. Every one of them. They always come back to Vermont too." Harry squeezed Marsha's hand before releasing it.

"So would you consider Vermont a good place to raise a family?" Lily shook her head as an image of Rick, Poe, and a blond-haired child playing in a grassy field snuck into her head.

Where did that come from? Lily traced the edge of her phone and focused on Marsha and Harry.

"It's the perfect place for that," Marsha said. "The boys got plenty of fresh air and exercise on our farm."

"Learned discipline too," Harry added. "We had those boys doing chores soon as they were able. No free rides here. Everybody contributes to running a family, running a life."

"They had wonderful experiences in school because their classes were small and there's a real sense of community around these parts. Neighbors help neighbors," Marsha said.

"Not like in the city," Harry said. "Neighbors are more likely to steal from you or kill you."

"Harold." Marsha's brows lowered.

"What? It's true." Harry pointed a finger at his wife, and she swatted it away, a grin on her face.

He then faced Lily. "What I like most about Vermont is that it's on its own schedule. People ain't in a rush. They do what they can in a day's time and don't worry about getting ahead of everybody else. You can just *live* in Vermont. No stress, no worries. Can't say that about many places these days."

"True enough," Marsha said. "We can work hard, relax hard here."

"I'll second that." Harry held up his beer and tapped it to Marsha's.

Lily had never met a more satisfied couple, and she'd met a lot of people in her business dealings. The guests that visited Utopia Resorts didn't appear this content. In fact, she'd witnessed outrageous fights between couples at Gems Utopia. Who cheated on who. Who gambled his money away. Who drank until she couldn't climb the stairs. Craziness. Lily wanted to bottle whatever Harry and Marsha had and sell it in Utopia gift shops.

"Where are you from, Lily?" Marsha asked.

"California."

Harry whistled. "So did you understand any of the words we just said?" He elbowed Lily and winked.

"Barely. Life in California is definitely not what you've described here."

"Suppose some folks like it though," Marsha said, a crinkle in her brow that said she found that hard to imagine. "Do you like it?"

"Yes… I love it." Lily's usual answer did not spill out automatically. God, she had to get out of Vermont. "I love California," she said again with more certainty. "It suits me."

"Person's got to be happy with where they live," Harry said.

"I am. Very happy."

"Good." Marsha studied Lily for a silent moment. "You know, Harry, she looks like Gail, doesn't she?"

"Spitting image," Harry agreed.

"Gail Hinsdale, the famous talk show host?" Lily smirked.

"Yeah," Marsha said. "A younger version, of course, but you have the same coloring, the eyes, the hair. You even interviewed us like she would one of her guests."

"I suppose I did." Lily hadn't meant for the encounter to feel like an interview, but perhaps she'd channeled her grandmother's spirit. Nice to know Grandma Gail would always be a part of her. "Gail was my grandmother."

"Was?" Harry put his beer down after taking a swig.

"She passed away." Lily folded and unfolded a napkin from the table.

"Oh, sweetheart." Marsha took Lily's hand, stopping her folding. "We're so sorry."

"So sorry," Harry echoed. "We were in here with Gail about a month ago, right, Marsha?"

Marsha nodded. “About that time, yes. Remember she got the band to play Sinatra songs all night?”

Harry barked out a laugh. “For a couple of young kids, they sounded pretty good.” He tossed his thumb toward the band on the stage now. “Of course Gail wouldn’t let them not sound good.”

“Told the boys it was a sin to butcher Sinatra songs.” Marsha smiled at the memory, and Lily could picture her grandmother directing the band until they sang exactly the way she wanted them to. Like Lily, Grandma Gail was a perfectionist.

“You staying at that beautiful house of hers?” Harry asked.

“Yes. She left it to me.”

“Oh, you’ll enjoy it, Lily. It’ll be a nice break from the city.” Marsha let go of Lily’s hand.

“You going to move here?” Harry asked.

“I’m not moving. I can’t.” Lily rolled up the sleeves of her sweater and glanced toward Hope and Sage. Two men were sitting with them now. One was the drummer, and he was saying something that had Hope laughing. Sage appeared to be weaving a spell on the guy across from her too.

Lily was on her own.

“Can’t?” Harry scoffed. “Who says you can’t?”

"Me." Lily closed her phone, hoping that would end the otherwise pleasant conversation she'd had with Harry and Marsha.

"Don't ignore the possibilities, Lily." Marsha swept her arm out in a wide arc. "Plenty of nice boys here to settle down with."

"In fact," Harry started, "there's a fellow over there that's been eyeing you for the last five minutes." He pointed to the bar.

Lily followed Harry's finger. Her gaze rested on a pair of blue eyes. Nervous eyes. Like those of a deer.

"Thanks for your time, Harry, Marsha. Lovely meeting you both."

She shook both their hands and collected her phone. That blue gaze tracked her as she slithered through the crowd toward the bar. A finger tapped on the neck of a beer bottle. He still had on the blue thermal shirt, but had replaced the flannel shirt with a brown corduroy jacket. The color of it made Lily think deer again. She slowed her step, worried that a fast approach would make her appear too eager to be near him. She didn't want to scare the sexy buck away.

When she was two feet in front of him, Lily said, "You came."

"I came." Rick raised the beer bottle to his lips and tipped his head back. Lily liked how a short crop of golden blond hair covered the underside of his chin. She remembered the feel of that beard against her lips when they'd kissed earlier. What would it take to feel that again?

Why do you want to feel that again? Be logical, Hinsdale.

Rick turned to set the empty bottle on the bar behind him and swiveled back to face Lily. His casted leg rested on the rung of the stool, while the other made one long line to the floor. He was trying for casual, but Lily could tell he wasn't comfortable in the bar.

But he'd come anyway.

"The next drink is on me." Lily pushed the sleeves of her sweater up farther. Not as a signal to Hope or Sage, but because someone had raised the heat in the bar. Maybe the scarf had to go.

"You don't have to buy me a drink." He shed his coat. A good sign he planned to stay a little while.

Why do I want him to stay? I shouldn't. I absolutely shouldn't.

Lily moved to lean against the bar. She needed something to support her as she got a prime view of how well that thermal shirt showcased Rick's body. He had definitely been hiding things under the flannel.

"You kept me from cracking my skull on your coffee table. That earns you at least a drink." Lily forced herself to focus on Rick's face, but the things she found there were as pleasing as the things she found elsewhere. Those pale blue eyes of his hypnotized her, pinned her in place next to him.

"What was I supposed to do? Let you damage my table? I built that chest myself. Anybody would have tried to catch you."

"But anybody didn't. You did." Lily sat on the stool next to him. "So I'm buying your next drink."

Rick motioned to Jake and ordered another beer. Lily dug in her jeans pocket where she had stashed a few bucks and paid for his drink.

There. Back on equal ground. She no longer owed him anything.

Rick tipped the bottle toward Lily in salute and took a sip. "What are you drinking?"

"Soda. It's at the table with Hope and Sage."

"Along with the drummer I see." His lips formed a straight line as his cousin flirted with the band member.

"Hope's a big girl," Lily said.

"Mmm-hmm." His gaze didn't waver from Hope's suitor. "Who's the guy with Sage?"

"I don't know," Lily said. "I was in the corner speaking with Harry and Marsha Frideway."

"Bet they gave you a good glimpse into how people feel about Vermont. They're practically the founding members." He took another sip of his beer. How many beers would it take to get Rick to truly relax? He was trying, but why should he have to try? They were just two people chatting in a bar about nothing too important.

"Yeah, they stopped shy of showing me their 'I heart Vermont' shirts."

Rick laughed and the sound washed over Lily. She closed her eyes for a moment and let the deep, raspy noise flood her senses.

"I went to high school with two of their boys, Tim and Steve. Nice guys."

"Harry and Marsha would say it was because of the fine Vermont upbringing they received." Lily found the old couple at their table. They'd gone back to holding hands. Did the grins on their faces ever fade?

"Harry and Marsha would be right." Rick put down the beer and crossed his arms as if he were gearing up to fight.

"I'm not saying they're wrong, Rick," Lily said. "Look, we're not on opposite sides, okay? I don't want to put a resort here anymore. Selfish thinking gave that notion power. Actually, nervous thinking. The vice president of Utopia backed me into a corner to give her a nature-based resort idea. I had just had the conversation with my father about my grandmother's property. The two events combined and… exploded. Do you know how many people would kill for my job? I've got to supply ideas and make them work, or I'll be replaced. That's how it works."

Lily shifted her phone from hand to hand. "I've rethought the situation, and you've seen the new designs I came up with when I had time to think, when the big boss wasn't thumb-tacking me to the wall. I'll put what I gather here tonight with the photos Hope and Sage took and use it all to convince Utopia's upper management to go with the new design in some other location. Alaska, maybe."

Isn't there pristine wilderness there that people won't want developed either? That thought concerned Lily. She'd always thought everyone was for progress and innovation, but maybe that wasn't the case. Maybe there were more tree-huggers than she'd realized. Maybe there were more people like Rick.

Lily reached out and grasped Rick's forearm. He didn't shake her hand away, but he didn't attempt to hold it as Harry had done to Marsha.

"I'm probably a moron for believing you," Rick said, "but I do believe you."

"You're not a moron." Lily patted his forearm then dropped her hand. Her fingers itched to be intertwined with his, and she didn't exactly know what to do about that.

Deciding she needed more time to think—and more time with Rick—Lily was about to ask him to join his cousins' table when a band member sidled up next to them.

"No, no, no. Tell me someone's slipped some powerful drugs into my beer." The man held his bottle up to the lights and pretended to inspect the liquid inside. "I am not actually standing in front of *the* Rick Stannard, am I?"

"Knock it off, Josh." Rick tapped his bottle to Josh's in greeting.

"Aw, c'mon. I'm allowed to give you some hell. Where have you been, man?" Josh took a solid stance in front of Rick and Lily, his legs about shoulder-width apart and his arms crossed over his chest. He wasn't going anywhere until he got his answer.

"Same place I've always been. Busy this time of year. You know that." Rick brought his other leg up on the rung of the bar stool and repositioned himself.

His brow creased then relaxed. How much trouble was his ankle giving him? He hadn't complained about it, but he didn't strike Lily as a guy who did much belly-aching about things. He either dealt with a situation or avoided it completely. Which was his style? Lily had a feeling it depended on the situation. Try to take his land, Rick was going to fight. Try to get him to open up, he was going to hide.

And why the hell do I want to massage him until that crease of pain in his brow goes away? Lily focused on Josh, but couldn't erase the image of a naked Rick sprawled out like a buffet for her hands.

"Dude, you have to play with us." Josh clamped a hand on Rick's shoulder and shook him.

"Not tonight." Rick shook his head.

"C'mon, man." Josh shot a look to Lily. "Wait a minute. Are you on a date?"

"No," Lily and Rick said at the same time.

"Josh, this is Lily," Rick said. "She's here on business."

"Pleasure to meet you, Lily." Josh shifted his beer to his left hand and shook Lily's hand.

"Likewise, Josh. You guys sound great." She gestured to the stage where the band's instruments stood waiting.

"Thanks. We'd sound better if this guy would stop being so damn shy and join us." Josh waved a hand toward Rick.

"What do you play?" Lily asked, a new curl of intrigue spiraling inside her.

A frown appeared on Rick's lips. Clearly he didn't want to elaborate on this secret Josh had tossed out into the open.

Too bad. Lily was determined to find out what she could.

"Guitar."

Lily waited for Rick to say more. When he didn't, Josh said, "Rick doesn't *play* the guitar. He makes love to it."

"All right," Rick said. "That's enough, Josh. Shouldn't you get back to the stage? Your fans are waiting." His cheeks were a lovely shade of pink making him super adorable, and Lily wanted to run to her purse to get her camera.

Ignoring Rick, Josh turned toward Lily as if he were excluding Rick from the conversation. "This kid doesn't read music, but I've never heard anyone do what he does with those strings. He's amazing. It's like his fingers were made to pluck and press and go crazy on those strings."

Lily absently fanned herself with a napkin from the bar. Josh's description had images chasing each other around her head in which Rick's fingers were plucking and pressing her, going crazy on her. She needed something cold to drink. Right now.

She signaled to Jake and ordered a hard cider. Josh threw money on the bar between Lily and Rick.

"Allow me," he said. "I just noticed you're the prettiest gal in here tonight. I make it a point to buy a drink for the prettiest gal."

"Thank you." Lily didn't have time to protest that she'd buy her own drinks. She needed cooling off immediately before she threw herself at Rick, full bar watching or not.

The drink slowly worked its magic as she swallowed the first gulps. Its frostiness slid down her throat, cooling her inch by inch, sip by sip. Blaze extinguished. Crisis averted.

She glanced back at Rick, imagined him playing the guitar on that tiny stage, and a five-alarm fire flared back to life.

Get yourself under control. She normally didn't have to remind herself of such things. Lily couldn't remember the last time she'd been so aroused. God, she was a mixed up bottle of hormones someone had shaken and threatened to uncork.

"One song, Rick. Please," Josh begged. "The crowd would love it, and so would Miss Lily here." He tipped an imaginary hat.

"I really would," Lily said. She grinned when Rick looked at her.

"Should have let you nosedive into my coffee table," Rick mumbled, but a half smile played on his lips. He finished his beer and stood. Pointing a finger at Lily, close enough to almost touch her nose, he said, "You owe me another drink for this."

Rick limped after Josh through the crowd. He waited at the edge of the stage while Josh got him a stool. The two men appeared to converse over Rick's ankle, then Josh shot one glance back at Lily. Rick shook his head at whatever Josh asked him, and Lily wished she had mutant hearing.

Josh stepped up to the microphone while Rick shook hands with the other band members already on stage. They all looked more than pleased he had joined them.

"If our drummer would stop flirting with Hope Stannard at table six, we could get the music rolling again for you folks," Josh said.

The bar patrons laughed as Sam slowly rose to his feet. Hope had her face buried in her hands. The drummer leaned down and whispered something into her ear, and she looked up at him with a dreamy, blissful look. Again, Lily wished she had her camera handy. These little moments would add to the Vermont charm she hoped to convey to Drew, Rita, and Webster at Utopia.

Lily made her way back to the table where Sage's male friend had also left to play pool with some other guys.

Sage grabbed Lily's arm and pulled her down into the seat. "What the hell did you say to Rick to get him to go up there?"

"More importantly," Hope said, "what did you promise him if he did?"

"I didn't do anything." Lily dug her camera out of her bag. "And I certainly didn't promise him anything. He decided on his own to go up there."

Sage and Hope shook their heads. "No way," Sage said. "He's only gone up there in front of a crowd one other time that I can recall."

"For our mom's fiftieth birthday and only because she promised to give him money toward buying new sugaring equipment," Hope said. "He doesn't perform for the hell of it."

"He hates being up there," Sage said. "He won't even play just for us in his own home."

Rick rested the guitar in his lap, and that cork on Lily's bottle of hormones loosened a bit. Why was he up there if he hated it? Just because she'd said she would like to hear him play?

What else would he do for her? What else did she want him to do?

****

Rick had to admit he liked the feel of the guitar in his hands even if it wasn't his own. What he absolutely loathed, however, was the blinding spotlight and the entire crowd eyeing him, waiting for him to play. His stomach was knotted, his heart pumping. If he thought about merely playing in the solitude of his house, he could perform in the bar without impeding his health. He could do this.

But why am I doing it?

Because Lily had said she wanted him to? Rick pushed that thought aside as the drummer got behind his set, and the band discussed what to play next. It would really irritate him if Lily were the reason he was up there.

"You up for a little Bon Jovi?" Josh asked.

"Sure." Rick squinted under the spotlight to look at Josh.

"Okay, take it away, brother." Josh stepped behind the microphone.

The bar lights dimmed, and Lily was the last thing Rick saw before the spotlight on him intensified. She had her camera out and a smile on.

Dammit, she is *the reason.*

As the rest of the stage lights faded leaving only the spotlight on Rick, he inhaled and focused on the guitar in his lap. Or tried to anyway. He ran a finger along the body of the instrument, but could only think of Lily's curves. The way her body had felt in his lap this afternoon. The way her hair had fanned out on his thighs.

Grinding his teeth a little, he played the opening segment for "Wanted Dead or Alive." Gradually, his jaw relaxed and by the time the rest of the band joined in, he was a little more comfortable. Not much. Though he couldn't see it, he knew that audience was out there, watching, demanding, expecting.

Lily was out there too. She probably thought he was pretty hokey playing the guitar with this band of bumpkins. She'd no doubt wanted to see him on stage so she could solidify her belief that the woods were full of countrified nuts. He'd bet Lily was accustomed to rock star performances. Hell, she probably knew the real Jon Bon Jovi. She had to think this band was a joke.

They'd reached the part where he was supposed to let loose on the guitar in the middle of the song. He did, Josh finished up the vocals, and soon Rick found himself playing the ending part. The audience erupted in applause, thunderous and floor shaking. Rick slid the guitar off his lap, preparing to put it down, but Josh grabbed his shoulder.

"No way you're leaving us now, cowboy," he said. "You heard the same applause I did. A few more songs. C'mon."

"Rick, Rick, Rick," chanted the crowd.

Rick knew Sage had started the chant. He'd choke her later. "One more song. That's it."

"I guess I'll take what I can get." Josh conferred with the rest of the band and after Rick switched to an electric guitar, they all dove into "Deja Voodoo" by Kenny Wayne Shepherd. When the song ended, Rick stood, rested the guitar against the stool, and made an exit before Josh could coerce him into another song.

"Rick Stannard, everybody," Josh called over the applause.

The spotlight followed Rick's retreat so he headed for Hope and Sage. And Lily. He would have liked to head for the door, but not with everyone watching. He was a hermit, not a jerk.

Sage popped up from her seat and stretched up to throw her arms around Rick's neck. "You rocked!" She dropped a kiss on his cheek and let Hope wiggle in for an identical hug and kiss.

"I wish you would play more," Hope said.

"I play plenty." Rick noted his jacket had been hung over the chair beside Lily.

"She meant out in public, stupid." Sage rolled her eyes.

"One minute I rock, the next I'm stupid. Nice, Sage." He shuffled between chairs to get to the one marked with his coat.

"You still rock," Sage said. "You're just as dumb as one too." She stuck her tongue out at Rick then picked up her drink. Angling it toward the pool tables, she said, "I'm going to play with some balls."

Rick looked to the pool tables and saw the guy Sage was with before. The dude waved her over, a mischievous grin on his face. Rick turned to Hope and opened his mouth, but his cousin held up a hand.

"She'll be fine, Rick. You know Sage doesn't take shit from anybody." Hope looked to Lily then to Rick. "Well, I need a refill and a closer look at my drummer." She got up and disappeared into the crowd.

Rick was alone with Lily. As alone as two people in a stuffed bar could be.

"I enjoyed your performance," Lily said. "I've captured it here. Want to see?" She nudged her camera toward him.

"Absolutely not." He picked up the camera and dropped it into Lily's purse hanging on her chair.

"I can see why Josh wants you to join the band. He had an okay sound when I first walked in, but with you up there? Well, it became something way better."

She brought her glass up in a small salute, and Rick watched her throat move as she swallowed. He wanted his lips on that throat and everything connected to it.

"Doesn't compare to what you see in California though, does it?" Rick positioned Sage's empty chair so he could heft his ankle onto it. The burn was getting to be a bit much. He had to stop overdoing it.

"I don't go to concerts," Lily said. "I'm more into movies for entertainment."

"You have a favorite movie?"

"All of them." Lily grinned, and Rick wanted more than his lips on her now. "You want another drink?"

He shook his head. Two beers were enough, and the way he was feeling right now—the way his body was reacting to Lily—he was afraid to get even a little buzz going. He'd gone on stage without much of a fight. What else would he give in to if he were liquored?

"Actually, I should head out." Rick pulled his jacket off the back of the chair. He had to get out of there. Away from Lily. Take a cold shower. Alone.

"I'll compile my notes from tonight into a case against having a resort here," Lily said. "Maybe I could run the presentation by you tomorrow?"

The hopeful look on Lily's face, combined with that lion mane of strawberry blonde hair, had Rick nodding. How could he say no to seeing her again?

He couldn't, but he needed some rules, something that put meeting her on his terms, on his schedule. "Come by in the afternoon. I plan to check taps in the morning with my aunt. She won't let me walk in the woods unattended." He rolled his eyes and motioned to his ankle still propped on the chair next to him.

"Smart lady. One that cares about you," Lily said.

"One that thinks I'm going to find my death in the woods." Rick slid his leg off the chair and fidgeted into his jacket.

"Like I said, smart lady." Lily stared at her empty glass as Josh and the guys finished their last song.

"Why don't you come with me and my aunt?" *What are you doing, stupid?* Rick tasted the fear coming off Lily at the mention of death in the woods, and for some unknown reason, he wanted to do something about that fear.

Lily's eyes, huge blue-green seas, flicked over to him. She clamped both hands around her glass as she spoke. "No. Thank you. I'll leave you to your work. I'll meet you after." Her voice had a hint of a quake in it as if it were taking all her energy to remain calm.

"Okay, how about—"

"Lily," Josh interrupted.

In nearly drowning in Lily's eyes, Rick hadn't seen Josh approach their table. Their table. As if he was *with* Lily tonight.

He wasn't.

"Enjoy the show?" Josh rested his hands on the back of the chair opposite Lily.

"Yes. Lovely." Lily's hands relaxed on her glass, and she sent Josh one winner of a smile.

"This kid is something, huh?" Josh jutted his chin toward Rick.

"Talented," Lily said. "For a hermit."

Josh laughed and for some reason the sound of it got on Rick's nerves.

"I keep telling him to join us. It's fun, the extra money from gigs is good to have, and the chicks dig us." Josh's smile was sunshine bright, and an uneasy feeling wormed its way into Rick's stomach at the way Josh looked at Lily.

"Chicks do dig you guys." Lily pointed to Hope sitting behind the drum set. The drummer stood behind Hope, curling her hands around the drumsticks and explaining something.

Josh turned to look at the stage. "I think that right there is more a case of Sam digging Hope. He nearly broke a drumstick in half when he saw her walk in. He almost didn't come tonight, but he switched his shift. He's an EMT in real life."

"For the record, I think Hope's doing some digging too," Lily said.

Josh pulled out the chair across from Lily, turned it around, and straddled it as if it were a horse. Rick found himself wishing it would buck him off then hated that he wished that. He needed to leave, yet his legs wouldn't do the job. They refused to leave Lily at the table with Josh.

"Hope said you're writing something about how great Vermont is?" Josh leaned his elbows on the chair back. Rick could have sworn the kid flexed his biceps as he waited for Lily's response. He was like a bird, puffing out his feathers in an elaborate mating ritual. Where was a hungry cat when you needed one?

Or better yet, a coyote?

"That's right. A quick presentation." Lily waved a hand.

Something about Lily's short response pleased Rick. Was she not impressed by Josh's plumage? Was she interested in another bird, perhaps?

"Well, this place is okay to get a snapshot of Vermont, but I know a few places that would really give you something to write about. I have to help the guys pack up, but I have my own truck tonight," Josh said. "Can I be your tour guide for what remains of this evening, Miss Lily?"

Where do these guys get the balls?

Lily gave Rick a quick glance. One he was sure said, "Help me."

He didn't have time to think about what came out of his own mouth next. It just came spilling onto the table in front of him.

"Lily's leaving with me." Rick pulled her coat and purse off her chair. "You're ready, right?"

"Yes, thank you." Without hesitating, she slipped on her coat and took her purse from Rick as if they had pre-planned this exit together.

Red washed across Josh's face. "I'm sorry. I thought you said you two weren't on a date." He volleyed glances from Rick to Lily and back to Rick.

"We're not," Rick said. "We weren't." *Holy hell, it feels like a date now.*

"I came with Hope and Sage," Lily said, "but they seem to be otherwise engaged, and I'm ready to leave now. I'm tired and still have some work to do." She smiled pleasantly at Josh when she stood. Extending a hand to him, she said, "A pleasure meeting you and hearing you play. Thanks for your offer to show me around, but I think I've got enough material for my presentation."

Polite. Clear. Rick had to admire how she didn't cut the man down. She was probably used to having to turn guys down all the time. She'd gotten good at it. Didn't have to get bitchy. Could make it seem as if she would like to go out with them, but truly didn't have the time for such activities. What other strategies did she have in her toolbox? Had she used any on him yet?

"C'mon." Rick stood.

"I'm going to let Sage know I'm making an exit with you." Lily patted Rick on the chest as she brushed by him. That one touch, even through his shirt and jacket, was like getting zapped by a defibrillator, which he knew all too well was life-saving, but scary as hell just the same.

When Lily reached the pool table, Josh came to stand in front of Rick. "I'm sorry, man. I didn't know you wanted her."

As if Lily were the last Snickers bar in a vending machine. Rick let out a slow breath. "I'm giving her a ride home, Josh. That's it. She said she's got work to do and didn't want to wait for my cousins."

"Right." Josh looked back at Lily who was leaning against the pool table by Sage. The position made a denim-clad showcase of her ass and long legs. "Somebody needs to sample that, my friend."

"Get out of here." Rick nudged Josh away and walked to the door to wait for Lily. If he went within reach of Sage, she would give him hell over this. He didn't need that right now.

He needed to leave. So much for the alone part of that plan.

Lily gave Hope a wave, and when she turned toward Rick, Hope threw her hands up over her head and pretended to be a cheerleader. Rick wanted to raise a fist to her, but couldn't do so without Lily seeing. He'd get Hope later. Always later.

Rick held the door open for Lily, and again, she hesitated before passing in front of him, a little grin on her lips.

"What's so funny?" Rick asked.

"You are." She stopped on the wooden ramp outside leading to the dirt parking lot and turned to face him. She zipped her coat and shoved her hands in her pockets. "You're a gentleman."

"And that's amusing?" Rick led the way to his truck.

"Yeah," Lily said as she fell into step beside him. "I think California is classy, but I may be wrong about that."

Rick unlocked the passenger side door, mentally cursed at the mud caked on his truck, and opened the door. "You may be wrong about a lot of things."

He closed her door after she got in and walked to the driver side. He paused with his hand on the door handle, not sure if he was ready to be in the close confines of the pickup's cabin with Lily.

Don't be an idiot. It's just a ride home. He opened the door and settled in behind the wheel.

"Thanks," Lily said as Rick put the key in the ignition and started the truck.

"For what?" He backed out of the parking space and headed for the main road.

"For not leaving me with Josh." She rested her arm on the center console next to Rick's, and he fought to keep his arm from reaching over to her.

"He's an okay guy," Rick said, "but you didn't seem as if you wanted to go with him."

"I didn't, and yes, Josh did appear to be an okay guy, but his guitar playing wasn't up to snuff if you ask me."

Rick glanced at Lily, something warming in the center of his body as she smiled back at him.

"You were a musical genius up there," she continued, "and, if we're being honest, you were really… hot playing that guitar." She rolled down the window and leaned toward it, pretending to need air.

"A trick of the stage lighting," Rick said, though he couldn't stop the smile coming onto his lips now.

“I don’t think so.” Lily shifted closer to him and put her hand on the back of his seat by the headrest. “I think it was all you, Rick.”

He didn’t know what to say. He did know he wanted her hand to make the leap from the headrest to his shoulder, his neck, his face, anywhere. The memory of kissing her in his living room came flooding back like a white-hot blaze capable of setting the truck on fire.

Rick pulled over to the side of the road and shut off the truck. Lily’s eyes widened as she looked out into the complete darkness surrounding them.

“Nothing will hurt you out there,” he said just before he reached over and crushed his lips to hers.

Chapter Twelve

One minute Lily was paranoid about the nighttime woods closing in around the truck. The next she didn't care if Bigfoot ripped open the passenger door and dragged her through the forest by her hair. Rick's mouth possessed her, took her breath away, made her want more. So much more. His hand on the back of her neck kept her within his reach, and the captivity of it further excited her. She wanted to be hunted by him, trapped, tamed.

Rick ran his other hand along Lily's thigh, but his lips never left hers. While his hands roamed as far as the tight space in the truck would allow, Lily yearned to explore all of him.

She pushed back for a moment after he nipped at her earlobe.

"What's the matter?" He went suddenly still, his nose still buried in her hair.

"Nothing," she whispered. "I just want more room so I can properly throw myself at you."

Rick laughed into her neck then kissed a line along her jaw. He caught her lips once again and brought her to the breaking point.

"I think I can make it to your place in ten minutes." He sat back and turned the key.

"Try to make it in five."

The truck bounced over ruts in the road as they neared Grandma Gail's house. In seven minutes, Rick opened the passenger door and scooped Lily out of his truck. She let out a squeal as she held on to her purse in her lap. Being six feet tall had pretty much kept other men from attempting to literally sweep her off her feet.

"You shouldn't be carrying me with that ankle," she said, though she snuggled a little closer to Rick's chest as he shuffled to the porch steps.

"What ankle? Nothing hurts right now," he said. "Everything feels excellent." He gave the back of her thigh a squeeze and slowed down to take the steps one at a time. When he reached the front door, he set Lily down.

She opened her purse to get her keys, and while she searched, Rick pressed himself up behind her. Her legs went to jelly, and she had to reach out her palm to the door to steady herself.

"I'll never get us inside at this rate." She attempted to angle her purse toward the porch light, but ended up dropping it to turn around in Rick's arms.

"The porch will do." He braced his hands on the threshold, corralling her between him and the door. "It's not that cold out here." He lowered his head and teased her lips with a few slow kisses.

"Not anymore it isn't." Lily liked the way the porch light illuminated Rick's features and got caught in his eyes.

As they kissed, something rustled in the trees behind Rick, and Lily glanced over his shoulder. "But it'll be nicer inside."

She stepped out of his hold and retrieved her purse. Rick scanned the tree line as her hands closed around her keys. *Hurry up, hurry up. Get inside.*

"Squirrel probably. Something small." He massaged her left shoulder, and she closed her eyes at the gesture. That one, brief touch brought her exactly the right dose of comfort, as if with him nearby she didn't have to be afraid of anything.

She pushed the key into the knob, but before she opened the door, she turned to face Rick again.

"Bear attack."

"What?" His eyebrows drew together, and he angled his head.

"I'm afraid of the woods because a bear attacked me when I was ten." There, she had said it, but she shivered all over.

"It happened here?"

Lily nodded. "My parents were working out their divorce, so I stayed here with Grandma Gail. I was in the hot tub around back when this mammoth beast came barreling out of the woods. I screamed and ran. The bear roared and charged, and well… she was faster than me."

Rolling her shoulders, she tried to keep the memory from filling her mind, but it was too late.

"I'd heard some crunching in the woods, but figured it was a bird or something so I didn't get out of the hot tub. Grandma Gail said she'd just be a moment while she put on her swimsuit and grabbed towels for us. I remember gazing up at the summer night sky. There were so many stars, too many to count. It was nothing like the California sky where the only sparkling things came with an electric buzz, you know?"

Rick nodded, his blue eyes focused on her as he listened.

"I was starting to maybe realize why Grandma Gail liked the woods, and then that rustling got louder. Just as I had made up my mind to go into the house, a gigantic, black monster shot out of the shadows with its teeth bared. Sometimes I can still hear its growling."

She hugged herself and ran her hands up and down her arms.

"I let out a shriek and bolted for the house, but that pissed off bear was so fast. It raked its razor sharp claws across my back as I tried to climb the porch steps." She closed her eyes, her scars tingling as she remembered. "I fell and my blood was hot as it flowed out of the slashes in my skin. The bear's breath huffed in my ears as it bent over my body and sniffed me."

Every detail was vivid as if she were going through the whole ordeal all over again.

"My grandmother screamed my name as she flew out of the house. She banged two metal pots together and shouted obscenities at the animal. The bear let loose one more horrible growl before lumbering off the deck and disappearing back into the woods.

"The next thing I remembered was being scooped up by Grandma Gail and taken into the house right before I passed out. When I woke up, I was in the hospital stretched out on my stomach. My father and grandmother were there and fussing all over me."

She'd thought they'd never leave her alone, and truthfully, she didn't want them to. They'd surrounded her in a steady noise—a noise that drowned out a growling bear that had taken up residence in her mind. In the quiet, that damn bear got damn loud.

"Lily."

At the sound of Rick's voice now, she became aware that she wasn't in the hot tub. She was, in fact, still on the porch with him.

He cupped her face in his hands and kissed her lightly on the forehead. "That was a freak thing, you know. Bears don't usually behave that way."

"I know." She shrugged. "Doesn't keep my mind from replaying it every time I see the woods. Every time I hear something crunching around out there, I think it's happening all over again."

"That's the way the human mind works, isn't it? Damn thing." Rick paced away from Lily and leaned against the porch railing, his back to her. "I don't leave Vermont because New York gave me a heart attack at age thirty-one."

Lily set her purse by the door and put her arm around Rick's waist from behind him. She snaked her hands up until her left palm rested where his heart would be.

"My secretary found me keeled over on my desk. She called 911 and when I came to, I wished I hadn't. I was in a too bright hospital room, and it felt as if someone had taken a sledgehammer to my ribcage." He let out a slow, even breath and curled his hand around Lily's still on his chest. "An orchestra of beeps and clicks filled that room while machines kept me going. The smells of bleach and death..." He shook his head, unable to finish.

"Everything all right in there now?" She gently patted his chest as she pressed her cheek into his shoulder.

"Since I moved back to Vermont, not one problem, but it's pretty easy for me to imagine pain shooting down my left arm and a tightness in my chest. As if someone had taken my heart and put it in a vise." Rick leaned his head against Lily's on his shoulder.

"Guys my age aren't supposed to have heart attacks. They have skiing accidents, fall on extreme rock-climbing expeditions, drown in the rapids of a whitewater rafting trip. Their hearts don't decide to up and quit on them like mine did."

She gave him a squeeze. "It didn't completely quit on you. You're still here, right?" She dropped her hands and leaned her butt against the railing next to Rick. "The lifestyle here keeps you calm and healthy, right?"

"Yeah. The city's a killer," Rick said.

"So are the woods." She pushed off the railing. "But even though there could be a bear out there watching me right now, I still want you tonight, Rick."

"I want you too." He tugged on her hand, brought her to the door. "I'll bet we can make each other forget all the reasons we shouldn't do this."

After a kiss that made Lily wonder if she'd been alive before this point in time, Rick opened the door and pulled Lily inside. He shut the door, backed her up against it, and shed his jacket, letting it drop to the floor. He lowered the zipper on her coat while teasing her neck with his lips. What else was that fantastic mouth capable of? Lily looked forward to finding out tonight.

"Found something to keep you warm this evening?"

Lily gasped, and Rick whirled around. He kept his body in front of hers, his arms out to his sides further shielding her.

Drew stood in the kitchen, his shoulders squared, his arms folded across his chest. He still wore his work clothes—navy dress pants and a powder blue dress shirt. His tie was gone, but Lily figured he came straight from the office. Had to have left early this morning.

He was much shorter than Rick, but that didn't mean he wasn't a worthy opponent. Drew did

Jujitsu and other martial arts. He competed, and he was good. Lily had been to a few of his matches. Very Jean-Claude Van Damme in *Bloodsport.* Drew had made her watch that movie. She hadn't cared for the fighting, and Lily didn't want any blood on the marble tile of her grandmother's floor.

Especially not Rick's blood.

"Hey, Drew," she said. *Friendly, keep it friendly.* No need to get Drew's testosterone level up any higher.

"Hey, Lily," Drew said, mocking her tone. "Hey, whom I assume is Mr. Rick Stannard. Have a nice night out, you two?"

He was about seven layers deeper than pissed. The firm set of his jaw, the defensive stance, the glower. He was ready to blow. Lily had never seen Drew this upset.

She maneuvered out from behind Rick, but not without having to silently convince him to let her. "What are you doing here, Drew? I thought we decided I'd finish up and see you in California in a few days."

"*You* decided that," Drew said. "Not me. I'm your boss, so I decided to see for myself why Vermont was suddenly not the place for a resort." He let out a short huff as he stared at Rick. "And I see the reason is exactly as I predicted."

"Look, buddy," Rick started.

"We're not buddies, Mr. Stannard," Drew interrupted. "I wouldn't be buddies with someone interfering with my work and trying to fuck my woman."

Rick took two quick steps forward, the air cast banging against the tiled floor. He stayed steady on his feet as he said, "That's not the way you speak around a lady."

"Don't tell me how to speak around a lady. Lily is probably the first lady you've ever seen." Drew edged forward and so did Rick.

Lily wiggled between them and forced Drew back a couple steps. "Let's all settle down here, all right?" She turned to face Rick. "Maybe you should go."

"If I recall," Rick said, "I'm the one with the invitation to be here. Not him." He glared at Drew then looked at Lily, his eyes full of blue fire. Even mad he was ultra-sexy.

"I don't need an invitation," Drew shot back as he pushed Lily out of his way. He stood nose to chin with Rick, but that didn't diminish his confidence. "I've known Lily much longer than you have. We've been all over the world together. We've made love on almost every continent."

Lily cringed. "That's enough, Drew. Go into the great room while I see Rick out. I'll deal with you in a minute." She grabbed Drew's arm and pulled him back toward the great room.

"See?" Drew said. "I get to stay."

The smug look on Drew's face made Lily want to toss him out, but he was her boss and he was usually reasonable. She needed to calm him down and make him listen to some logic. He was an intelligent man. He'd come around to her way of thinking on this project, but not while he was all fired up. Not with Rick standing here, his lips still swollen from the mega kissing they'd done on the porch.

Drew settled on the couch as Lily walked back to the kitchen. Rick shook his head. "I don't think I should leave you alone with him."

"I don't want you to leave me alone with him." Lily coaxed Rick to the door. "I want to be alone with you, but we can't do that with one angry boss in my living room, now can we?"

"Let's get rid of him then." Rick looked over Lily's shoulder. "Or come to my place." He ran his hands down her arms, and she closed her eyes, let her head drop back a bit.

"Tempting," she admitted, "but I need to sort the project out with Drew so he'll get on the next plane back to California."

"He's not going to leave you here now that he's seen me with you."

Lily thought the same thing, but didn't say so.

"Let me stay," Rick said. "You can talk to him, but let me be around. Just in case."

"No, your presence is what's making him nuts right now. In fact, it's making me nuts, but in a very different way." She dug out a smile and relaxed a little when Rick grinned back.

He leaned down and rested his forehead against hers. “We’re not done. You and me. You know that, right?” His voice was low, and the rumble of it burrowed deep into her soul.

“I know,” Lily whispered as she backed Rick into the foyer out of Drew’s sight. “We haven’t even started yet, have we?”

He pulled her against him and feasted on her lips. Lily fought not to moan aloud as he ran his hands along her hips, wrapped his arms around her, raked his fingers over her back. His kiss was hot, hungry, all-consuming.

Why am I making him leave?

She had to break away to catch her breath. To keep herself from stripping down naked in the foyer and offering herself to Rick right here, right now.

He took a step toward her. “I still don’t feel right leaving you here with him.”

“It’ll be fine. I’ll talk to him. Make him see. He’ll come around. He’s usually pretty reasonable.”

Lily rested her hand on Rick’s chest. How horrible it must have been to have a heart attack so young. Her fear was avoidable. Stay out of the woods. His, however, was inside him. Sure, staying out of the city helped, but he must live with a continuous ticking time bomb feeling.

Yet, he had come out to the tavern tonight, because she’d asked him. He’d played guitar in public, because she’d asked him. He was leaving right now, because she had asked him.

She pressed a kiss to Rick's cheek. "How about if I do join you and your aunt tomorrow to check the taps?"

"What?" Rick's eyes widened. "You want to hike into the woods?"

"I want to be with you. If that means hiking in the woods, then yes." She'd probably freak out over this later, but now it felt absolutely right.

"If you're sure…"

"I am. What time are you heading out?" She picked up Rick's jacket from the floor where he'd dropped it, stole one more look at that wonderful blue thermal shirt, and handed him the jacket.

"Eight o'clock too early?"

"Nope."

"Come to the store. I'll get Aunt Joy to make us her famous coffee." Rick traced a finger along her cheek.

"Sounds good. See you then." She opened the front door.

He threw a glance toward the great room, but Lily lifted a hand and cupped his cheek. "I can handle Drew. Don't worry. I know how his mind works."

"I could send Poe over," Rick said.

"I thought she wasn't vicious." She wagged a finger at him, and he swatted it away.

"She's not, but she can look the part when necessary." He walked through the door, but poked his head back in to leave behind one more kiss. "I'm right next door, Lily."

"Thanks." She watched by the open door as Rick got into his truck and started it up. Soon, he was nothing more than fading taillights in the dark.

"This is better."

Lily jumped at the sound of Drew's voice in her ear. She closed the door and turned around to come face-to-face with him. "Back up, will you?"

"C'mon, honey." He rested his hands on her hips right were Rick's hands had been moments ago.

She pried his fingers off her and pushed him back. Made him give her the space she'd requested. "The couch. Now." She pointed to the great room.

"How about the bed now? The couch later. Maybe the kitchen table, the hot tub too." Drew tried to take her hand, but she sidestepped out of his reach.

"Drew, we're not having sex." Lily entered the great room and sat on the couch, mulling over the fact that she had been perfectly ready to have sex tonight.

With Rick.

Maybe several times.

"No, we'd be making love, honey." Drew lowered his knees onto the couch and pressed on Lily's shoulders to get her to lie down.

She clamped her hands onto his wrists to stop him. "I'm serious, Drew."

"You were going to fuck him though. You were ready to tear into Stannard." He threw his arm out toward the foyer as a vein bulged on the left side of his forehead. Lily had never noticed that before. Probably because she'd never seen Drew this wound up.

"Maybe I was," she said, "but I have that right. You and I are not a couple. I've told you this. We have our work relationship, and we're good friends, but that's all. That's all I can give you."

Red washed over Drew's face, and Lily braced herself for… for what? Was he going to scream at her? Hit her? Why hadn't she gone with Rick?

No. This is my place. I don't need to run away. My rules. Not Drew's.

"Look, you're here." Lily put her hand on his shoulder, and his body relaxed under her grip. Some of the red dimmed on his face. "Let's discuss business. I've been working on evidence to support why this isn't a place for Utopia. You must have seen for yourself. You had to drive through to get here." Lily paused. "Wait a minute. Where's your car?"

"I parked it around back." Drew sat on the couch beside her and traced the crease in his dress pants. "I wanted to surprise you."

Mission accomplished.

"How did you get in?" He didn't have a key, and she hadn't told him the security code. Her mind just now registered the fact that she hadn't had to disarm the house alarm when she and Rick had entered.

"That lock on the front door was easily picked." He shrugged as if it weren't a big deal.

"And the alarm?" Lily's stomach felt as if she'd filled it with sour milk.

Drew reached into the pocket of his dress pants and tossed a small piece of paper into her lap. When she unfolded it, she recognized it as stationary from her desk back in California. Drew had used a pencil to reveal the impressions from what she had written on the sheet before this one. The security code was right there in a small leaden rectangle.

"You snooped on my desk?" Lily never thought Drew would do something like this. He never appeared to be that… that desperate.

"No, I had Tam snoop."

Of course. Why snoop yourself when you can get someone else to do it for you? Tam was technically *her* assistant, but Lily had seen the woman gazing at Drew from across conference tables. She'd snoop if it meant pleasing Drew.

"I needed to be with you, Lily. Get everything back on track. The project. Us." He picked up the paper Lily had dropped on the coffee table. "This was the only way."

"Why couldn't you trust me to handle things over here?" She tried to keep a lid on her rising anger. She knew it would do her no good. If she stayed calm, so would Drew.

"Because we're a team." He put his hand on her knee. "This deal wasn't going right, because we weren't together."

Lily shook her head. "It wasn't going right, because I was wrong about Vermont." She scooted to the edge of the couch and opened her laptop. After pulling up the photos Hope and Sage had taken, she turned the computer so Drew could view the screen. "Utopia can't build here. Look."

Drew scrolled through the pictures. Lily watched over his shoulder, and when the bear shot came up, she looked closely at the creature. Why didn't it cause her to drop unconscious now? It made her uneasy, but her heart wasn't racing in her chest, her body wasn't coated in a sheen of sweat. Instead, the memory of Rick squeezing her shoulder out on the porch this evening when something had rustled in the woods filled her mind.

Lily leaned forward to get a better view of the computer screen. She hadn't seen any of the photos beyond the bear one and chuckled at the last shot.

"Who are they?" Drew pointed to two blonds hugging a maple tree and pretending to kiss it.

"Hope and Sage." Lily pulled the computer into her lap. "Rick's cousins."

"So you know his entire family, do you? How much time have you spent with the lumberjack?"

"He's not a lumberjack. He owns a maple syrup company."

Drew waved a hand as if he didn't see the difference.

"It's actually divine syrup." Lily clamped her lips closed. *Idiot. Why don't I tell Drew everything?* "That's what folks around here say anyway. I went to a tavern tonight, and everybody knows his syrup. We can't take his land, Drew."

"Sure we can. We're Utopia Resorts. We can do anything we want."

"You saw the pictures."

"Big deal. A couple of tree photos aren't going to stop Utopia. Guests want the great outdoors. These pictures just show how great the outdoors is up here, and we're the company to bring it to the guests."

"Guests don't need us to bring it to them. All they need is a tent, some hiking gear, whatever. They don't need a fancy resort that'll cut the woods down and impede the beautiful view."

"Beautiful view?" Drew grabbed the laptop from Lily and flipped back to the bear photo. "You call that beautiful? This thing looks ready to eat a man. I thought you were afraid of the woods."

Lily shivered, but took a deep breath at the same time. "Most people like it."

"People who have never experienced a suite in a Utopia Resort." Drew stood and paced away from the couch. "My God, Lily, these people don't know what they're missing. That's all. They need us to show them how to vacation."

"They need us to leave them alone." Probably what Rick needed too. If she'd never shown up here, he wouldn't be caught in the middle. He didn't need to be worrying about his land, his business. She didn't want to be the cause of any stress that might be unhealthy for him. No, she had to get Utopia to fold on this one.

"Look, I'm tired," she said. "I'm going to take my laptop upstairs to bed and work on my presentation. I'm going to make Rita and Webster see. Make you see."

"Don't be like this, Lily." Drew followed her into the hall, started up the stairs with her.

"You're not coming to bed with me, Drew. You can have one of the guest rooms if you've got nowhere else to go, but you're not sleeping in the same room with me."

"Dammit, Lily. We're supposed to be together. You know it." He retreated a step, and Lily continued up. When she got to her room, she found Drew had put his suitcase next to hers. He'd been in her room when she wasn't here.

Now that's annoying.

She placed her laptop on the bed then wheeled his suitcase out into the hallway. She listened for a moment as Drew opened the refrigerator downstairs and clanged some silverware.

He just doesn't get it. She shook her head, considered going to the kitchen and telling Drew to leave, but decided against it. She really was tired. She'd work on the presentation, get some shut-eye, then send Drew on his way tomorrow morning if he hadn't already left.

After a quick shower—being naked with a still peeved Drew downstairs unnerved her—Lily climbed into bed and booted up her laptop. While she waited, she threw an arm out and drummed her fingers on the empty side of the bed next to her. A side that could have had a naked Rick draped over it right now if things had gone differently.

Just as well. They'd both admitted being together would be a mistake. Better off they didn't do it. Lily was in a big enough mess without adding new problems.

And had she actually agreed to hiking into the woods with Rick tomorrow morning? What had she been thinking? That was the last thing she wanted to do, but she'd said she would.

"How bad could it be?" Broad daylight with two other people, one over six feet of mountain man muscle. It'd be fine.

A soft knock on her door had the mountain man muscle fading from her mind.

"Lily?"

"What?"

"I wanted to say good night. Can I come in?"

She heard Drew's hand on the knob. "No, Drew. I'm working. Help yourself to whatever you need."

"I need you." His voice was raspy, almost whiney.

"You're exhausted from your unnecessary flight out here. Get some sleep." Lily hoped he wouldn't try to come in. Sometimes his confidence had him doing things that overstepped the bounds, and right now he didn't have tight control of his emotions.

Drew pounded his fist on the bedroom door, and Lily jolted at the sound. "I'm a patient man, Lily," he growled, "but I have my limits. I'll give you tonight to yourself, but that's it. Tomorrow we go back to the way things were between us. How things are supposed to be."

She listened as he marched down the hall. She had a feeling sleep would not come easy for her tonight. First, she had an angry man staying in her guest room. One that thought she was his. Second, her body had been all stirred up by Rick. When he'd kissed her in the foyer, she'd wanted him so much it hurt. She didn't usually react that way to people, especially ones she barely knew. Rick fell into that category. She could count the number of things she knew about him on her two hands. He owned a maple syrup business, hated the city, liked solitude, kept a coyote in his house, played the guitar but mostly in secret, had an aunt and two cousins that cared about him deeply, loved the woods.

Had a heart attack.

Wanted her.

How could that be enough information to want him beside her right now? In her bed? In her?

Drew was the one who knew her, and she knew him. They'd been acquaintances, business associates, friends, for years. Lovers on and off throughout those years. It made sense, she and Drew.

But it wasn't what she wanted. Not even a little bit.

Lily flicked on the TV. *When Harry Met Sally* was on. One of her favorites. Meg Ryan was faking an orgasm in the diner as a demonstration for a doubting Billy Crystal.

I could have had the real thing tonight.

She sighed and shut off the TV. For the first time in her life, a movie hadn't brought her peace.

Chapter Thirteen

For the second time in the last few days, Rick found himself deliberating over his choice of clothing. He didn't like this new format. One in which he was concerned with his appearance and about the reaction of a female—a tall, strawberry-blonde female to be exact.

Poe barked from her position on his bed.

"Yeah, hurry up. I know." Rick scratched the coyote's ears and walked back to the closet. He chose blue jeans, a gray T-shirt, and a heavy, gray sweater that zippered from the neck to mid-chest. He wouldn't need a jacket wearing that sweater. Less clothes to take off later.

When he was with Lily.

Coming home by himself last night had sucked. He couldn't get to sleep. Every time he closed his eyes, he pictured Lily on top of him, her long legs on either side of his body, her hands doing things to him he almost couldn't handle. Things that reduced him to his primal instincts. He'd never been so charged up.

He'd paced his bedroom. Tried to read. Strummed the guitar. Played fetch with Poe. The coyote had been delighted. The man, not so much.

Nothing could settle his mind or his body. When he finally surrendered and climbed back into his bed, only light sleep came, and even that was riddled with dreams of Lily.

Better that than nightmares of New York.

If only Drew hadn't shown up. Rick stuck by his initial assessment of the guy from the phone conversation he'd had with him after Lily passed out. Typical asshole. Overconfident. Possessive. Irritating. What kind of a man flies across the country after a woman has told you not to? And if Drew had such a great relationship with Lily as he'd said, why didn't he trust her to be doing her job?

If Lily was Drew's, why had she been willing to sleep with me?

Another bark from Poe, who was now waiting by the bedroom door, propelled Rick into the hallway.

"Sorry, girl." He patted his thigh, and Poe followed him to the kitchen. He fed the coyote and had a quick breakfast, which would have been a big breakfast had he and Lily had their fun last night. "There'll be another chance," he told himself. Why he wanted there to be another chance was a complete mystery.

With Poe by his side, Rick headed for the store and found the females of his small family puttering around. Hope rushed over with Sage right behind her.

"Soooo? How was your evening?" Hope said, a dopey grin on her face.

"Lonely." Rick let his nose lead him to Aunt Joy's coffee while Poe sat in front of the pastry case. That coyote remembered what went in there, and she was waiting for her favorite, Sage's signature maple peanut butter cookies. Rick once witnessed a genuine fist fight between two customers over the final batch of those cookies last season. That was how good they were.

"How did you screw this up, Rick?" Sage said, her hands on her hips. "It was in the bag. I saw the way Lily watched you play the guitar last night. She was a smitten kitten. Primed and ready."

He prepared his coffee and when he turned around, both his cousins leaned on the pastry case on either side of Poe, waiting.

"I didn't screw it up, Sage." He sipped his coffee and mentally saluted his aunt's brilliance once again. "When I got Lily home, she had company."

"Company? Who?" Hope asked. "She doesn't know anyone around here but us."

"Her boss from California showed up."

"Uh-oh," Sage said. "That Assburn guy? The one from the phone?"

"*Ash*burn." Rick ground his teeth. "That's the one."

"I didn't like him just from his voice." Sage crinkled up her nose in disgust.

"Not much better in person." He pulled out a chair and sat at one of the tables. His ankle felt pretty good this morning, but he wanted to conserve that comfort for the hike. Wanted nothing to cut short his time with Lily in the woods today. This was his chance to show her everything he loved about this land. Her chance to see that the forest meant her no harm.

"I'll bet he didn't like you much either," Hope said, sitting next to him.

"Nope." He chewed on his bottom lip as he eyed his cousins. "Lily didn't say anything about him, did she?" What if Lily and Drew did have a relationship deeper than work and friends? What if he *was* getting in the middle of something still in progress? Was Lily just using him to pass the time while she was in Vermont?

"When we watched movies with her," Sage said, "the only thing she said was she wished she could find love like they have in the movies."

"I took that to mean she didn't already have it. Not with her boss or anyone else." Hope patted Rick's hand on the table.

"Lily doesn't strike me as a player either," Sage said, as if she were following where Rick's silent thoughts were traveling. "There's an honesty about her."

"She's backing off trying to take all this away." Hope gestured to the store.

"A cold-hearted, two-timing, lying bitch wouldn't back off," Sage said. "What's Assburn look like?"

"Short, but in good shape, as if he does karate or something. Dark hair." Rick shrugged. "I didn't check him out thoroughly, but he doesn't wear flannel, I can tell you that much." He didn't think all the clothes in his closet plus the ones in his cousins' closets could match the price tag on one of Drew's shoelaces. He peered down at his jeans and rubbed at the faded denim on his thigh.

"Now don't lose all your confidence because you're not what Lily's used to," Hope said. "She likes you, Rick."

Does she?

"She agreed to check the taps with me today even though she doesn't like the woods." Rick couldn't help but smile at that.

"Well, guess you won't need me then." Aunt Joy came around the pastry case to stand behind Hope's chair. "I think Lily can chaperone you." She walked to Rick's chair and squeezed his shoulder. "Besides, you don't need an old lady cramping your style."

"What style?" Sage asked.

"I don't know, Sage," Hope said. "He must be doing something right."

"I don't know what the hell I'm doing," he admitted, "but I guess I'll try anyway." His body had already decided it wanted Lily. His mind was slowly being convinced as well. How long would it be before his heart thought it was a good idea too?

Aunt Joy clapped, leaned down, and hugged Rick. "About time, sugar. About time."

His aunt and cousins returned to their tasks while Rick and Poe checked the storage tanks by the sugarhouse. Getting full. Boiling would commence soon. He could almost smell the syrup already.

At eight o'clock, Rick meandered back into the store and peeked out the front windows. No sign of Lily yet.

She'll be here. He neatened the book swap area and placed walking sticks by the front door. A walking stick was much sexier than a freaking cane. He refreshed his coffee.

Still no Lily.

His impatience irritated him. If he had been with Lily last night, they would have most likely awakened in each other's arms and been ready to start the day together. Instead, he had left her with her furious boss who wanted to be more than her boss. He should have stayed.

Maybe Lily changed her mind. He understood why she was so afraid of the woods. Being attacked by a bear at such a young age had to be terrifying. He'd been a grown man when he'd had his heart problems, but he'd still been scared shitless. Looking death in the face changed a person. In one sense, it made him stronger. A "hey, I survived" mentality. In another sense, it made him worry about how his body would fail him next. Maybe Lily woke up this morning and couldn't face the woods today.

Rick waffled between giving her more time, calling her, and driving over to her grandmother's place. The first option seemed the most logical. The other two reeked of desperation.

"For God's sake." How had he gotten mixed up in this? His rule was to keep it simple. Trying to decipher why a female was late was not keeping it simple. He was now delving into areas about which he didn't want to be concerned.

He retired to the small office he kept in the sugarhouse. If Lily showed up in the store, his cousins would make enough noise that he'd hear. He finalized some orders, readied some packing boxes, and hoped Drew had left Vermont.

But mostly, Rick wondered if Lily would have dinner with him tonight… and breakfast tomorrow morning.

****

Lily had stayed in the master bedroom, hoping to hear Drew wheeling his suitcase down the hall, her front door opening and closing, his car—wherever he'd hidden it—starting and traveling down the driveway. She'd dressed in clothes from her grandmother's closet. A pair of faded blue jeans, a green, long-sleeved T-shirt, and a blue and green flannel shirt. She'd pulled out a pair of work boots that looked suitable for hiking in the late-winter woods. Looking at the assembled outfit, Lily shook her head.

I've finally lost my mind.

What scared her even more was she was comfortable in those clothes. Really comfortable. The fabrics were soft and moved with her. They were warm and cozy, like a hug from Grandma Gail.

Trying to hold onto her sanity, she had put the finishing touches on the presentation early this morning. She'd done a damn good job at highlighting the simplicity of Vermont. Utopia couldn't want to build here. She'd made it seem like a lost chunk of land that was no doubt beautiful, but a commercial black hole. She hoped it would be enough to convince Utopia to target some other place.

She paused in her email correspondence with Tam back in California. "Did I just admit that Vermont is beautiful?"

Lily shook her head and answered Tam's nine thousand questions about various office matters. She'd let things build up while fooling around over here and now had to dig out of a hole. Figured she'd get some of it done while she waited for Drew to leave. That'd been two hours ago. She was on Tam's last question now. A question asking if Drew had shown up.

Tam had left a message that he was on his way, but Lily had been ignoring her phone and email while she collected information about Vermont and Rick's business.

"Oh, be honest," she told herself. "You've been doing more flirting than working." Totally unlike her. She never let work pile up. Never ignored emails. Especially not for distractions of the tall, blond, and handsome type.

Lily sifted out a breath as she replied to Tam.

Drew is here and pretty upset. Waiting for him to leave. Attaching a presentation for you to proof and tell me what you think. No hotel here. Not right. Presentation is evidence. Does it do the job?

She attached the presentation, hit send, and checked the time. Shit. Past eight. She was late, and Drew was to blame, dammit. She'd have to go down and deal with him if she wanted to head over to Rick's.

And she wanted to head over to Rick's.

She'd wanted to wake up and have him beside her after what she was fairly certain would have been an amazing night. Yes, Rick wasn't like any of the men she was usually drawn to, but she wanted him anyway. She wasn't sure if it was the gentlemanly manners, the simple outlook on living, the way he'd shown her his business, how he wanted to help her with her fear of the woods, or the fantastic guitar playing, but something about Rick Stannard spoke to her.

Spoke enough that she was willing to deal with Drew so she could hike with Rick.

"This is so messed up."

She packed up her laptop and dumped it into her bag. She couldn't wait to show Rick the presentation. Hoped he liked it, hoped it did his business and home justice. Did him justice.

Lily closed her hand around the doorknob, but her camera on the bedside table stopped her. She picked it up and turned it on. Leaning against the door, she found the video she'd taken of Rick playing the guitar last night. As she watched, the way his fingers moved along the strings got her hot all over again. Who would have expected that such a quiet, reserved man possessed this amazing talent? His uncasted foot tapped to the beat, keeping time, while his hands made that guitar sing. His golden hair fell across his forehead as he looked down at the instrument and when Lily zoomed in, she noticed that his eyes were closed. He was probably imagining himself alone in his cabin, the sexy hermit.

Wanting to see Rick even more now, Lily dropped the camera into her bag, opened the bedroom door, and nearly ran into Drew. She stumbled back a few steps, but he caught her by the biceps. He backed her into the bedroom until the back of her legs touched the bed.

"Drew." Lily tried to maneuver out of his grip, but he only tightened his hold.

Her bag fell off her shoulder and landed on the bed just before he pushed her back. Lily sat only because he gave her no room to do otherwise.

With his hands still on her arms, he said, "I wondered how long you would wait in here."

"Let go of me." Lily brought her hands up and tried to break free, but Drew's hold was solid. *Kickboxer.* She couldn't out muscle him even if she had paid attention to Jean-Claude Van Damme's fighting moves.

"No, I'm all done letting go of you, Lily." Drew moved his hands to her shoulders and shoved her until she was flat on her back. "I know you don't think we should be a couple, but you're wrong. I'll show you."

He put his knees on either side of her and sat on her thighs, pinning her to the bed. He kept his hands on her shoulders so she couldn't sit up. She struggled against him, but he used his body to immobilize her.

Lily's mind raced as she realized for the first time Drew might actually try to force himself on her. His face was so red. His hands were so rough.

His eyes looked so feral.

"You don't want me this way, do you? You know this isn't right." Lily hated that her voice wavered. "If you back off me now, we can talk about this. We're friends first, Drew. Friends talk things over."

His grip loosened, but he didn't get off her. "You've done your talking. I've done my listening. Time for action." He lowered and pressed his ready body against hers.

Lily squeezed her hands between them and pushed at Drew's chest. "Get off me."

Drew slid off the bed, but grabbed her wrist and pulled her with him. "You're right. Not here. Downstairs where I've prepared everything."

He yanked Lily out of the bedroom and dragged her down the stairs. She nearly fell twice, and her bag that she'd managed to take with her clunked against the railing. When Drew stopped in the great room, Lily crashed into him.

Then she got a look at the room.

Candles occupied every surface. On the coffee table, the end tables, the mantle, the hearth. Drew had closed the blinds and unbound the thick curtains shrouding the room in a nighttime darkness. Candlelight flickered over everything. In the middle of the room, the quilt from the couch had been laid out on the floor. Orange juice, fruit, toast, eggs, and coffee sat on a wooden tray on the corner of the quilt.

Lily walked into the room then turned to face Drew. "What are you doing?"

"What a lover should do. I was wrong to let you come here alone. You need me, Lily." He stepped to her, and she shuffled back.

Mistake.

Drew's jaw clenched. "You didn't mind the lumberjack's hands on you. You weren't afraid of him."

"I'm not afraid of you." She managed to keep her voice steady though her heart slammed against her ribs. "Friends, remember? I know you won't hurt me."

Drew's jaw relaxed, a faint smile tugging at his lips. He stepped forward again, and this time Lily forced herself to stay where she was. He pushed her hair aside and cupped her cheek. "Have breakfast with me." He buried his face in her hair, let his lips trail along her neck while she stood like a statue.

The clock on the mantle read 8:30. Rick was going to think she wasn't coming. Maybe he'd come here looking for her.

Please, let him come.

She didn't want Rick to get caught in the middle, but she didn't know what else to do. She could run for the door, but Drew was as fast as her. They'd gone jogging together along Pearl Cove in the past. He could keep up. While Drew continued to explore her neck with his lips, she searched around the room for something heavy, something sharp, but the thought of actually hitting Drew made her stomach flop. She wasn't a violent person. She didn't even like to watch violence in the movies. All her treasured films were romances and comedies. She didn't do *Silence of the Lambs.*

Drew came up for air, edged her to the quilt, and motioned for her to sit. She put her bag on the couch and hesitated at the corner of the blanket.

"This food is only going to get colder," Drew said. "I expected you downstairs sooner than this. Didn't know you'd be playing so hard to get."

He kneeled and picked up a strawberry, held it up to her.

Lily stared at the berry. “Where did you get all this food? I didn’t have any of this stuff.” She’d only bought a handful of supplies, not expecting to be in Vermont this long.

“I stopped off after my plane landed. I know you can only make pancakes.” He chuckled as if he found her lack of cooking skills adorable. “That’s why you need me, Lily. To take care of you.”

He pulled on her arm, the muscles in his biceps flexing in silent warning. She kneeled beside him. Drew snaked his hands under the flannel shirt. “You also need me to get you out of these dreadful clothes.” He fingered the fabric. “Flannel? Really, Lily. What is this state doing to you? What would your grandmother say if she could see you now?”

In one swift movement, Drew jerked the flannel shirt off her shoulders, tearing one of the sleeves. Lily immediately stood and backed off the quilt. She righted the shirt and ran a hand through her hair.

“For your information, this is my grandmother’s shirt,” she said. “I wear it proudly.” She fisted and unfisted her hands as she stared at Drew. “You need to go. Now.”

She shook with anger. At Drew. At the situation he was creating. At what Vermont *was* doing to her. She was fucking Lily Hinsdale, Senior Hotel Designer for Utopia Resorts. She decided what she wore, what she ate for breakfast, who she ate it with, and by God, who she slept with. Stronger than her or not, Drew wasn't getting what he wanted.

"Get your suitcase, and get out of my grandmother's house. I'll see you back in California."

Lily picked up her bag, but Drew grabbed it and pulled her down, bringing her knees crashing onto the hardwood floor. She let out a yelp of pain as he ripped the bag off her shoulder, opened it, and took out her laptop.

"You think this will stop Utopia?" He waved the laptop in her face.

Lily shielded herself with her hands and slid away from him. He followed her until her elbows touched the wall across the great room. She had nowhere to go.

"It won't. A stupid documentary about how quaint and charming this place is won't stop the company. Won't stop me."

"You haven't even seen the presentation." Lily tried to get the laptop back, but Drew whipped it out of her reach. "Let me show it to you." *Work, get him focused on work.*

"I don't want to see it, Lily. I don't want to see any of this bullshit."

He hurled the laptop at the fireplace where it exploded into plastic bits against the stones. The pieces fell like electronic hail onto the hearth and wood floor. The following moments of silence were deafening. Lily held her breath, waiting to see what

Drew would do next and hoping she could avoid injury. Fortunately, she'd saved all her work to her flash drive and had emailed a copy of the presentation to Tam and herself.

Drew turned to face her, all the red drained from his skin. "I'm sorry, Lily. I don't know what happened. I just… I don't know." He shook his head, and his hands trembled. He was so not in control.

"You need to go back to California, Drew." She somehow got to her feet, walked over to him. "It's this place. Vermont. It's no good for people like us. It squeezes the life out of us."

Drew nodded. "All the quiet gets to you. You can't think straight."

"Exactly." She retrieved her purse, cringed at the shattered remains of her laptop, and said, "I've got a few things to finish up with here." She gestured to the house. "Regardless of what happens to this land, I need to box up some things. Personal stuff of my grandmother's. You understand." She used a voice she would use with a small child, comforting, reserved.

"Of course." He looked exhausted as if he'd surprised himself with the level of anger he'd displayed. "I can help you."

"No." Lily actually reached out her hand and patted Drew's arm. "It's something I need to do on my own, and you need to get back to California." She led him to the stairs, started him on his way up.

"You'll be coming back soon too, right?" He looked at her over his shoulder.

"Soon as I can." She managed to give him a little smile, and Drew's shoulders relaxed as he continued up the stairs.

"We belong in California," he called.

One of us belongs in a padded cell.

As soon as Drew hit the upstairs hallway, Lily bolted for the door. She didn't even think about how many animals were watching her as she ran for the Jeep. She started the vehicle, hit the gas.

How could she be more wary of what was inside that house than outside it?

Chapter Fourteen

Rick stood outside the store with Poe. 8:45. Lily wasn't coming. He should have known better than to think she'd choose him over Drew. To go hiking no less.

"Stupid, Poe. Just plain stupid." He walked into the store to get his walking stick. "That's what happens when you let your dick be in charge." He puffed out a breath and considered asking Aunt Joy if she still wanted to check the taps with him. He seriously shouldn't go alone with his ankle, but alone was exactly what he wanted. No conversations. No questions.

Poe let out a bark and rose to her hind legs to look out one of the store's front windows. By the time Rick arrived at the window, Lily's Jeep skidded to a halt, mud churning up under its tires. When she got out and headed for the store, his heart skipped a little in his chest—a good skipping, an alive skipping.

He grabbed the other walking stick and met her outside. She wasn't wearing a jacket, but what she was wearing had him stopping in his tracks. Flannel and work boots? God, she was perfect.

Except for the panicked look on her face and a torn shirtsleeve.

"What happened?" In two big steps, he was in front of her. The walking sticks dropped to the ground. "Why is your shirt ripped?"

Lily stared at the woods, and Rick thought she wasn't going to answer.

"Sorry I'm late." She squinted at him in the morning sun. "Drew needed a little convincing to go back to California."

"Did he do this?" Rick fingered the tear in her shirt.

She looked at the rip until he used his finger to lift her chin.

"Lily, did he do this?" He said the words slowly, trying to contain his rising anger.

When she blinked, a few tears chased each other down her cheek, and Rick saw red. "Is he still at your grandmother's?" He took Lily's keys from her hand and headed for her Jeep.

"Rick, no!" she said. "He's leaving. He's packing up and leaving." She wiped her cheek. "Let's go on our hike. He'll be gone by the time we get back."

"I can send the police over there. Only take a minute to make a call." What he really wanted to do was march over there and pound on Drew's face.

"No." Lily twisted the strap of her purse. "He needs to cool off. He'll fly back, focus on work, and by the time I get to California, he'll be fine."

"If he's not..." Rick rested his hand on her shoulder. She flinched. She wasn't telling him everything. "If he's not, promise me you'll get the police involved." He wasn't sure the police shouldn't be involved now. What else had Drew done to rattle her so?

She nodded then rolled her shoulders. "It'll be fine." She dug in her bag and pulled out a flash drive. "Can we load the presentation on your computer before we go? My laptop is... no longer functioning, and I want to have copies in different places." Her voice wavered for a moment, then she appeared to collect herself and put aside whatever had happened at her grandmother's place.

Rick took the drive, picked up the walking sticks, and led her through the sugarhouse to his small office. He pulled out the desk chair, made her sit then powered up his computer.

"Do I want to know what happened to your laptop?" He grabbed a bottled water off the supply shelf beside his desk and handed it to Lily.

She took the bottle and drank in long, slow swallows. Some of the color returned to her cheeks, but she shivered as she set her purse on the floor and stared at the bottle. Rick reached behind the office door and pulled a flannel-lined denim coat off a hook.

"Here. Put this on." He handed the coat to Lily, and she shrugged into it. She looked lost in it, but he loved the sight of her in his clothing.

"I left without a jacket," she said as if she'd just noticed. "I needed to get out of there."

Rick crouched in front of her, rested his hands on her knees. "Lily, look at me."

She raised her gaze. Some of the blue-green fire he'd seen in her eyes last night had fizzled.

"Did Drew hurt you? Please tell me." He braced himself for an affirmative answer.

"No." Lily shook her head. "No, he didn't, but I think he could have." She rubbed her own arms. "I think he wanted to, but then he came to his senses."

She told Rick of her morning encounter with Drew as he uploaded her presentation to his computer. When she finished her tale, he gathered her in his arms. She stiffened at first, but then let her body go limp in his hold.

"Please let me call the police," he said. "At the very least, Drew broke into your grandmother's house."

"I don't think Drew meant to be… a… a…"

"Lunatic?"

"Yeah, okay, lunatic." Lily sifted out a breath as she folded and unfolded her hands in her lap. "He just forgot how to be reasonable for a minute. He wouldn't hurt me."

"He won't touch you," Rick whispered. "You're staying with me today." He backed up and looked at her face. The thought that someone would treat her in the way she'd described made him have thoughts about the Browning Buck Mark Hunter pistol he had locked in this office.

"It's okay if you don't want to tackle the woods," he said. "I can send Hope and Sage."

"No." Lily cleared her throat and appeared to mentally file away the morning's events. "No, I want to go, Rick." She pointed to the computer. "Then I want to show you my fabulous presentation. The one that will get me out of your hair. And out of your coat." She stood and cuffed the sleeves so they didn't hang below her hands.

"There's no rush on getting you out of my hair or my coat, Lily." He offered her a smile and patted himself on the back when she smiled. "We'll check the taps along the fringe of the property. If they're doing okay, the rest are probably fine too."

Rick handed her a walking stick, and they ventured out with Poe galloping ahead and sniffing at absolutely everything in sight. He could tell Lily didn't want to talk any more about Drew, and that was fine with him. He still thought the police should be called, but he would respect her decision. He just hoped his unwillingness to relinquish his property didn't cause Lily harm. He didn't want that.

They walked quietly, side-by-side, until they hit the tree line. Poe trounced around in the leaves that had been revealed under the snowmelt. She poked her nose into rock crevasses, turned over leaves, picked up fallen twigs. Lily laughed at the coyote, and the sound floated through Rick.

"She's a puppy at heart." He took the stick Poe had dropped at his feet and threw it a distance away. The coyote dashed off in a flurry of leaves after it.

"How old is she?" Lily leaned on her walking stick. She waited for an answer, but her eyes tracked everything around them as if she were waiting to be ambushed.

"Poe is seven." He took Lily's hand and continued walking.

"How long do coyotes live?"

"Roughly the same as dogs, thirteen to fifteen years," Rick said. "In captivity, that is. They don't last as long in the wild. Most coyotes die before reaching their second year."

Poe raced back to Rick, dropped the stick again, and wagged her black-tipped tail, ready to go another round.

"She has you to thank for making it past two then." Lily picked up the stick. "May I?"

"Go for it. She doesn't care who throws it as long as it gets thrown." Rick held his breath as Lily hurled the stick across the clearing in front of them. Sure enough, Poe darted off like a red-gray blur.

"She's kind of a sloppy runner and noisy," Lily said.

"She hasn't had a proper coyote mom to show her how to run without making all that ruckus. I played with her right from the start, always had her running around, but she knew it wasn't hunting. No need to be stealthy."

The coyote started back toward them, but something caught her attention by a boulder. She sniffed around, dug in the leaves, but never put the stick down. Rick led Lily to the boulder, amazed that she didn't object to going deeper into the woods. How much had Drew scared her this morning? Apparently enough that she'd risk the woods to stay by Rick's side.

He used his walking stick to edge Poe back from the boulder. After setting the stick down, he bent to peer in a little hole and found what had the coyote so curious.

"Look." He tugged Lily over and pointed into the hole.

"Bunnies." She whispered the word.

"Have you ever seen live bunnies?"

"No," she said, lowering beside him and putting her own stick down. "They don't make a habit of hanging out on the streets of La Jolla."

"Is that where you live in California?"

"Yes, by the water. Pearl Cove."

"That explains the tan."

"Only have that because I run on the beach in the mornings. No time for the beach otherwise." She inspected the backs of her hands. "The tan's already fading from being here."

"Ah, yes, dreadful Vermont." Rick scooped up one of the bunnies that had tried to make a run through his feet. The bunny settled into his hands as if it had meant to end up there.

"It's not afraid of you." Lily shuffled a little closer. "Isn't it supposed to be terrified?"

"Probably," Rick said, "but it's been this way with me and animals since I was a kid. Ask Aunt Joy. She had a continuous stream of critters in her house when I lived with her. Poe's not my first unusual pet." He stroked the soft brown fur, and the bunny pressed its tiny body into his palm.

"What kinds of critters?" Lily reached out a finger and stroked the bunny's back. She rested one hand on Rick's shoulder as she did so, and he wasn't sure who enjoyed her touch more, him or the bunny.

"All kinds of critters. Hold out your hands." Rick transferred the fluffball to Lily's cupped palms, and she didn't move a muscle as the bunny sniffed her wrists. "Two raccoons, a skunk, groundhog, owl, fox, and a red squirrel. Most of them were hurt in some way, and Aunt Joy and I nursed them, but they couldn't go back to the wild. They wouldn't have survived."

"You're a regular wildlife hero, Mr. Stannard."

The bunny nibbled on the cuff of Rick's coat at her wrist.

"Seems you're capable of making friends too." He motioned to the bunny.

"It's easy to make friends around here. Hope, Sage, Poe." Lily leaned over and pressed a light kiss to Rick's cheek. "You."

After letting the bunny hop off her hands, she picked up her walking stick and stood. "Show me more." She waved a hand to the trees around them.

Rick used his walking stick to get to his feet. "I think you might actually like it out here."

Lily scratched Poe between the ears. "Maybe." She started walking, the coyote sticking by her side. Rick wished he had a camera to preserve that moment. A beautiful woman, a gorgeous animal, a pristine setting.

Treasures.

They spent a good portion of the morning wandering through the forest, inspecting taps here and there. Rick pointed out different kinds of trees and plants while Lily asked him questions about all of it.

"Boy, you really are a clone of your grandmother," Rick said as they headed back to the sugarhouse. "So many questions, just like when she let me lease her trees. She wanted to know how it was going to work, does it hurt the trees, would there be… let's see, how did she say it? Random, attractive men wandering through her property."

"Was the answer to that no?"

"It was."

"I'll bet she was disappointed." Lily smirked.

"Very."

"I learned to appreciate watching men from Grandma Gail. She never missed an opportunity to admire a good specimen."

"Specimen? You make it sound like a science."

"Oh, but it is." Lily brushed a few curls out of her face, and the movement put Rick in a trance. "I'm sure once I go through some of my grandmother's things at her place, I'm going to find secret notes on all the ogling she's done over the years."

"Would make a good book," Rick said.

"Or a movie. Hell, half the men she ogled were movie stars anyway."

"So what's your definition of the perfect specimen?" He took her walking stick and let Poe into the sugarhouse before them.

"Tall," Lily said firmly. "I feel like a beast next to a guy shorter than me, but it's a lot to ask, I know."

Rick made a point of standing close to her and having to look down a few inches at her face from his 6'3" height. "Doesn't seem like much to ask to me."

She grinned and slid her hands up to his shoulders, clasped them behind his neck. He dropped a light kiss on her cheek.

"What else?" he asked.

"Beards. I definitely like short, stubbly beards."

He rubbed his whiskered chin along her neck, and when she shuddered against him, he nipped at her ear.

"What else?" God, she felt so right in his arms.

"If you'd asked me last week, I'd have said I liked expensive suits and cologne and fast foreign cars." She arched her neck back as Rick kissed a line down her throat.

"And this week?" He drew in her scent, a little less grapefruit-coconut-sunshine and a little more thawing woods, pine needles, and damp earth.

"This week…" She pushed back and gave him a once over. "This week, I'd say faded jeans, a gray sweater, and a pickup truck are the right recipe."

"See, and Poe thought I took too long picking my outfit this morning." Rick eyed the coyote then caught Lily's lips with his own. He pushed aside all thoughts of how this was crazy. How it would never work out in the end. How they were so completely wrong for each other.

He tucked all that away and kissed Lily as if their lives depended on it.

****

Lily threw away logic, all that made sense in her world, and gave herself over to the fully awake dragon roaring for attention inside her. Her lips held onto Rick's as they explored each other's mouths with a blazing need rising between them. His hands tangled themselves in her hair. Her hands drew him closer. She hung on to him, his body supporting hers, keeping her from sliding to the floor in a boneless heap as he deepened the kiss, deepened his tasting of her.

Rick paused for a moment, and she let out a small, begging sound.

"Don't worry," he whispered. "I'm so not done." He picked up her purse and handed it to her. "Let's go to my cabin."

He turned to head out of the sugarhouse, but stopped and gazed down at Lily's face. "I'm sorry. Are you sure you want to do… this?" He gestured between the two of them. "I mean, after Drew this morning."

Lily grinned. A gentleman all the way. She reached up and dropped a light kiss on Rick's lips. "I want to do this. With you. Definitely."

He took her hand and gave it a quick squeeze. Lily followed him out of the sugarhouse. For a man with a casted ankle, he crossed the distance to his cabin like an Olympiad. Poe took off in the other direction. Had Rick sent the coyote a silent message to scram?

Once inside, he took his coat off Lily and hung it by the front door. Very much the host. All perfect manners. He slid her purse off her shoulder and set it down on his kitchen table.

"Your phone's in there?" He peered inside.

"Yes."

"Shut it off."

"It is off."

"Good." He stepped back and locked his front door. "No coyote, no phone, no distractions." He took Lily's hand and pulled her down the hallway. He pushed open a door with his casted foot, and Lily followed him inside.

His bedroom. A full bed with a solid, navy comforter and two plump pillows cased in shams sporting pictures of wolves in snow. A single bureau lined the far wall, a closet in the other, and two huge windows on the third wall framed a glorious mountain view. Books littered the bureau and the nightstand where a lamp made from a short, narrow log stood. The last piece in the room was an acoustic guitar.

"It's a small room. I know, but Poe and I don't need much space." Rick pulled his sweater off, leaving Lily with a tremendous view of him in a plain, gray T-shirt and jeans.

"It's perfect, Rick." She backed him up to his bed and lightly pushed on his shoulders until he sat. She took some time to investigate his biceps with her fingers, tracing along his contours until goosebumps appeared on his flesh.

He slid his hands to the backs of her knees and pulled until she had to position a leg to either side of his waist. Rick scooted back on the bed as she joined him on it. He was on his back and looking up at Lily.

"I've never met anyone like you." He hooked some of her curls behind her ear.

"You mean someone who barges in and tries to sell your world to a hotel chain?" Lily pursed her lips and attempted to roll to Rick's side, but he stopped her with his hands firmly on her hips.

"Do you still want to do that?" He didn't move while he waited for her response. Didn't breathe.

"You know I don't. If my new designs don't dazzle, or that presentation doesn't work, I won't stop, Rick. Utopia will not build here or on my grandmother's land." Lily cupped Rick's cheeks as she looked down at him. "In fact, I had Tam, my assistant back in California, email me sale documents for Grandma Gail's property. Not a sale to Utopia, but to you."

"Really?" Rick raised himself to an elbow.

"Really." She stared out the window and drew in a breath. "Those documents, however, were on my laptop that is now in a bazillion pieces, and I didn't save them to the flash drive. I'll text Tam later today and get her to email the documents to you directly."

Rick's gaze slithered over her like hot fudge. "Thank you, Lily."

"Least I can do after wreaking all this havoc on your peaceful existence." She shrugged.

"Seems I could stand a little havoc." He reached his head up and captured Lily's lips again. As he kissed her, he leaned back on the bed, taking her with him. In a quick motion that had her laughing, he rolled her to her back so he was on top.

He peeled the torn flannel shirt from her shoulders, and Lily slid her arms out.

"Your grandmother's?" He laid it gently, reverently, on the comforter beside Lily.

"Yeah. She's got an entire wardrobe I knew nothing about." She gestured to the rest of her outfit.

"It looks good on you." Rick moved to sit on the end of the bed. He reached for her feet and undid the laces of her boots. The shoes knocked to the wood floor, one at a time, and he leaned over her. "I'm betting it'll all look good *off* you too."

"Only one way to find out." Lily pulled her T-shirt over her head and heard Rick's swift intake of breath. His smile widened as he ran a finger along the lace edge of her purple bra. His fingertip was rough, but the sensation had her pressing into his touch, wanting more.

"I thought the woods, the mountains, offered a great view, but this… you… you're something." He flattened his palm against her stomach, and she closed her eyes at the warmth of his skin against hers.

"The back view isn't as pristine." Lily silently cursed the bear attack scars. Four deep gouges. Eternal reminders.

Rick removed his T-shirt and peered down at his chest. He traced a rough line of skin down between his ribs. "We've both had our battles."

Lily pushed to sitting and ran her finger along the light pink track of damaged skin. "The important thing is that we won, and we're here now." She pressed her lips to his, and he wrapped his arms around her. Lily couldn't be afraid of anything in his embrace. Nothing could touch her, but Rick. She only felt him, only wanted him.

The rest of their clothes came off, and Lily was sure she had never seen a more beautiful man. Muscles in all the right places. Long, lean, but powerful legs. Strong, yet comforting arms. Rick's body fit against hers as if it were made to do just that. His touch brought her need to the surface, screamed at that dragon to come and conquer. There were times she felt as if she were climbing a mountain, the air getting thin, her muscles straining at the challenge. Other times, Lily was falling, down, down, drowning in a pool of pure bliss. She was hot, yet she shivered. She was cold, yet she burned. Every sensation Rick caused in her, she felt soul deep, as if she'd never felt anything before.

"Hang on," he said around a very male groan as she ran her fingers along his abs.

He reached over to the nightstand and fumbled with opening the single drawer. After rummaging around for a few seconds, he pulled out a box of condoms.

"A hermit with condoms?" Lily asked. A moment passed where she wondered if the shy, quiet guy persona was just a ploy to lure women into his bed.

"Sage bought them for me last month on my birthday," he said as he wrestled a packet out of the formally *unopened* box. "She said if the box wasn't empty by Christmas, she was going to get me a prostitute. She thinks she's so funny."

Lily took the condom and eased it on him, loving the feel of him in her hand, loving how ready he was for her. "Remind me to thank Sage for these."

When he slipped inside her, she lost herself. Lily Hinsdale, Senior Hotel Designer for Utopia Resorts did not exist. She was only a woman. A woman sharing an unearthly experience with a man. A remarkable man with the power to make simplicity feel like so much.

This is what I've been waiting for.

Rick was tender, making love to her in slow, easy strokes. His lips explored her territory, left no surface unclaimed. Her body matched his movements, thrust for thrust, caress for caress, kiss for kiss. Rick somehow knew exactly what she liked, what she would respond to, as if they had done this a thousand times, had the choreography memorized. Only Lily knew this wasn't a dance she'd done before. Not like this. Never like this.

Her breath came in gasps as Rick sought deeper, hidden places. He said her name as if it were the only word he knew, the only word that meant anything to him. When she cried out on a wave of euphoria, and her desire reached its peak, he was right there with her. Timed to perfection. Giving her a pleasure so great her body became drunk on it.

Rick collapsed to her right side, his chest rising and falling. Lily was certain neither of them would be able to walk a straight line. She put her hand on his chest and found his heart was beating as hard as her own.

"Are you okay?" She was suddenly concerned they'd overdone it. What if he'd gotten too excited?

"*Okay* is so not the right word." He turned his head to face her, his eyelids closing over those sky-blue eyes.

"Your heart is racing."

Rick put his hand over Lily's on his chest. "Yeah, and for once, I don't give a shit if it explodes."

He took a few deep breaths then turned Lily so he could scoot up behind her. A second later, his lips and tongue teased the scars on her back. She closed her eyes, and the bear attack became a distant memory. One that would plague her no more.

With a final soft kiss to her shoulder blade, Rick folded his arms around her waist. His hands rested on her stomach, and he pulled her against him.

"I may have enjoyed you more than pancakes," he whispered into her hair.

Lily snuggled into his hold. If they could stay like that forever, nothing could hurt either of them again. Nothing.

Chapter Fifteen

Rick stopped in his bedroom, his hair wet from the shower he'd taken. He only wore a towel around his waist and the cast on his ankle. He paused to look at the rumpled sheets and quilt on his bed where only an hour ago he'd had the most spectacular time of his life. He'd been intimate with a couple of women in New York, but none of them compared to what he and Lily had shared. Such synchronicity, as if they had each known what the other was looking for, what the other needed. His breath caught in his chest just thinking of being inside her, of having her wrapped around him so perfectly, so completely.

God, he felt so alive. Invincible.

He threw his clothes back on and noticed Lily's torn flannel shirt still at the foot of his bed. Rick curled a fist around the shirt as he thought of Drew having his hands on Lily in such a way as to cause that rip. How could anyone touch her that way? That bastard better be on his way back to California.

Lily clanged around in the kitchen, and Rick smelled pancakes. He never thought he would admit this, but it was a nice feeling to have a woman making herself at home in his cabin. A woman who made his heart dare to hope it could beat forever.

He peeked out into the hallway, taking in a deep inhale of fresh coffee. Lily hummed something as she mixed batter, and Poe sat in the middle of the kitchen. They seemed to be getting along well.

He closed his bedroom door and noticed the hooded sweatshirt he kept hanging on the doorknob was gone. An image of Lily wearing it—and hopefully nothing else—as she cooked flashed into his mind. On that thought, he crawled across the bed and picked up the phone. He dialed and watched the minute change on the alarm clock sitting on the nightstand.

"Danton Police Department, Avaline speaking, how may I direct your call?"

"Avaline, Rick Stannard." He hoped she could hear his low voice.

"Hey, darlin'," she said. "Joy tell you how I cleaned house at Bingo the other night?"

"She may have mentioned how you got all the lucky cards." Rick didn't have time for the small talk, but Avaline was his aunt's closest friend and fiercest Bingo competitor. She'd been running the office down at the police station for as long as he could remember. He was pretty sure once she retired, a massive breakdown in Danton law enforcement would immediately follow.

"The Bingo Gods were with me, Rick." She let out a little laugh. "What can I do for you?"

"Looking for a favor."

"Name it. I do you a favor, then Joy owes me one later."

"Sounds good to me. Could you send an officer to Gail Hinsdale's place sometime today?"

"Something amiss with the granddaughter who's staying there?"

Rick rolled his eyes at the small town knowledge of everybody's doings. "No, Lily's all right, but she had an unwanted guest. She told him to leave, but I want to make sure he's gone. I also don't want her to know I called you."

"A secret white knight," Avaline said. "How romantic! You finally find a gal to pull you out of your shell, sweetheart?"

Rick could picture his aunt telling every aspect of his nonexistent love life to Avaline as they placed Bingo chips on B-9. "Maybe. I don't know. Will you send someone?"

"Of course. Billy and Walt ain't doing nothin' important anyways. I'll send them over for a look-see. Tell them to be discreet too. Hush, hush. This unwanted guest got a name?"

"Drew Ashburn." Rick didn't want to give out more information than he needed to. Just wanted the police to check out Lily's place. Not that he planned to let her go back there tonight. He smiled over what he did plan for her.

"I'll give you a call back only if this Drew guy is still there. How's that sound for keeping it under wraps?"

"Sounds perfect. Thanks, Avaline." He got ready to hang up.

"One more thing," Avaline said. "If he is there, any reason we should take him into custody?"

Rick thought about that. Lily didn't want to make a big deal out of Drew getting rough, breaking and entering, or destroying her personal property, all of which were excellent reasons to take him into custody.

"If he's still there, maybe a police escort to the airport could be arranged?" Less likely Lily would find out he'd made this call if Billy and Walt just enforced Drew's flying back to California.

"Easy enough," Avaline said. "Tell Joy I'll see her at Bingo."

"See her and whip her ass, right?"

Avaline's laughter filled the receiver as she said good-bye. Rick hung up, feeling a little guilty about going behind Lily's back, but thinking he'd done the right thing anyway. Boss or not, Drew had crossed the line in his treatment of Lily. Rick wished he had been there. He wasn't sure what he would have done, but was certain Drew would have known he wasn't welcome in Vermont.

Casting aside the dark thoughts, Rick opened his bedroom door and shuffled down the hallway. He was getting tired of the sound of the cast scratching along the wood floor. From the ache that still radiated from his ankle, he still had a ways to go in the healing department. With his heart, recuperation had taken an eternity. He could stand a few more weeks in the cast for something as trivial as a severely sprained ankle.

When he entered the kitchen, he spent a few silent moments watching Lily as she moved around the tiny room. He was disappointed she was completely dressed under his sweatshirt, but loved how that garment took on another level of comfort with her in it. Her hair was drawn up in a high ponytail that spilled red-blonde curls still wet from her shower. She turned around toting two plates heaped with pancakes and almost dropped them when she saw him.

"Shit, Rick." She quickly put the plates on the table.

"Sorry. I didn't mean to scare you." But she did look adorable with her eyes bugging so wide and her mouth slightly opened. God, he wanted those lips on him again.

"What are you doing over there when the pancakes are over here?" She pointed to the two places set at the table, and he liked the balanced look of it. "I hope you don't mind pancakes again or that I rifled through your entire kitchen, but I was absolutely famished."

"I told you I could eat pancakes at every meal," Rick said as he walked over to her. He caught her lips in a long, deep kiss, and she actually licked her lips when he stepped back. "And I'm just as famished."

"For pancakes or something else?" She leaned toward him and raked her fingers through his damp hair.

He grabbed her around the waist. "Both."

"Sex and pancakes. It's all we need." Lily freed herself from Rick's hold, but not before he kissed her again.

"I can't argue with that." He sat across from her and took in a whiff. "Banana pancakes?"

"I like to mix it up." Lily shrugged one shoulder. "Maybe we can have chocolate chip pancakes for dessert later." She grinned at him. "Or would that be overdoing it?"

"No such thing." He covered his dish in syrup and offered the jar to Lily. As she doused her own dish, he watched the amber liquid creep along the pancakes, and he got some creative ideas for that "later" she'd mentioned.

He ate with several breaks to look up at Lily. What an odd thing to be happy someone else was sitting with him. He'd spent so much time alone he never thought it could be another way. He should be terrified. Anxious that Lily was going to spoil his tranquility, shatter the harmony he had established in living by himself apart from all the things that try men's souls.

But looking at her, eating pancakes in his sweatshirt with coils of soft hair framing her face, he couldn't find the fear or the anxiety. Not a drop of it.

Foolish. This little snapshot was not representative of the real world. An isolated, post-sex contentment was what it was. Something that tomorrow would shine a spotlight on and reveal all the impossibilities.

But that was tomorrow. Today was today.

"You want to look at the presentation," Lily said as she took their plates to the sink when they were done eating.

Tomorrow was closer than Rick cared to accept.

"Sure." He helped her clean up and they went into the living room. After powering up his laptop, he took the flash drive from Lily. He rested his ankle on the chest in front of the couch and sat back with the computer on his lap. Lily snuggled up next to him. The couch was quickly becoming his second favorite spot to be with her.

Rick watched the presentation with Lily pointing out various things she would say when she shared it with Utopia.

"It's the best we've got," she said when it was over. "I hope it's enough. I'll launch right into my Arctic design after I show this. Hopefully I can suck them into an idea they can make more money on."

"That's what it's all about anyway, isn't it? The money." He closed the presentation and opened a set of barn blueprints.

"Utopia speaks in money. It's the only language they understand." She craned her head to see the screen. "What's this?"

"The Tramtons' barn." Rick slid the computer to Lily's lap, and she leaned forward to study it, chewed on her upper lip, and tapped her fingers on the edge of the laptop. He got a glimpse of what she must look like at her desk in California working on designs. Had he ever seen a more beautiful woman? Not even the female characters in some of his favorite books could compete with Lily.

"Is this an oculus in the ceiling?" She pointed to the eye-like opening in the barn's dome-shaped roof.

"Yeah. The owner wants to let natural light in, save on electricity. The barn's going to be in a pretty open area, lots of sunshine." Rick scrolled through a few more schematics for the oculus. "Ted Tramton hired me to design their barn over the winter and start building it after the syrup stops running. That time is fast approaching."

"This is beautiful, Rick." She waved a hand toward the bookshelf where he kept the photo album of the barns she'd already looked at. "They're all barns yet they look as if they've been made by a dozen different people. That's not easy to do. Designers usually fall into a certain style, but yours are all unique."

"I imagine you have to do the same thing with all the hotel themes." He took the laptop back, closed it, and set it on the chest.

"That's how I know it's not easy. To get that level of originality in a one room construction like a barn is even more challenging."

"It's about the art of it."

"Exactly. Not the money it'll make from rich tourists."

"I thought you liked rich tourists."

"I did." Lily shook her head. "I do."

Rick fought not to smile at her uncertainty. Was the city girl warming up to the woods?

"I need to go to the Tramtons' and measure up a few things now that the site has thawed some. You up for a ride with me?" He slid his leg off the chest and tried to seem as if he didn't care if she came or not. But dammit, he did care. More than he wanted to.

"I suppose I need some way to work those pancakes off." She knocked her knee against his. How, even fully clothed, could she jumpstart him like she did?

"I've got a way we can work them off." Rick grinned at her as he stood and offered her a hand.

She accepted his hand and stood beside him. "Then I guess I'll keep feeding you pancakes."

****

With Poe jumping ahead of them, Lily and Rick stopped into the store where Rick's aunt insisted they take some leftover muffins she'd experimented with to the Tramtons.

"Becky will love these," Aunt Joy said as she held the kitchen door open and directed Rick inside. "Then she'll blab about them to everyone she knows, and we'll have customers throughout the season sniffing around for these babies."

"Probably not a marketing plan you'd use in California, right?" Sage peered up at Lily from one of the tables where she was ordering baking supplies from a catalog.

"Word of mouth is the strongest form of advertisement." Lily scratched Poe between the coyote's oversized ears. "We may not use the word 'blab,' but the idea's the same."

"East coast or west coast, consumer psychology is an important part of any good business." Hope stepped down from the ladder she used to dust the various artifacts displayed above the bookshelves.

Lily hadn't noticed them before and wandered over to have a closer look. Old farm tools mostly, wrought iron and rusty. Some copper cans and tin buckets. A few lanterns with old beeswax candles inside. They would have been perfect in the log cabin resort. The one she was no longer designing.

Career suicide. Refusing to carry out a deal Rita and Webster had both approved would not be earning her high marks on her annual evaluation. As good as her presentation and new designs were, it'd be a miracle if they were enough ammunition against building in Vermont. Utopia saw dollar signs in these woods, and rich tourists *would* come if a resort were built here. Hell, Utopia had people slugging it out to the middle of the Chihuahuan Desert. Why should these quiet woods be any different?

She needed something else to save Rick's land. Land she'd put in jeopardy with her own insecurities. She could have told Rita she needed time to put something together and research a suitable location. She could have been not quite so worried about dealing with her grandmother's land. Holding that bunny this morning in the woods with Rick had made her see the woods weren't all bear attacks and blood and pain. Some of it was soft and warm and gentle.

"That one on the end," Hope said, tugging Lily over to her side and pointing to a photograph of two men in a twig frame. "The one on the left is my father, and the one on the right is Rick's. They were in their late teens there. Handsome chaps, don't you think?"

Lily squinted up at the picture. Two young men leaned against an aging barn. Both had blond hair, one light like Hope's and Sage's, the other a little darker like Rick's. They looked like sturdy farm boys with muscles where they should be and easy smiles on their faces.

"They were only a year apart like me and Sage," Hope said. "Mom says they were tighter than tight like me and Sage too. I don't remember them well. I was only four when they died, but I do remember when you saw one of them, the other wasn't far away."

Hope moved the ladder to the end, climbed up, and ran the feather duster over the frame. She blew the men in the photo a kiss, came back down, and stood next to Lily. "You have any brothers or sisters?"

Lily shook her head. "Nope. Not sure my parents even wanted me." That was something she rarely admitted out loud, but it came tumbling out now.

"They may not have planned to have you, but I'm sure once they saw you, they realized how lucky they were." Hope threw an arm around her shoulders while Poe pushed her muzzle into Lily's knee.

"My dad maybe." Lily looked at Hope. "My mom definitely not."

"No family's perfect." Hope gave her a squeeze before releasing her and patted Poe on the nose. "But I do know that when I marry the drummer and have me some babies, I'm going to love them to pieces."

Lily laughed at the love struck expression on Hope's face. "So, do tell me about the drummer."

Hope did a little dance around the nearest table. "We've got a date this weekend, which will probably just involve dinner at Black Wolf Tavern, but I don't care."

"That's because you're a cheap date," Sage said as she gathered up her catalogs. "Bet Lily could tell us about some real expensive dates."

Rick came out of the kitchen toting a plain, brown shopping bag. "Ready?" he asked as he passed Lily and headed for the front door. Poe scrabbled after him, her tail wagging.

Screw expensive dates. A ride in a pickup truck with a man who smells like maple syrup is just as good. Better actually.

"Sometimes it's not the money they spend on you," Lily whispered to Hope and Sage. "It's how hard they can get your tail to wag."

Hope and Sage burst into laughter, and Rick threw Lily a questioning look. He was about to say something, but Sage said, "Hey, is that Rick's sweatshirt you're wearing, Lily?"

At that, Rick gave Sage a look and ushered Lily out the door without letting her answer. "Sorry about them. They never stop." He led her to his truck.

"Would you really want them to?" she asked as he unlocked the passenger door and held it open for her. She leaned against the truck and looked up at him. The sun caught in his hair, reflecting gold, like found treasure.

"No, I guess they wouldn't be Hope and Sage if they didn't bust my balls every chance they got." He grinned, set the brown bag down on the floor of the passenger side, and trapped Lily with a hand on either side of her.

"What are you planning, Mr. Stannard?" Lily ran a finger along his bottom lip, and his blue eyes disappeared behind his lids for a moment.

"Well, the way I figure it, Hope, Sage, and probably Aunt Joy are watching us from the window as we speak." He leaned down and dropped two short kisses on Lily's lips. "We may as well give them a show."

In a quick motion that had Lily giggling, Rick pulled her away from the truck, spun her around, and dipped her low. He kissed her long and hard as he held her, and Lily could hear the women hooting and cheering from inside the store. Rick straightened so they were both standing again and planted one more kiss on Lily. She actually felt a little dizzy.

She somehow made it back to the truck and watched as Rick faced the store and bowed to his audience. When she looked to the window, three sheets of paper sporting the number "10" were on display.

"High marks," Lily said, letting Poe hop into the truck before she climbed in.

"They've never seen me behave in that fashion, I assure you." Rick started the truck and headed down the driveway. "Felt kind of good."

His cheeks were a little flushed, and Lily took the hand he rested on her thigh. Her day had started out like a scene from *The Shining,* all crazed Jack Nicholson, but Rick was rewriting the ending with each kiss, each look, each silent promise to treat her like something very valuable.

How long could she pretend that was enough?

Chapter Sixteen

After thirty-five minutes of driving along a scenic stretch of Route 91 while Rick pointed out various points of interest and a ton of cows, the truck came to a stop in front of a huge farmhouse with a wraparound porch. Behind the house, a dilapidated barn looked as if a swift breeze would knock it over.

"Hence the need for me," Rick said as he gestured to the barn. "That thing is not fit for equipment, never mind the horses and cows Ted wants to raise."

They got out of the car, and Lily grabbed the bag of Joy's muffins. As she followed Rick, she had a weird sense of being exactly where she was supposed to be.

How can this be right?

She was wearing faded jeans, a man's hooded sweatshirt, and work boots now covered in mud for heaven's sake. A coyote trotted along beside her, and she wasn't freaking out about it. She carried a load a muffins while she walked up the creaky steps of a farmhouse. Her laptop was destroyed, and her cell phone was back in the truck.

And the damn thing was off! She didn't even care how many messages she was missing.

What's happened to me?

"Lily?" Rick touched her shoulder. "You okay?"

"I think so, yes." She let out a little laugh and reached up to kiss Rick's cheek.

"What was that for?" He shifted a notebook of graph paper from one hand to the other.

"I'm not sure yet. Just felt you deserved a kiss." She rang the doorbell, and a howl erupted from inside. Lily froze as Poe answered with her own howl.

"Don't get nervous." Rick immediately took Lily's free hand. "The Tramtons' dog is big, but he's even gentler than Poe."

Another low canine cry sounded beyond the front door. "How big?"

"Great Dane big. I'm sorry. I totally forgot about him."

The door opened, and Lily thought she was looking at a pony. "How do you forget about that?"

Poe walked right in, past a short, square woman who stood by the door, and touched noses with the mammoth dog.

"Old friends," the woman said, angling her head toward the two animals. "Hey, Rick. C'mon in."

"Becky, this is Lily," Rick said.

"Yeah, I figured. Just got off the phone with Joy." Becky pushed her long, brown braid off her shoulder then shook Lily's hand.

"Of course you did." Rick glanced at Lily as if to apologize.

"Those would be the muffins she was yapping about?" Becky pointed to the bag.

"Yes." Lily held the bag out to her. "Nice to meet you."

"Likewise." She wiped her hands on the red and white-checkered apron around her waist and took the bag. "Ted's out back by the site, Rick. You can cut through the house. Lily will come with me, and we'll bring out some cider."

Rick saluted Becky. "Becky makes fresh cider from apples they grow in the orchard behind that eyesore of a barn."

"I'll be so glad to watch that thing crumble." Becky raised one hand to the sky as if she were thanking God. "C'mon, Lily. Kitchen's through here."

Lily followed Becky, but stopped when Poe headed her way instead of Rick's.

"Real nice, Poe." He shook a fist at the coyote who pushed her nose into Lily's hand. "Traitor. That's fine. I'll be friends with Brom here instead." He patted the Great Dane's back and winked at Lily.

As Rick disappeared deeper into the house, Becky said, "You succeeded in tearing Poe from

Rick, her daddy, and Brom, her boyfriend. That's mighty impressive for a tall, skinny city girl."

Had Joy described her as a tall, skinny city girl? Probably. "Poe just knows we've got the food." She rubbed the coyote's ears, and golden eyes squeezed closed.

"Don't think it's got anything to do with the food." Becky set the muffins on a table made from scarred barn wood. "Animals get a sense 'bout people, and Poe's got a good sense 'bout you."

"Maybe." Lily shrugged and ran a hand over the top of the table. The wood was fantastic. Tongue and groove with a rich, dark stain. Stout, square legs supported the top and two benches were tucked under either side.

"Like furniture?" Becky got out a basket and lined it with a blue linen napkin.

"I like themes," Lily said. "This table suggests a time period."

Becky pushed the basket toward Lily and tapped the bag of muffins. After pulling up the sleeves of Rick's sweatshirt, Lily filled the basket as Becky said, "My great-great-great-great-great granddaddy made a table like this when he bought this land back in the 1700s. When we took over the land, I found an old picture of that table and had Ted make me one just like it." She pressed her palms to the top. "I love this table."

"It's gorgeous." Lily folded the empty brown bag and Becky took it.

"Gorgeous as my new barn will be. Have you seen the designs?"

"I have. It's a masterpiece." Lily looked out a door leading to the backyard where Rick stood in a cleared field with a dark-haired man in overalls and calf-high rubber boots. Rick was a giant next to the man who appeared to be shorter than Becky.

"Wouldn't expect anything less than a masterpiece from Rick," Becky said following Lily's gaze. "Man's syrup is good, his designs are good, and I'll bet his kissing is good too."

Lily's face grew hot as she tried not to look at Becky. She focused on Rick who bent over to rest his tape measure on the ground, but that only made her warmer. Really, a spectacular ass. Grandma Gail would so approve.

"That pink in your cheeks answers that." Becky laughed. "A man that can do that to you is a good man to have around. Gets cold around here come winter."

She picked up the basket and handed it to Lily. Becky toted a tray of drinks and used her bottom to push open the door. In the enclosed, four-season porch, they set the basket and tray on a small table surrounded by a wooden bench and two wooden Adirondack chairs. Poe settled down at Lily's feet like a rug.

"Ted make this set too?" Lily asked as she sat on the bench so she could face Rick and still watch him.

"Yes, he did. He's great at furniture, but the barn project completely baffled him. Plus, we don't have the equipment to get rid of the old one and erect a new one, but Rick does."

What equipment was needed, and where did Rick keep it? Lily didn't remember seeing another building besides his cabin, the sugarhouse, and the store. But then again, she hadn't seen the barn on her grandmother's property either.

Rick and Ted walked across the field and up the steps to the porch. Ted walked through the door first and gave Lily a friendly smile.

"Afternoon, miss," he said. "I'm Ted."

"Lily." She shook his hand then pulled back when the Great Dane sloshed his tongue across her forearm.

"Oh, Brom." Becky popped up from her seat and searched the two trays on the table. "I forgot napkins. Be right back."

Lily stared at the wet strip on her arm. Rick stepped over to her and pulled the sleeve of his sweatshirt down then back up.

"There, all set. I've wiped way worse on that sweatshirt." Rick grinned as he sat in one of the Adirondack chairs.

"Wonderful." Somehow Lily didn't care what Rick had wiped on the sweatshirt. Who was she right now?

Becky came back and dropped the napkins on the table. "Let's see what all the fuss over these muffins is about." She handed out paper plates and offered muffins to everyone. Moments of silence followed as everyone took bites.

"Well, she's done it again," Ted said. "Joy could mix mortar, cow manure, and cat litter into her muffins and the darn things would still taste heavenly."

"That's the truth." Becky nodded. "Woman's got a gift for coffee and pastry. Can't deny it."

"You're going to supply us with cider again, right?" Rick asked after drinking some.

Lily took a swig, and it was as if she were drinking liquid apple pie. So tasty. Not a great deal of cider being served in La Jolla.

"You want cider, you got cider, Rick," Ted said.

Lily thought of the business meetings she had back in California. Conference tables, fluorescent lighting, slideshow presentations, paperwork, and sometimes three hundred dollar meals at fancy restaurants. But Rick and Ted had accomplished the same thing over cider and muffins on a back porch. No legal consultations, no signatures. Just neighbors trusting neighbors.

Utopia Resorts would never understand a thing like that.

"So what's the plan for the barn?" Becky dusted muffin crumbs off her lap.

Rick grabbed his notebook and slid out copies of the blueprints Lily had seen earlier. He had views of the outside and the oculus in the roof.

Becky took the papers and studied them. She nodded at each one and set them on the table for Ted to look at. "Mighty fine, Rick. Just what we wanted."

"Good. I have questions now on the interior. How many stalls you want, what size tack room, loft or no loft, that sort of stuff?" Rick fished a pencil out of the binding of the notebook.

His strong fingers curled around his pencil. Those fingers had brought Lily such pleasure earlier today. She had to bite her bottom lip to keep from sighing aloud.

"Twelve by twelve tack room ought to do it," Ted said. "Would love a loft, but won't that cut down on the natural light we got coming in through the top?"

"Don't make it a full loft." Lily tore her gaze from Rick's hands and focused on the blueprints. "If you make it so it lines the inside perimeter of the barn, but only juts out maybe three-fourths of the width of the stalls beneath, you'll still get plenty of light."

"I like that," Ted said. "Gives me extra storage above the stalls too."

Rick scribbled the idea into the notebook and looked up at Lily.

"I'm sorry," she said. "I shouldn't have butted in like that." She put a hand over her mouth. This wasn't her meeting.

"I'm all for butting in when the idea is good," Rick said. "And this is a good one. Easy enough to do." He gave her a half-smile.

"You two make a nice team," Becky said. "Don't they, Ted?"

"Sure enough do. Two heads are usually better than one." Ted went back to studying Rick's designs.

"Especially when one of those heads is as pretty as Lily's here." Becky elbowed Lily and winked at Rick.

"Can't argue with you there, Becky." Rick tapped his pencil on Lily's knee then continued writing in the notebook. "How many stalls?"

"Eight, right, Becky?" Ted looked to his wife.

"Eight ought to do it." Becky nodded and refilled Lily's cider glass.

As Lily drank, she marveled over how in sync Becky and Ted were. Rick asked them about other little details, and they agreed on everything. Shared the same vision. Wanted the same end product. Lily had never been so completely on the same wavelength with anyone like that. What was it like?

Rick walked his customers through the process expertly. He recorded all their wishes, re-sketched a few parts of the barn on the copies until the Tramtons were happy, and made a plan to come back to demolish the old barn. He may have claimed to live a simple life, but he had a deep understanding of business. He knew what needed to be done, how to do it, and how to cater to his customers' needs.

Is he that different from me? Didn't Lily do the same thing for Utopia? Maybe her world was faster-paced, more technologically advanced, and rang up a bigger bill, but in the end, weren't the basic facets the same?

Rick built barns. She built hotels. The space between their worlds wasn't that big.

Lily finished her cider and wished it had included alcohol, because now her thoughts were all over the place. She couldn't let Vermont suck her in. She had a successful life in California. One she needed to get back to even if it meant facing Drew.

Drew. Lily checked the clock on the wall to her left. 4:00 p.m. Drew should be on a plane back to California by now. She should check her phone for messages from him or Tam. Lily put her hand into the pocket of Rick's sweatshirt, forgetting for a moment her phone was in the truck. She couldn't remember the last time her phone had been more than a foot away from her person for any length of time. She had to get back into the swing of things. Had to focus on selling her grandmother's property to Rick, cleaning the house out, and getting back to California. She'd spent enough time flubbering about in Vermont.

She purposely tried not to look at Rick as he finished up with the Tramtons. The more she looked at him, the more she wanted the ridiculous.

Instead, she turned her attention to Poe still resting by her feet. Part of the coyote's front paw was on her boot, and when Lily moved her foot, Poe raised her head and let out a puff of air. She rose to all fours and stretched out her legs. First the back then the front. Lily expected the animal to head over to Rick or the Great Dane sleeping at the other end of the porch, but Poe didn't do either of those things.

The coyote sat on her haunches and pawed at Lily's knee instead. Lily scratched Poe's neck as the animal looked up at the porch roof. When the coyote lowered her head, she angled her face at Lily, giving the distinct impression she was thinking something pretty heavy. Poe's big ears twitched toward Rick as he spoke with Ted, then twitched back toward Lily. With a big coyote yawn, Poe rested her head in Lily's lap and closed her eyes.

"Bet you never had a coyote in your lap in the city." Becky reached over and rubbed Poe's muzzle.

Lily shook her head. "Can't say I have." Against her leg, a contented hum vibrated in the coyote's throat, sending an odd comfort throughout her body.

"She bothering you?" Rick asked.

Lily made the mistake of looking at Rick. Between his pale blue eyes wondering if she was okay and the warm fur of Poe in her lap, Lily couldn't help but think this was all a girl needed. Fancy galas, penthouses, even her precious movies didn't fill her like sitting on this porch was right now.

What am I going to do?

"Lily?" Rick reached over the table and touched the knee not covered by Poe's head.

"Yeah." She looked at Rick again, then at Becky and Ted, all three of them studying her with concerned looks on their faces. "I'm fine, but I think I'm going to head to the truck and check my messages while you finish up here." She stood, and Poe whined a little.

"Come here, Poe." Rick patted the armrest of the Adirondack chair he sat in, and the coyote whimpered at Lily, but did as Rick asked. She sat by his chair then lowered to her belly.

"Thank you, Becky, Ted," Lily said. "Nice meeting you. Wonderful cider. Good luck with your barn."

She didn't wait for them to answer. Instead she opened the porch door and stepped into the house. She didn't stop until she was at the passenger side of Rick's truck. She leaned against the door. The sun was a fading ball of orange in the sky. A small chill rattled Lily's spine as dusky gray crept through the woods. Everything was still. Quiet.

She needed noise and right now. Lily climbed into the truck and closed the door. She fished around in her purse until her hand closed around her cell phone. God, it had been off for hours. She turned it on and waited for the screen to announce an insane number of messages.

"Shit, ninety-seven." Lily hung her head. She scrolled through them, responding and deleting accordingly, until she only had two messages left. The first was a text message from Tam.

Got presentation + designs. Look great. Don't know if Utopia will bite. Sent sale docs. When r u coming back? Marilyn Monroe has no one to talk to in office.

Marilyn wouldn't even recognize Lily in her current ensemble. She'd roll her eyes from that poster that hung in her office, and Lily would feel the need to don some pearls.

And Tam feared the same—a presentation and new designs weren't enough to stop the hotel plans. Damn. Lily texted back she needed the sale documents again, but sent to Rick's email instead. She told Tam she'd explain why later and conveniently left out when she would be returning.

The final message was from Drew. A voice mail. Lily hesitated over whether to listen to it or not. Curiosity won and she played the message.

Lily, I'm so sorry for the way I behaved this morning. I think I saw you with that Stannard guy and lost my mind or something. I don't know. I've always pictured you with me and no one else. No excuse for acting like I did. I understand if it's over this time, but I hope you can at least forgive me, and we can work together and be friends. I'm leaving your grandmother's house now. I'll see you when you get back to California.

Lily checked the time on the message. 9:30 a.m. Not too long after she'd left for Rick's. Good. She hadn't wanted Drew to hang around at her grandmother's while she wasn't there, especially while he was in the mood for smashing things.

She rolled her shoulders, glad that one problem had flown back to California. Now she just had to solve the resort problem and the falling for Rick problem.

Lily left her phone on and dropped it into her bag as Rick appeared on the front steps of the Tramtons' house. He gave them a wave and headed to the truck with Poe running circles around him. When he reached the driver side, he opened the door and let Poe jump in. The coyote immediately licked Lily's ear.

"She missed you." Rick slipped in behind the wheel. He nudged Poe so she slithered into the back of the cab behind the front seats. "I missed you."

"Sorry," Lily said. "I had to get out of there. I was feeling a little too… too…"

"Comfortable?" Rick put his notebook under the armrest and slid his key into the ignition. He rested his hands on the steering wheel and looked out the front window.

"I shouldn't be this comfortable, Rick. I don't belong here. This isn't my world." Lily threw a hand out to indicate the farmhouse and fields.

"Well, if it's any consolation, I haven't been acting like myself either." He ran a hand through his hair, and the strands fell back into place. Lily had an immediate desire to touch that golden hair. To feel it between her fingers.

Rick angled himself against the door and pointed at Lily. "I blame you for all this."

"Me?" Lily shook her head. "No, I definitely didn't want this to happen."

"Well, what's more believable?" Rick asked. "That me, a hermit with limited social skills, seduced you, or you, coming from a family of people known by the world for their charm, seduced me? Hmmm?"

"Let's call it even," Lily said, unable to hide a smile. "There are obviously forces at work beyond our control."

"Control. That's it right there." Rick started the truck. "Both of us are letting go of the control we usually cling to. I don't think it's necessarily a bad thing, Lily."

"I don't either, and that's what has scared the designer boots right off me."

Rick laughed, and Lily closed her eyes as the sound massaged her body. Did she have any sounds that did that back home? No. And she'd filled the silence with stupid parties and movie lines. And work.

"Come home with me, Lily," Rick said before backing out of the Tramtons' driveway. He tugged on the sleeve of her sweatshirt. His sweatshirt, technically.

How could she say no? She didn't want to. Lily wasn't in a rush to go back to her grandmother's house where she'd do nothing but remember the fury on Drew's face or start boxing up her grandmother's possessions. Neither activity held any optimism.

She huffed out a breath of defeat and said, "Oh, okay." She folded her arms across her chest as Rick eased the truck onto the main road. A light snow had started to fall, dusting the muddy road in a speckled whiteness.

"I'm not happy about it either," he said, pulling at her arm until the left one came free. He flattened her hand against his thigh. "I know we're both being stupid right now. This has nowhere to go besides down the shitter, but for once, I just don't care."

"Me neither," Lily said, "but somebody ought to."

Chapter Seventeen

Rick followed Lily and Poe into his cabin. He turned on the lights in the kitchen and gave the answering machine a quick glance. No messages.

Good, that means Avaline didn't call, and Drew is on his way back to California.

Lily had told him about the voice mail Drew had left her, but Rick liked knowing the police had checked it out as well. He let out a breath as Poe stood right by Lily and barked.

"Why is she doing this, Rick?" Lily thrust a hand down to the coyote. "She's glued to me."

Poe barked again.

"Hush, Poe." Rick tapped Poe on the nose, and she sat in the middle of the kitchen. When Lily walked to the counter to put her purse down, the coyote got up and escorted her. Rick stepped in front of Poe and kneeled down. "What's with you, girl? Give Lily some space, okay?"

He stood and filled Poe's food bowl. That distracted the coyote enough to allow Rick to take her place in front of Lily.

"Now *you're* in my space." Lily pressed her hands against Rick's chest but didn't push.

"Yes, I am, and I plan to be in it for the rest of the evening and well into tomorrow morning."

He dropped a few short kisses, teases, on Lily's lips. When she leaned her body into his, a rumble escaped from his throat. "It was getting increasingly hard not to touch you at the Tramtons' house." He ran his lips along her cheek to her ear.

"I felt the same. You're hot whether you're playing the guitar or scribbling on graph paper." She grabbed a fistful of Rick's sweater and backed them both into the dark living room.

Rick lowered her onto the couch and wished he could snap his fingers to start a fire in the fireplace. Doing it the old fashioned way would involve him having to leave Lily unattended for a spell, and he couldn't fathom doing that when her hands roamed down his back, tugged off his sweater. She arched up, pressing harder against him, as she trailed hot kisses down his neck. She slid her hands under his T-shirt and removed that too.

He kneeled back, one leg bent on the cushion underneath her, the casted one still trying to support him, but shaking at the strain.

"You're in no condition to have the top." She arched a devilish eyebrow at him and grinned.

"You want the top?" Sensitive areas tightened in Rick's body as he thought about Lily hovering over him.

"I'd like to give it a go, yes." She wiggled up to a sitting position.

"By all means." He grabbed her around the waist, pulled her to him, and gently turned around so they switched places. He leaned back on an elbow and watched her unzip his sweatshirt she still wore. She pulled the zipper down an inch at a time, slowly revealing the green, long-sleeved T-shirt she had on underneath as if unwrapping a gift, only it wasn't Christmas or his birthday. It was an entirely new special occasion. One he wanted to celebrate daily.

The sweatshirt dropped to the ground, and Rick made quick work of ridding Lily of her T-shirt. They slid off everything else until she wore only a pair of diamond stud earrings, and he just the cast. He was so glad he hadn't hurt his back on his snowshoeing blunder. That would have made all this fun impossible.

And, shit, he was having fun. More fun than he'd ever allowed himself to have. Even before New York and the heart attack, he'd always played it slow and careful. When you had lost your parents and learned about death at age eleven and your heart had thrown in the towel at thirty-one, life appeared to need a helmet. Danger was around every corner and waiting to take away what you loved most. Rick had forgotten, however, that life was also about taking risks and letting go. It was about following a path to see where it would lead. He liked this path he was blazing with Lily. It would no doubt lead him in a big circle, but what a ride on the carousel.

Lily sat on his hips, her bottom all soft and hot on his thighs. She reached up an arm and pulled out the elastic binding her curls together. They spilled about her naked shoulders in a red-gold explosion that had Rick's temperature soaring. Had he ever seen someone so spectacularly perfect?

No. Never.

He reached up and brushed his hands over her breasts, and she moved her hips just enough to completely undo him. Rick pushed to sitting and wrapped an arm around her. His fingers found the scars on her back, and he played them like the strings of his guitar, only the music she made came in soft moans and heated gasps. She was a glorious instrument, and for the moment, all his.

After digging a condom out of the pocket of his discarded jeans and putting it on, Rick covered Lily's breast with his mouth. She placed her hands on either side of his head then slid them down his back. He released her, only to find a new level of ecstasy when she parted her legs, took him in, surrounded him. She writhed in small circles with him inside her, and he was certain he'd reach his peak in seconds. Long before she would be ready. She knew exactly how to work him, exactly what movements would bring him to the edge.

Lily pushed Rick to his back, letting her fingernails glide over his chest, down his arms. She leaned forward, changing her angle and overwhelming him with sensations too good to be of this planet. Surely he had reached heaven in this angel's embrace.

Finding his mouth with hers, Lily nipped slowly at his lips then took what she wanted more forcefully, her tongue grazing along his teeth, dancing with his tongue. She tasted like apple cider and maple cinnamon muffins, and Rick wanted to live on her alone, eat nothing but her day after day.

He snaked his hands around her hips and drove himself deeper into her wet folds. When she threw her head back, shuddered, and whispered his name, he gave all he had to her. She spasmed, again and again, her eyes closed, her hands flattened on his chest right over his scar. With a final shudder, she lowered so her head rested on his chest, and she released him, slowly. He forgot how to breathe as each inch of him left her. They lay like that, Rick on his back and Lily using him like a beach towel, for several catching-their-breaths moments.

Finally Lily said, "Everything sounds good in there." She rubbed a hand where Rick's heart was returning to a steady beat. "I love that sound." She slipped her arms around Rick's waist and snuggled against him.

He gathered her as close as he could, let his legs tangle with hers, dropped a kiss on her forehead, and pulled a quilt from the back of the couch down over them. "I feel like it's guaranteed to beat forever with you around."

She raised her head and rested her chin on his collarbone while she kissed his jaw. He shifted to look at her face, illuminated only by the light spilling in from the kitchen. A face he could stand to look at for eons. Those big, blue-green eyes had him. He was trapped prey and perfectly happy to be that.

Right now.

Maybe longer.

Rick coiled some of Lily's curls around his finger, and her eyes closed again. When they opened, headlights outside made her pupils get small. Rick angled his chin up so he could look—upside down—out the window at the front of the house. He never closed the shades, but he'd never had a need with just him in the cabin. The only guests he had were Aunt Joy and his cousins.

"Shit." Rick wrapped the quilt around Lily's shoulders then grabbed his jeans. "Probably Hope or Sage come to annoy me. Again."

"Don't be mad at them. They didn't know you were going to be… entertaining this evening." Lily walked her fingers along his stomach, both tickling him and arousing him.

"Turn off the kitchen light. Let's pretend I'm not home." He indulged in a steaming kiss before picking up Lily's clothes and draping them over her shoulder. "Bathroom. Go. Unless you want to greet my cousins or aunt in this lovely quilt you're wearing."

She pressed another kiss to his lips and disappeared down the dark hallway. Rick waited until the bathroom light went on and the door closed before putting on his clothes and straightening the couch cushions and pillows.

"There," he said. "No funny business happening here. We were just… talking."

He knew the moment he opened the door Hope and/or Sage would know what he'd been doing. *Oh, God, what if it* is *Aunt Joy?*

Rick could take busting from his cousins, but Aunt Joy would want to know what in the hell he was thinking, and honestly, he didn't know. All he did know was Lily gave him back something he'd lost a long time ago.

Faith. In other people. In life. In himself.

When he reached the door, he heard footsteps coming up the front stairs. He turned on the porch light and opened the door.

The gun pointed at his gut was the last thing he expected.

****

Lily hummed quietly in Rick's bathroom as she dressed. She was simultaneously exhausted and exhilarated from making love with him.

And that's what it was. Making love. She ran her fingers through her hair, trying to calm the runaway curls. She'd only been having sex before Rick. Going through the motions, pleasuring her body, but not her heart.

Not her soul.

She looked at herself in the mirror above the sink. Something extra glittered in her eyes. A spark, and not one put there by work. Yes, designing was her life. She didn't think she could stop doing it if she tried, but there had always been something missing. She hadn't allowed herself to realize that before meeting Rick. She'd filled the emptiness with parties and movies, but had never felt complete. He had somehow managed to fill that intangible void.

"It's ridiculous, but you love him," she whispered to her reflection. Lily had a sudden urge to tell Rick, crazy as it was. She hardly knew the man, but she pulled on his sweatshirt and opened the bathroom door. She nearly tripped over Poe who sat right at the threshold.

"What are you doing, girl?" She scratched the coyote and tried to walk around her, but the animal kept corralling her back deeper into the hall as if it were herding sheep. "Stop being so silly, Poe."

Lily forced her way down the hall, zigzagging around the coyote and listening for Hope, Sage, or Joy's voice.

Instead, she heard nothing.

"Rick?" She entered the kitchen and rounded the wall separating the front door from the rest of the cabin. When she saw Rick's hands up and out to his sides, she clamped a hand over her mouth to stifle the scream.

"You lied, lumberjack." Drew pushed the pistol into Rick's stomach, backing him up. "I knew Lily was here."

She swallowed her shock. *Not the time to go all damsel in distress.* It was her fault Rick was in danger right now. Her doing. She should have just gone back to California when he said he wasn't going to sell his land to her.

"Why are you still here, Drew?" Lily stepped closer to Rick. "And where the hell did you get that gun?" She tried to get in front of Rick, but he wouldn't let her. He kept her at arm's length and away from the weapon.

"Stay over there, Lily." Rick backed up a couple steps.

Drew looked at the gun and waved it. "Do you have any idea how easy it is to get a gun around here? Another reason you don't belong in Vermont, Lily. It's too dangerous, honey. You need to come back to California with me. Where you belong. With me."

"I'm not ready to go back to California, Drew." Lily met Rick's gaze as he looked over his shoulder at her. She wanted to tell him she loved him right now. Just in case.

No. I'm going to get rid of Drew first.

She squared her shoulders and took a step toward Drew. She'd just back him up to the front porch, get him outside, and deal with him. He wouldn't shoot her. She was sure of it.

"Lily, what are you doing?" Rick tried to keep her back.

"She's coming to me, lumberjack. She's changing her mind about you." Drew's smile held all the smugness of a true villain. How could she have felt bad for not loving him? How could she have had sex with him?

Because I didn't know what making love was. Not until Rick.

She had to protect Rick, the man who had shown her the simple pleasures in life, the man who had opened her eyes. She took another step, but froze in place when Drew pressed the pistol into Rick's stomach and wiggled his finger on the trigger.

"No!" Lily yelled.

At that same moment, Poe came running from the hall. She arrowed right for Drew, and he moved the gun from Rick's gut to squeeze off a shot. The coyote whimpered and limped back on three paws, her front right one oozing fresh blood.

Lily went to the animal, but the gun was already trained back on Rick. Gathering Poe close, Lily took off Rick's sweatshirt to blot at the wound. It didn't look deep, just a graze, but it infuriated her.

"Drew, I thought you were on your way to California. Your message, your apology, you said you were leaving."

"Look, no one has to get hurt here." Rick shot a worried glance to Poe, and Lily knew he wanted to go to her, but Drew wasn't moving the nose of that gun.

"She's okay, Rick," she assured. "It's not deep." Turning to Drew, she said, "What is it you want?"

"You." Drew angled his chin toward her. "I want you, Lily. Always you."

"You can't have her," Rick said.

"Seeing as how I'm the one with your gun, I think I can have anything I want." Drew smiled and glanced at the weapon. "Nice piece, by the way. Think I'll keep it as a souvenir."

Lily thought about rushing Drew and knocking him off his feet, but she knew under his overpriced leather jacket muscles coursed down his arms and across his chest. She was taller, but he wouldn't topple easily and not without potentially hurting Rick in the process. No way she would take that risk.

She tied the sleeve of the sweatshirt around Poe's leg to stop the bleeding. The coyote rested its head in her lap. "You came for me, Drew." She eased Poe off her thighs and stood. "Put the gun down, and I'll go with you." Lily walked to Rick's side.

"No, Lily." Rick turned his attention away from Drew and grabbed her shoulders. "You are not going anywhere with him." Pushing her behind him, he turned back toward Drew and the gun.

"Seems as if Lily wants to come with me, Mr. Stannard." Drew craned his head so he could see over Rick's shoulder to Lily. "Better let the lady make her choice. The right choice."

Lily put her hand on Rick's waist, and Drew flicked his gaze to her movement. The gun never wavered in his hand, but he clearly didn't like Lily touching Rick.

"Rick, I brought this trouble here," Lily whispered. "Let me take it out of here too."

"You're not going with him." He reached his arms back and took Lily's wrists in his hands.

"I don't get Lily, you don't get to take another breath, lumberjack." Drew shifted the gun to his other hand, and Lily knew he could make the shot right or left-handed. She'd seen him shoot a bow and arrow with both hands, swing a bat, a tennis racket, a hockey stick. He'd always hit his mark with either hand.

"If I go with you," Lily started, "we have to leave right away. You don't shoot anyone."

"That's not as fun, but fine. C'mon, let's go." Drew held out his hand and motioned for Lily to come to him.

"Lily's not going anywhere with you." Rick pushed forward, letting the barrel of the gun press into his stomach again. "Put the gun down, and we'll fight fair."

Drew seemed to consider this for a moment, but Lily wasn't going to stand around and wait for them to duel to the death over her. This wasn't medieval times or the Wild West or Hollywood.

"Drew's right, Rick," Lily said. "I'm choosing him. You and I wouldn't have worked anyway. I mean, you're a hermit. Too simple for my tastes. The bathroom in my penthouse is practically the size of this entire cabin. You can't afford me with your little maple syrup business and building barns." The words burned her tongue. Lying never tasted right.

Drew backed toward the front door, a delighted grin on his face. "Got to love her spunk, huh, lumberjack? It's what makes her so sexy."

"You don't mean that, Lily," Rick said, but she could tell by his voice he wasn't sure.

Good.

"You won't move to the city. You'd rather hide behind the trees. I can't live like this." She threw her hands out to indicate the cabin and the woods outside. "Besides, I just wanted your land, Mr. Stannard. If I had to degrade myself to achieve that goal, so be it. I'd do anything in the interest of my career. To please my boss and company." Shaking her head, she said, "I belong with Drew in California."

"I'll second that," Drew said.

In a lightning fast movement and while Rick was looking at Lily with a dumbfounded expression on his beautiful face, Drew sent a roundhouse kick into Rick's stomach. When Rick bent over, Drew drove his elbow into the back of Rick's neck.

Lily struggled not to rush to Rick's side when he collapsed to the floor. "That wasn't necessary, Drew." She balled her hands into fists at her sides. "He would have let me go with you."

"It was taking too long. Besides, you should be happy I didn't kill him."

Drew nudged Rick's crumpled form with his foot, and Rick let out a groan as he rolled to his back. His eyes opened, and Lily let out a breath.

"See, he's still alive." As Drew reached over Rick's body and yanked Lily to his side, he trained the weapon on Rick again. "Hope you got a good taste of her, because you'll probably never snag a woman of this caliber again, lumberjackass."

Lily looked Rick straight in the eye though it killed her to do so. The hurt on his face tore her up, but how else could she keep him safe? If Rick thought she had made her choice—if she'd insulted him, made him think this was all a ploy to get his land—he wouldn't go looking for her. If he didn't go looking for her, he wouldn't encounter Drew again, and he'd stay out of danger. Nothing could happen to Rick. Lily wouldn't be able to live with herself if something did. Better to fly back to California with Drew and deal with him there, far away from Rick and his family.

Rick made a move to get up, but Drew waved the gun. "Get up and you're dead. Lily shouldn't have to see me kill you, but I will if I have to."

Lily watched Rick's right hand as it rubbed a spot between his ribs. Was this bullshit causing another attack? She juggled between kneeling beside Rick to make sure he was okay and getting Drew the fuck out of there. Deciding that Rick was conscious enough to get to a phone and dial 911, Lily slid her feet into her boots and tugged the bigger problem through the front door. The cold night air bit at her. Ripped through her skin. Made everything hurt.

"C'mon, Drew." With a final look back at Rick spread out on the floor, Lily climbed in the open driver's side of Drew's rented SUV and scooted to the passenger side as Drew got in. He closed the door and started the vehicle. Within moments, Drew had peeled out of the driveway.

Lily didn't say anything. She was too busy concealing the fact that she was crying. Her insides ached over what she had said to Rick, over the hurt she'd caused him. She closed her eyes and imagined saying what she had planned to say to him after coming out of the bathroom. That she loved him.

Now he'd never know.

But he'll be safe, she reminded herself. And that, above all else, was essential.

Drew patted her hand, and Lily struggled not to shirk away from him.

"Now, this is right, honey. You and me. Just like always." He smiled cheerily, and the range of emotions Drew exhibited in a small time frame seriously freaked Lily. "I've packed your suitcase. It's in the back with mine. I've organized flights and a limo to drive us back to Gems Utopia once we land. Figure you're tired of being carted around in a pickup truck like cargo." He rolled his eyes as they continued down Rick's long driveway.

"It's okay, Lily. You're allowed to screw up. You wanted to see what it would be like to have sex with a pity case. A poor, country simpleton. But was it worth it?"

Yes, good God, yes. "No. It was silly. I guess I got scared in the woods, and you weren't here to see me through it."

Drew tossed his arm around her shoulders, and Lily wondered where he'd stowed the gun. "I'm sorry, honey. I shouldn't have let you go alone. None of this would have happened if I'd come with you. It's okay now. We'll get you settled back in La Jolla, and I'll oversee the building of the resort here. We'll make plans. It'll all work out."

Not the right time to mention she still intended on changing Rita and Webster's mind about the Vermont resort. Lily definitely didn't want Drew traveling back here by himself. She could only imagine what methods he would employ to get Rick off his land.

Drew looked at her now and smiled. Lily marveled over his ability to seem like a normal person. He'd fooled her for years, fooled their clients, fooled the world. She shivered at the duality.

California was full of actors, pretenders playing parts, but Lily hadn't realized it was also full of liars.

"Keep your eyes on the road," Lily said, sounding more cranky than was probably safe. "It's slick out here." She looked out the windshield at the dusting of snow on Rick's driveway.

"Another reason to go back to California," Drew said. "It's always sunny. None of this cold, white shit to deal with."

Not long ago, Lily would have wholeheartedly agreed with Drew. Now she wanted nothing more than to be at Rick's, snuggling under a quilt next to his naked body, and watching snow fall over his woods. She wouldn't have thought it possible to become a completely different person in just a matter of days, but meeting someone like Rick could bring about such a transformation. Lily knew she would never be the same. She didn't want to be.

Drew reached for Lily's hand and pulled it over to his lap. He stroked her skin, and Lily had to bite the inside of her cheek to keep from telling him off.

Not yet. Once they got back to California, she'd tell him where to go and how to get there. Bastard.

"Come closer." Drew pulled up the armrest between them. "I want to be near you, and you must be cold without your jacket. Do you want mine?" He peeled his leather coat off his left shoulder.

"No, you're driving, Drew. I'm fine. Let's just get to the airport and we'll sort things out." Lily's teeth clenched together. She wasn't sure how she was going to endure a six-hour flight across the country with this man.

Drew slammed on the brakes and let out a growl. The SUV spun out just after the bend in Rick's driveway, and Lily clawed at the dashboard.

"Drew, what are you doing?" The words screamed out of her throat as she watched the woods swirl around them.

"You haven't chosen me, have you?" Drew shouted as the SUV skated toward the right edge of the driveway. "You're just protecting him!"

Lily focused on Drew's white-knuckled grip on the steering wheel. He wasn't driving anymore. Not really. His fingers were melded to the wheel, his arms rigid. There were little corrections he should have been making to keep the SUV from sliding into the two-foot deep gully lining Rick's dirt driveway.

Instead, Drew looked at Lily, realization that she'd been just telling him what he wanted to hear painted across his face. He opened his mouth to say something more, but the SUV careened over a small snow bank to the right of the driveway and into the muddy gully. The last thing Lily saw was the airbag deploy as the hood of the SUV rammed into a maple tree.

White filled her vision, but she managed to open the passenger side door. She peered back into the SUV and looked at Drew's body wedged between his seat and the airbag. He didn't make any noise, didn't move.

Is he dead?

Lily shivered. She had to call 911, but she didn't have her cell phone. It was back up at Rick's in her purse.

"Dammit."

She climbed around to the driver side of the SUV and opened Drew's door. His body slumped out, and Lily couldn't stop him from hitting the ground. A thin trickle of blood oozed into Drew's eyebrow from a cut she couldn't quite see in the darkness. One headlight of the SUV must have been broken and the other was only illuminating the maple trees in front of them.

Lily propped Drew against another tree and searched his pockets for a cell phone. And a gun. She didn't find either.

"This night is going to shit." She opened the back driver side door and dug into her suitcase Drew had so psychotically packed for her. She pulled out her short, black leather jacket, because it was the first one she found. Not the warmest, but now that she looked around, she saw that they were at the part of Rick's driveway that branched off and connected with her grandmother's. She could walk up to Grandma Gail's house and call an ambulance. Or the police. Or both. As much as she wanted to leave Drew there to bleed in the snow, she wasn't a completely heartless bitch.

Lily trudged up Grandma Gail's driveway. She'd thought about heading over to Rick's, but decided against it. She needed him to think she was gone to keep him safe. Besides, if she saw Rick again tonight, she'd never be able to leave.

And she had to leave.

Chapter Eighteen

Is Lily truly playing me to get my land for Utopia?

The thought of it clawed into his soul as Rick stared at the ceiling. He'd fallen in love with Lily as absurd as that sounded. Rick Stannard, spokesperson for clean, quiet, natural living, had fallen for a woman who dressed like a movie star and worked for a company that wanted to build a hotel where his house stood.

How the hell had that happened?

A wet tongue sloshed across his cheek and he turned his head to see Poe had crawled up alongside him. She used her teeth to pull at the sweatshirt Lily had tied around her paw.

"Are you okay, girl?" Rick picked himself up from the floor and took a few deep breaths. Nothing felt broken. Things were definitely bruised though. "Let's have a look at you."

He untied the sweatshirt and found the wound—only a small slice—had already stopped bleeding.

"You'll be fine, Poe. Good girl." He scratched her between the ears then shuffled to the bathroom and got what he needed to bandage Poe's paw.

Once he'd finished seeing to the coyote, he grabbed his keys and his jacket and limped to his truck, trying to move as fast as he could. His mind came back online with the sharp slap of cold night air outside. A dull ache throbbed in his chest, but it had less to do with his physical heart and more to do with worrying if Lily was okay. Even if she had meant what she'd said, that she didn't want to be with him, that she'd chosen Drew, Rick still wanted her to be safe. She couldn't be safe with Drew. The guy might be obsessed with her, but that didn't mean he wouldn't snap and hurt her.

As Rick started his truck, his pulse was in his ears, loud and fast. He had to calm down or he'd be no use to anyone. He hit the gas and followed the tracks Drew's SUV had made in the dusting of snow on his driveway. When he hit the part of his driveway that curved, he noticed the tire tracks swooped out in a wide, erratic loop. He pulled his truck over and got out. He followed the tracks until he found Drew's SUV against one of his maples. The tree didn't look any worse for wear, but the SUV's hood resembled an accordion and the passenger and driver side doors were open.

Please make Lily be okay.

Rick pulled out his cell phone and dialed 911 as he moved closer to the SUV hoping to find Lily uninjured somewhere close by. That was when he saw them.

Footprints.
In the snow.
Two sets.
Leading over to Gail Hinsdale's place.

****

Lily kicked the snow off her work boots as she climbed the steps on the porch. When she reached the door, she let out a groan.

"No key, genius." Her purse was still at Rick's. She leaned her head on the front door and stared at the tips of her boots. Good thing they weren't her brown suede ones. They never would have survived the walk up the driveway.

Huffing out a breath, Lily turned around. "Now what?"

A crunching of snow made her snap her head up. When a dark shadow lumbered toward her, she flashed back to the bear attack. She couldn't even get the scream to come out of her throat.

"Lily…" The shadow crashed into the stairs and reached out a hand to her. "Lily."

In the streetlight glow, she caught Drew's profile. His body was draped over the steps, his breathing coming out in loud gushes. Lily edged around him, wanting to get as far away as possible, but as she passed by, he grabbed her ankle. She tripped down the steps and smashed onto the driveway. Her shoulder took the impact the hardest and instantly the wet and cold of the snow seeped through her jeans to her skin. She looked up to find Drew standing over her.

"It takes more than a little bump on the head to do me in, honey. You should know that." He grabbed a handful of snow and pressed it to the gash on his forehead. After a few seconds, he dropped the bloody snowball and yanked Lily to her feet.

She tried to free her arm from Drew's vise grip around her biceps. "You're hurting me."

"You ran away from me." The words barely had room to come out from between his clenched teeth as he tightened his hold on her. Drew's other hand reached into his coat pocket, and Rick's gun made a reappearance.

"I was getting help, Drew. Did you want me to leave you there to—"

"Stop it. Just stop it, Lily." He shook her, and her eyes stung as Drew shined a flashlight into her face.

"Take this and come on." He forced the flashlight into her hands and used the gun to prod her into the woods. The dark, snow-covered woods. Past Grandma Gail's barn. The barn Rick had built.

After a few minutes of walking, Drew pushed Lily between two huge boulders. On the other side, a tiny log cabin stood covered in snow-dusted vines and surrounded by trees. She would have never noticed it if Drew hadn't directed her toward the decrepit structure. Inside, damp, moldy air assaulted Lily's nose. Fluttering sounded overhead, but she couldn't see what made the noise. She had to keep the flashlight focused on the ground to keep from tripping. She wasn't sure she wanted to know what was up there anyway.

She was certain of one thing. Something she'd learned when she was ten years old.

The forest was a killer.

Chapter Nineteen

Rick hiked up Gail's driveway, the footprints he followed illuminated by his flashlight beam. His ankle throbbed, the mother of all headaches slammed about in his skull, and his left arm felt slightly numb. He shook it all off and pushed ahead.

For Lily.

She *was* real, wasn't she? He hadn't imagined her. He'd talked to her, touched her body, eaten her pancakes. Loved her. What they had shared, not once, but twice, in his cabin had been more real to him than any encounter he'd ever had with another human being. Granted, he didn't make a habit of having encounters with folks, but Lily was different. Yes, she came in ready to wipe the floor with him to make way for her hotel, but something happened between them that had just fit into place so perfectly. Lily had made him see there was such a thing as too much solitude. She made him want to leave behind the way of the hermit, take chances.

He had to find her.

Police sirens howled in the distance as Rick reached Gail's house. The footprints led up the front steps where the snow was matted. As he climbed the stairs, his flashlight picked up something in the snow. He backed up and kneeled down.

Blood. And more footprints leading toward Gail's barn.

Rick took off through the woods. He managed a clumsy run, but his ankle screamed with each pound of his heel to the ground. He was aware of the police cars skidding into the driveway, the blue and red lights swirling against the leafless trees. Officers yelled at him to stop, to put his hands up. Rick imagined how it all looked. A man running awkwardly through the woods, but he didn't stop. Every minute that passed was a minute Drew could be hurting Lily.

His legs burned as he climbed the hill leading to Gail's barn. What if he was too late? What if Drew had done something rash?

What if the blood on the snow was Lily's?

****

Lily's face slammed into the cabin wall, splinters of rotten log sticking into her cheek like tiny daggers.

"You called the police," Drew growled in her ear as he held her head against the rough wall. His body crushed her from behind like a wall of steel.

The sirens were loud now. Close. Maybe not too late.

"I didn't call them," Lily said. "I don't have a phone."

"Liar!" Drew pulled her away from the wall so quickly her flesh ripped from her cheek. "I had nice plans for you and me. Life plans, but you came here, and Stannard ruined everything. Why did you let him, Lily? Why would you lower yourself to his level? You come from stars. Stars!"

His voice had reached a hysterical range, and his body shook with anger. The flashlight had dropped to the floor. Now the cone of light reflected across uneven wood boards illuminating strange, mushy piles scattered around. Lily had originally thought the floor was covered in dirt, but now she wasn't sure.

And what was that odor?

Probably fear.

"I'm with you, aren't I, Drew?" she said with more calm than she thought possible. God, her cheek was on fire.

"But it's a trick. You ran away." Drew shook his head. "You just want to get me back to California. You don't want me. You want him!"

Drew was screaming now, and something bristled in the darkness overhead. A light breeze ghosted over Lily, sending tendrils of her hair back and stirring up a new scent. Very organic and sharp.

"What is that?" Drew turned his head wildly in all directions. "Pick up the flashlight. Do it. Now!"

Lily reached down, her eyes still locked on the gun in Drew's hand.

"Shine it up to the ceiling." Drew poked the barrel of the pistol into Lily's shoulder, and she had a moment to think if this were a movie she would have shut it off a long time ago. Probably have thrown up her popcorn too.

When the flashlight beam made an arc up to the ceiling, Lily shrieked. Hundreds of tiny, dark bodies hung in clusters from the worn rafters of the cabin. Furry bodies with leathery wings and big ears writhed above her like an undulating black wave.

As the word *bats* formed in Lily's mind, the dilapidated door of the cabin was torn out of the threshold. She dropped the flashlight again and as it rocked back and forth on the ground, a work boot and a cast came into view at the doorway.

Rick charged in, and Lily tried to get between him and Drew before that gun fired. Rick's arms came around her, spun her around, and pushed her toward the doorway.

"Get out of here!" he yelled.

Lily stumbled forward, but caught herself before falling. She turned to see Rick face Drew as the gun lifted.

"You're not going to win this, lumberjack. She's mine. She'll always be mine." He aimed the gun at Rick's chest.

With movement akin to Hollywood special effects, Lily reached down, picked up a pile of what she now realized was bat shit, and hurled it at Drew. It hit him square in the face with a gloppy splat sound, and he immediately started coughing and spitting.

Rick sent his fist into Drew's jaw and backed him up into the wall. He knocked the gun from Drew's hand as armed police officers filed in.

"Everyone, freeze," the closest officer shouted.

No one moved, but Drew continued to choke on his mouthful of bat feces.

Lily held her breath, sure any sudden movement would cause something catastrophic. Guns were trained on all three of them. If she got out of this alive, she swore she'd only watch animated Disney movies from now on. Nothing with even the slightest bit of tension or danger.

"Which one of you is Rick Stannard?" the officer asked.

"I am," Rick said, backing away from Drew.

The officer's gun pinning Rick in place lowered.

"She's Lily Hinsdale." Rick pointed to Lily, then to Drew. "He's the asshole you're looking to arrest."

Rick pulled Lily up against him, and she instinctively buried her face into the curve of his neck.

"You just made the wrong choice, Lily." Drew rushed at Rick, but the police officer covering Drew shot first. One hit to Drew's thigh.

Bat wings flapped in unison around the cabin, the thunderous boom of gunshot sending them into flight.

Lily shielded her head with her hands as Rick used his body to cover her from the frenzied bats. A gunshot sounded over the squeaking animals, then another. Another.

When everything fell silent, Lily dropped her hands and wiped bat excrement off her fingers. The last of the bats soared out the open cabin doorway, and Drew lay on the scat-covered ground, Rick's gun in his hand and blood pooling under his body.

The officer who had first shot Drew was on the ground as well.

"Are you hit?" another officer asked.

"Yeah. Shoulder. Perp picked up his gun while the bats went crazy. I couldn't see. Is he dead?"

"Yes," a third officer confirmed. "Get the EMTs in here." Turning to Rick and Lily, he said, "Mr. Stannard, Ms. Hinsdale, we'll need statements from each of you. See one of the officers outside."

Rick thanked the officer and ushered Lily out the doorway. He didn't loosen his grip on her, and she marveled over how subjective touch was. Drew had held her tight, and she'd desperately wanted her freedom. Rick had an even tighter hold, and she never wanted him to let go.

Not ever.

Chapter Twenty

After talking to the police, Lily let an EMT tend to her scraped cheek inside her grandmother's house. No stitches, but a shit load of splinters had to be removed from her face. Hurt like a bastard.

Could have been so much worse.

Alone now, Lily took Rick upstairs to the master bathroom. In the bright vanity lights, she got a good look at him. He looked as if he'd been in battle with mud streaking his jeans. Lily leaned to catch a glimpse of herself in the mirror. Her face wasn't much cleaner. Angry red gouges grooved her left cheek. Somehow seeing it made it hurt more.

"Hot water ought to make that feel better." Rick ran a hand through his disheveled hair and shook his head.

Pushing off the threshold where he leaned, he joined Lily at the mirror. He winced at his reflection. "We look like hell. Let's share a shower and wash this night away."

He limped to the stall, reached an arm in, and turned it on. In a few seconds, hot steam curled along the ceiling of the bathroom and called to Lily.

So did the naked man tugging at her T-shirt and jeans.

Lily got into the shower behind Rick after he slid off the air cast and drew the curtain closed. He moved over so the spray hit Lily too, and she stepped a little closer to the water. To Rick. When he took the soap, turned her around, and ran his lathered hands over the scars on her back, she didn't know what to do with herself. Part of her wanted to grab him. Grab him and never let go. Forget everything that had just happened and selfishly take what she wanted.

Another part of her knew better. She had to keep her distance. She'd put him in danger. Nearly gotten him killed tonight.

"Lily, you're shaking." He backed her up against his body and wrapped his arms around her. "No one's going to hurt you now. I promise."

Rick's lips pressed to the back of her neck, and Lily couldn't stop her hand from reaching back, hooking it on his hip, pulling him closer. His hands came to her stomach, slid down to her thighs, then up to her breasts. His caress, combined with the hot shower water, made Lily's guilt slough down the drain.

If Rick could want to touch her right now, perhaps she wasn't evil incarnate for bringing trouble his way. Perhaps she could have this man she wanted so much more than anything in the world.

Perhaps she could just have tonight.

Lily slowly turned around to face Rick. Her hands, slick with soap, slid up his abs, along his chest, over his scar, then down his arms. His blue eyes disappeared behind his lids as Lily circled her hand over his arousal. He let out a soft moan and lowered his lips to hers. Before Lily could think too much about it, she was losing herself again in his kiss.

"Lily," Rick breathed.

"I didn't mean what I said," she blurted, tears streaming from her eyes. "This wasn't a trick to get your land. I swear. What I feel for you, Rick, is real. More real than anything I've ever felt in my life. I just wanted Drew to leave you alone."

"I know." He brushed the tears away with his thumb and kissed her again. "All I want to do is make love to you."

Lily cried, and she wasn't sure if she was overjoyed or miserable. Rick wanted her, but she knew it couldn't last. Tomorrow would come, and he'd hate her for ruining his quiet, safe corner of the universe.

Water beaded up on Rick's skin. When Lily focused back on his eyes, she couldn't deny him anything he wanted. Especially when it was exactly what she wanted too.

Lifting to her toes, she caught Rick's mouth with hers and, aware that he was favoring his hurt ankle, eased him down to the seat that lined the back of the shower. She massaged his shoulders, traced the muscles on his chest, arched back when he kissed a line across her stomach. She accepted him inside her as she lowered to his lap, and each inch she took had her body celebrating in the sensations.

Rick kneaded her hips, settling inside her more possessively, more completely. He stood and she wrapped her legs around his waist. They moved as one entity, small movements that sent shockwaves through Lily's body. A few hours ago she never would have thought she'd be here, feeling this… loved.

How could one person, whom she'd only known for a week, mean this much to her? Why was it that every time Rick touched her she reached a new level of peace? What made it so easy to picture loving him forever?

Rick covered her breasts with hot, demanding kisses. Each stroke of his tongue along her nipples made her body shudder with wild pleasure. The smell of citrus soap, trees, and man swirled around Lily, pulled her into another place, another time, another level of ecstasy. She didn't want to be anywhere else. Ever.

When they reached their peak, Lily let out a cry, which Rick mirrored with a husky sigh. After he sat again, she collapsed against him and listened to his heart beat steadily in his chest, thankful that it did.

Only one way to make sure that it kept on beating.

After catching her breath, she slid off Rick's lap and they finished washing. Rick applied some ointment to Lily's cheek to help it heal. He slid his jeans, T-shirt, and sweater back on while she put on a pair of her grandmother's sweats in a pretty shade of lavender. After another heated kiss in the master bedroom, Rick asked for Lily's car keys so he could check on Poe.

"Come with me. I don't want to leave you alone." He dropped a kiss on her forehead.

"I don't think I'm ready to go back outside just yet." A chill zigzagged down Lily's back. "I'll wait for you here. You'll be right back."

He was about to protest, but the doorbell rang.

"Are the police still out there?" Lily asked.

Rick peered out one of the front windows. "Yes." He walked to the door and opened it.

"Oh, thank God!" Aunt Joy spilled in with Hope and Sage right behind her. She hugged Rick, then gathered Lily in an embrace. "You both all right?" She stepped back to look them over and winced as her gaze settled on Lily's cheek. "Oh, dear."

"We're okay," Rick said.

"I went to your house," Aunt Joy said, turning to Rick, "and saw Poe was injured. My mind got all filled up with horrible, horrible pictures of what may have happened to you two." She hugged them both again, putting a little extra squeeze into it.

"Yeah," Sage said. "We weren't prepared to find someone else to pick on, Ricky." She gave him a light shove, but Lily saw the tears in her eyes.

"Don't call me Ricky." He pulled his cousin into a hug and kissed the top of her head.

"Oh, you guys." Hope squeezed both of them, kissed Rick's cheek, then did the same to Lily. "What happened?"

"Come in and I'll tell you." Lily nudged Rick to the door. "Go get Poe. I'll be fine."

He nodded. "I'll be right back."

He left and Lily stood at the door watching him hobble to her Jeep.

"You're letting the cold in, sugar." Aunt Joy took Lily by the arm and led her to the kitchen. "Sit and start from the beginning."

She told them everything and when she was done, she actually felt better. As if she had just told a story that had happened to someone else. She was able to separate herself from the fact that she could have died. Forgetting that Rick could have died was a harder task.

Aunt Joy, Hope, and Sage sat at the kitchen table in stunned silence until Sage said, "Bat shit? In the face? Classic, Lily. Classic. Assburn got what he deserved, if you ask me."

Lily felt guilty for agreeing. She had to remind herself that the man who had basically kidnapped her this evening wasn't the man she had known for years. He had turned into something else entirely, and it had gotten him killed. How was she supposed to go back to work in California and forget what had happened in that decrepit cabin?

"I don't know about anyone else, but I'm ravenous," Aunt Joy announced. "It has been my experience that food heals all wounds."

Sage nodded and opened Lily's refrigerator. "Wow, well-stocked. I was about to suggest heading back to our house, but screw that. We've got enough in here for a feast."

Lily came to the refrigerator and realized where the food had come from. "Drew bought this."

Sage's hand dropped off the door handle. "On second thought, maybe we should go to our house." She started to close the refrigerator.

"No, there's nothing wrong with this food. Drew was going to eat it too. After the crap he put me through tonight, the least we can do is have a meal on him."

"The bastard." Hope put her hand over her mouth.

"This is what it takes to get my sister to swear." Sage threw an arm around Lily's shoulders as Hope came to stand in front of the refrigerator on Lily's other side.

Sandwiched between them, Lily allowed the tension in her shoulders to loosen. Grandma Gail would have loved these women. Loved them as much as Lily did.

"Are you three going to stare at the enemy food or start making something?" Joy pushed them aside to look inside the refrigerator.

"I only know how to make pancakes," Lily said.

"Pancakes would be perfect," Joy said. "Solid comfort food." She reached in and grabbed the milk.

Sage took out the eggs, while Hope reached for some apples.

"Apple cinnamon pancakes?" Hope asked.

"Sounds good to me." Lily pulled out a mixing bowl and the rest of the needed ingredients.

The four women worked like a well-oiled machine. Chopping, mixing, pouring, flipping. By the time they were done, a sizable stack of pancakes graced the kitchen table.

"Let's eat in the dining room," Lily said.

"It's fancy in there." Hope followed Lily and stood at the threshold to peer into the elaborate room. "What if we spill something?"

"We'll clean it up." Lily shrugged and looked at the long mahogany table with ten high-backed chairs around it. An African bubinga wood inlay in a delicate, maple leaf design ran down the center of the table and was highlighted in the sparkling chandelier lights overhead. They all deserved some fine dining tonight. "Grab the food."

They brought everything into the dining room and when they were ready to sit down, the front door opened. Lily couldn't stop herself from going to Rick, but he wasn't alone when he stepped into the foyer. He and another man carried Poe to the great room and set her down on the fluffy rug by the fireplace.

"Lily, you remember Sam, right?" Rick indicated the man standing behind him.

"Of course," Lily said as she recognized the EMT by day/drummer by night from Black Wolf Tavern.

"He responded to my 911 call," Rick said as he patted Poe's back, soothing the coyote.

Sam answered Lily's unasked question. "Mr. Ashburn has been taken to the morgue. He'll be transported back to California this week. His brother, Ryan Ashburn, has been contacted."

Lily nodded. She'd met Ryan a few times. He lived in Germany. Drew and Ryan hadn't been close, and she wondered if there was a childhood trauma she didn't know about. An abandonment issue, perhaps. Something that could explain why Drew had gotten so possessive of her and completely lost it tonight.

Poe whimpered at her feet, and Lily kneeled. "How's our girl here?" Poe licked at the bandage wrapped around her paw.

"Just a graze," Sam said. "I gave her a couple of stitches. She'll be as good as new in a few days."

Lily scratched between Poe's ears, and the coyote rested her head on her paws while a satisfied rumble buzzed in her throat. "Glad Poe's been well taken care of. We were about to sit down to apple-cinnamon pancakes. Want some, Sam?"

"I'd love some chow," Sam said. "If you don't mind me joining you."

"I don't mind," Lily said, "and I'm fairly certain Hope won't mind either."

Sam's cheeks pinked, and Lily thought the dark-haired drummer/EMT was a perfect match for Hope. He had that same gentleness about him that Hope had.

"Dining room is right through the kitchen there." She gestured with her arm.

"Thank you." Sam headed to the dining room, and Sage busted Hope up about nearly choking on her coffee after he walked in.

Alone in the great room now, Rick kissed Lily's forehead then sniffed the air. He pointed to the dining room. "Pancakes. This way. Come on." He tugged her along behind him, his limp significant.

Lily pulled him to a stop just shy of the dining room. "How bad does that hurt?"

"It's killing me. You'll make me forget the pain after everyone leaves." He arched an eyebrow.

Dammit. How could she do what was best for him if he kept looking at her like that?

****

Rick watched Lily as she ate her pancakes. How could she still look like a runway model in purple sweats with a sliced up cheek? How had he lived without her? Yes, his property had been his sanctuary for the past couple of years and had kept him and his heart healthy, but he hadn't been living.

Not really. Not until he'd made love to Lily. The wheel of his life had started to spin again when she touched him. He didn't want it to stop. He wouldn't let it.

Tonight he would show her exactly how thankful he was that she had cured him. He'd thought solitude was the only answer for his situation, the only thing that would keep him breathing. Now he knew how wrong he'd been. He needed the exact opposite. He needed companionship and not just the four-legged kind.

All I have to do is think of a way to keep Lily.

"These pancakes are freaking awesome," Sam said as he helped himself to a few more.

"Lily has quite a talent for pancakes," Aunt Joy said.

"Nothing hard about making pancakes." Lily shrugged and finished her coffee.

"No," Sage said, "but these are like the mother of all pancakes." She held one up. "Perfect circles, golden coloring, a muffin-meets-cookie phenomenon happening. These are superior pancakes. We should serve them in the store." Sage smiled as if a light bulb had gone off in her head.

"I suppose if you can only cook one thing, you'd better be good at it." Lily offered Rick another pancake, and after a wary glance from his aunt, he nodded. Tonight he could eat a million pancakes and his heart wouldn't give a good goddamn.

They finished eating, none of them discussing the evening's events until Sam said, "Those bats that came out of the cabin were using the place as their hibernacula."

"Their what?" Lily asked.

"Hibernacula. Spots to hibernate for the winter." Sam popped another bite of pancake into his mouth, chewed, swallowed. "They were Indiana bats."

"Aren't those endangered in Vermont?" Hope asked.

"Yep," Sam said.

"Which means…" Rick began.

"This property is protected by law," Sage finished.

Lily's eyes widened. "Which means if a hotel wanted to build here, it totally couldn't."

A cheer rose up from everyone except Sam who looked from Lily to Hope. "Why the hell would a hotel want to build here? This is nowhere."

"It's somewhere to us," Sage said. "And now we get to keep it that way."

Hope explained the details to Sam while she walked him out, and Sage, Aunt Joy, and Lily cleaned up. Lily ordered Rick to a kitchen chair, and Aunt Joy seconded it when she saw how bad his ankle hurt.

"You'll be in that cast forever at this rate, sugar." Aunt Joy pulled another chair over for him to prop his leg on. Though her tone had been scolding, she patted his cheek before going to the sink to wash dishes. Sage dried while Lily put away. When Hope came into the kitchen—a bit flushed—she took a broom and a washcloth into the dining room.

Rick enjoyed watching the women in his family treat Lily as one of their own. She came from miles away—hell, it may have been a galaxy away—but they joked with her, showed her sisterly and motherly affection, talked with her as if they'd known her for years. Was it possible they had fallen in love with her just as he had?

When everything was back to its original tidiness, Lily showed Hope, Sage, and Aunt Joy to guest bedrooms upstairs. There had been talk of Aunt Joy and the girls going back to their house, but Lily said, "Let's all stay here. Safety in numbers and all that crap."

"A slumber party sounds wonderful," Aunt Joy said, shooting Rick a look that said she knew Lily needed to be surrounded by people. Bless Aunt Joy. "Besides, this place is huge!"

When Lily came back downstairs to the kitchen, Rick stood and asked, "Come to show me to my quarters?"

"I'm afraid only the master bedroom is left," Lily said. "Unless you want the couch."

Rick caught her around the waist and clasped his hands at the small of her back. "I want to be wherever you're going to be."

"Good," Lily said. "I want to hold you and be held tonight."

"That can be arranged."

Lily pulled him to his feet. He held back the groan of pain as he took a step.

Note to self, running in air cast through the woods is a mistake. One he hoped not to have to make again.

He climbed the stairs slowly with Lily under his arm, close and secure. When they got to the master bedroom, she undressed herself first then proceeded to remove his clothes. Lily pulled the blankets down on the bed and backed Rick onto the sheeted mattress. He scooted over and she climbed in next to him, pulling the covers over them.

Despite his nakedness, Rick had never been warmer. Lily's body was hot, like a soft, curvy wood stove right beside him. He wrapped his arms around her and loved when she burrowed deeper into his embrace, all her contours fitting against his. He nibbled at her bare shoulder, and she hummed her approval of his attention. Her hair smelled of that grapefruit-coconut fragrance, but she also smelled like apple cinnamon pancakes and maple syrup, and the mingling aromas lulled Rick.

"Good night, Rick," Lily whispered.

He wanted to say good night back to her, tell her that he loved her, but he was already someplace else, where the edges of reality blurred and dreams could make a man's heart feel brand new.

Chapter Twenty-one

Rick rolled to his back, feeling suddenly cold without Lily pressed up against him. She'd kept him warm all night, but now streaks of sun spilled in through the blinds on the bedroom windows announcing morning. He slid his hand over to the other side of the bed and found nothing but rumpled blankets.

Rising to an elbow, he scanned the bedroom, but Lily was not in there. He pulled back the covers and swung his legs over the side of the bed. As blood rushed to his feet, a slow burn emanated from his ankle up to his knee. His entire left leg was swollen.

"Wonderful." He stretched his arms out and yawned, not ready to get up, but wanting to find Lily to drag her back to bed where they could hopefully spend the entire day tangled up with one another. If he had to stay off his leg today, he was going to need someone to keep him entertained.

Lily was that someone. The perfect someone.

He pulled on his jeans and limped to the door. He checked the master bathroom, but didn't find Lily there either. Could she be making more pancakes in the kitchen?

He painfully made his way down the stairs, holding onto the railing with a death grip as he took each step. The kitchen was as they'd left it last night and empty. A nasty feeling seeped into Rick's stomach.

He went to the hallway. "Lily," he called. "Lily!"

Sage appeared at the top of the stairs, looking ready to kill him for disturbing her slumber. "What's with the shouting, Rick? You lose your teddy bear?"

When he didn't laugh, Sage's expression immediately sobered, and she came down the stairs, stopping on the last one so she could look Rick in the eye. "What's the matter?"

"Have you seen Lily this morning?" Rick skirted around Sage to go back upstairs.

She followed him. "I haven't exactly been up taking attendance. It's only 5:30 in the a.m. You know how I hate the a.m."

He went back into the master bedroom and scanned the room more carefully. No suitcase, but Lily had said Drew had taken it. Was it still in his rented SUV, which had been towed to the police station? The sweat suit she'd worn was no longer on the floor where she'd dropped it last night, but the rest of his clothes were.

He flicked his gaze to the bed. That was when saw it.

On the nightstand.

A small, white envelope with his name on it.

"Dammit." Rick picked up the envelope and sat on the edge of the bed.

Sage took a step backward into the hall.

"No." He looked up at his cousin. "Stay. Please." He rubbed his fist down his scar and let out a slow breath. He hadn't even read the letter and his heart ached.

Sage came into the room and sat beside him on the bed. She rested a hand on his shoulder. "You sure you want to open that, Rick?"

"I have to." He ran his finger under the flap and tore the envelope open. He pulled out the folded paper inside. Lily's handwriting was the neatest he'd ever seen. The letters looped together as if her pen had glided along the paper to some ballroom tune.

Dear Rick,

This house and property are yours. I'll mail you the proper documents. Do whatever you want with the house. Live in it, sell the stuff inside, tear it down. Doesn't matter. Just by staying in the house this week, I feel as if I know my grandmother on a whole other level. I now understand why she loved this place.

Last night was truly awful, but at least we can be sure Utopia Resorts will leave you alone now that there are endangered animals making their habitat—or whatever that hibernating word was—in the area. And now that I'm gone, you should be safe to continue your peaceful life that I so selfishly interrupted.

If you're asking yourself if you meant anything to me, the answer is yes. In capital letters, YES. No one has ever meant more to me. I don't know how it happened. We're so completely wrong for each other, yet I never felt more right than when I was with you.

I wish you all the best. Tell Hope, Sage, and Joy I said good-bye.

I stole a jar of your maple syrup. Call it a souvenir.

I love you.

Lily

"If she loves you, why would she leave?" Sage asked.

Rick stood and dropped the letter on the bed. "I think she left *because* she loves me." He stooped down and picked up his T-shirt and sweater. After donning them both, he found his sock and put on his one work boot.

"You're going after her, right?" Sage stood as Rick finished tying his laces.

"Lily doesn't get to decide how the rest of my life goes." He kissed Sage's cheek and headed down the stairs.

****

The airport was a tomb at this hour, and Lily was grateful. For once in her life, she didn't wish for a crowd, for the noise. She needed quiet. Sitting in a chair by her departing gate, she started to dig out her cell phone, forgetting she didn't have it. She had left her purse at Rick's after Drew... stopped by. Just as well. There would have been messages from Tam, probably from Rita or Webster too. She had to tell them about Drew and didn't think that was a conversation for texting back and forth. She also had to tell them the Vermont land was out of the question, but at least she now had something solid to convince them. Utopia Resorts would not want any bad publicity related to building on land holding endangered bats. The granola-eating, tree-hugging types would have a field day on a big corporation like Utopia.

Tree hugging. Lily guessed she could understand the sentiment a little better now. The woods could be dangerous with its bears and bosses-turned-psycho, but it also had people with the kindest hearts she'd ever encountered. Real people who didn't hide behind fancy clothes and fast cars. People who took you in and treated you like family simply because you needed them to.

She thought of Hope, Sage, and Joy. Three of the finest women she'd probably ever know next to Grandma Gail. She knew they'd take care of Rick if she'd hurt him with that letter.

It had been the right thing to do. She was sure of it. He needed to stay away from her. She was poison to someone like him. She belonged in California where she could surround herself with rich tourists looking to spend their money to feel like movie stars. She would go back to catering to their needs and ignoring her own. Everything that could fill her needs was still asleep back at her grandmother's house.

Leaving Rick this morning was the hardest thing Lily had ever done. He'd held her all night just as she'd asked. His arms kept all the nightmares—and she had new ones to choose from—away, and Lily had slept as if under a wizard's spell. When she awoke, she'd spent a few moments watching Rick sleep beside her and knew she had to leave.

Sighing, Lily rubbed her temples. She'd thought her return trip to California would be a time to celebrate. She felt like crying instead.

Gradually, the area near the gate filled with more travelers. Lily checked her watch. Maybe she should skip this flight. Take the next one instead. Perhaps she needed more time to think things through.

She shook her head. She had to go home and get on with her life. If she could call it a life anymore.

Finally the attendant opened the gate and started calling rows for boarding. Lily gathered the suitcase she'd found on her front steps this morning. One of the police officers must have salvaged it from Drew's wrecked SUV before towing it. Luckily, she'd stowed some cash inside the suitcase and had her license in her jacket pocket. She located her seat in coach with the rest of the regular customers. She always flew first class on Utopia's dime, but when she'd booked her own flight early this morning, she'd asked for coach. Today, she just didn't feel like it. She didn't want the attendants making her feel comfortable. She deserved to be uncomfortable. Perhaps she should have asked for a seat near the engines or next to a screaming baby.

Lily pulled out a bag of jellybeans then stowed her bag in the overhead compartment. She opened the candy as she settled in her seat by the window. Gnawing on sugar-coated antidepressants, she watched as the workers drove the luggage carts around on the tarmac. They looked as if they were having fun.

Her definition of fun had changed over these past few days in Vermont. She had more of an urge to go for a hike than dance at a gala. Surely spots to hike existed in California. She'd just never looked for them. Maybe it was time to. Hiking alone would suck though.

She folded the bag of jellybeans closed and wedged it in the seat pocket in front of her. They weren't doing shit for her today. A stop at the Rocky Mountain Chocolate Factory was definitely in order when she landed in California. This situation called for the big guns—dark chocolate double fudge cookies. She glanced at the screen at the front of the plane. Maybe the in-flight movie would offer her solace.

She doubted it.

She pressed her forehead to the cool glass of the small window by her seat. She wished for ice for her cheek, which looked and felt a lot worse today than it had yesterday. Lumpy purple bruises mixed with the cuts making for a lovely rainbow of pain. She hurt physically and was lost emotionally. How could she go from someone who knew exactly what her role in life was to someone who didn't have a clue what her next step should be?

She still loved designing. In fact, her fingers itched to draw something up, but doing so for a monster hotel chain interested only in making money didn't have the appeal it used to. Sure, working for Utopia was a glamorous job, but it didn't *mean* anything. Not to Lily. Not anymore.

"You're a pathetic mess, Hinsdale." She closed her eyes and knocked her head on the window several times.

"Careful. If you break that, you're going to compromise the integrity of this craft and seriously delay our flight."

Lily's eyes shot open. She turned her head and stared into the pale blue eyes of the man standing in the aisle. "Rick?"

"I believe so, yes." He sat, let out a small groan, and rubbed his left knee. He fastened his seat belt, pulling on it to check that it was locked.

"What are you doing here?" She wanted to crawl into his lap, but dug her fingernails into the armrests instead. Rick couldn't really be on this plane with her. Had she hit her head too hard on the window? Eaten too many jellybeans? Slipped into a sugar-induced haze?

"Figured it was a good time for a little vacation. Time to travel. See the world." He traced a finger along her hand on the armrest between them.

"I thought you didn't travel." Lily was slowly losing the battle of keeping her distance from Rick as she inched closer. The look of him, the smell of him, the heat of him called to her.

"I don't," Rick said, "but someone suggested that I should, and I'm willing to if it means I get to spend more time with you, Lily. Besides, I think you need a vacation too. If I remember correctly, you said you travel, but always for work and never for yourself."

"I did say that. So you're coming to California?"

"As a starting point," Rick said. "Then we're figuring out a destination we're both interested in, and we're going on a true vacation. I demand drinks with little umbrellas in them, good reading material, and lovemaking. Lots of it."

"Sounds perfect. And how long would this true vacation last?" Lily's mind was already constructing a list of possible destinations.

"Got a week or two to spare. I want to make the maple syrup like I always do, but my ankle is not in favor of me doing anything right now besides reclining on a beach chair under a tropical sun. In fact, we'll probably need to make a hospital stop when we land and before we officially begin our vacation. My entire leg is killing me." He tapped his left thigh and lowered his eyebrows. "Then I have only one goal, Lily Hinsdale—to figure out how to get you to come back to Vermont with me."

"Why would you want that, Rick? Life with me is likely to give you another heart attack." She pressed her palm to his chest, felt his heart beating in time with her own. Would she ever feel this connected to anyone? Was Rick her Tom Hanks?

Absolutely.

He caught her hand and brought it to his lips. "Life without you is likely to *break* my heart. That's worse, Lily. So much worse." He kissed her fingertips. "Can you honestly tell me you hate Vermont?"

She shook her head. "Despite what happened with the bear when I was a kid and what Drew did yesterday, I'm still remembering the wonderful things I experienced in Vermont. Wonderful things that have everything to do with you, Rick."

She leaned closer and caught his lips. Lips she didn't think she'd be tasting again once she'd left the bedroom this morning.

"Think you could use a barn-building partner?" she asked.

Rick smiled and Lily's insides danced. "I could use a barn building partner as well as someone to make pancakes in the store. And for me, of course. What good is maple syrup without fantastic pancakes?"

"I could send you a resume. You'll see I'm qualified for such positions." Lily rested her hand atop Rick's and traced his knuckles before sliding her fingers between his, right where they belonged.

"You can have those positions, and I have others in mind too."

Lily pulled up the armrest separating them and put her arms around Rick's waist. "I would love to hear more about all available positions." She dropped a light kiss on the tip of his nose.

Rick squeezed her against him. "Just one thing." He pushed her back a bit. "If you ever write me another letter like the one you left this morning…" He clenched a fist and shook it at her.

"I thought I was doing the right thing by leaving." Lily arm-wrestled his fist down to his lap. "I was being stupid."

"Yes, you were. Fortunately, I'm an intelligent man who came looking for you."

"Hey, I wouldn't fall for an idiot." She squeezed his hand.

The pilot announced they were ready for departure, and Lily fastened her seatbelt. Rick had gone stiff and quiet beside her.

"Are you all right?" she asked.

"I hate flying. We could end up dead like my parents and my uncle."

"We almost ended up dead on the ground," Lily pointed out.

"True." Rick touched below the bruises and cuts on her cheek. "I'm going to need someone to keep an eye on my heart while I'm on this plane, while I'm taking the first vacation I've had in years. Maybe you could do that?" His eyes opened extra wide as the plane began rolling into position on the runway.

"No, I don't think so," Lily said.

Rick's mouth turned down at the corners. "No?"

"I don't want to keep an eye on your heart just while you're flying or on vacation." Lily pressed her lips to Rick's and kissed him slowly, gently at first. She deepened the kiss and felt as if she'd taken off without the plane.

"I want to keep an eye on your heart forever," she whispered.

"My heart is yours, Lily." Rick cupped her cheek.

"I'll take good care of it and of you. I love you, Rick."

The airplane's engines roared as Rick ravaged Lily's mouth with a kiss hotter than a California afternoon and sweeter than a gallon of Vermont maple syrup.

"I love you too," Rick said. "I love you more than pancakes."

Epilogue

Three weeks later...

"And you really got Ricky to stay still on a beach under the California sun?" Sage asked as she looked at the pictures Lily had organized into an album on her phone.

"Yes, I did. And three beaches in Mexico too." She smiled, feeling pretty proud of herself for accomplishing the mission of making a mountain man enjoy flashy California and a true vacation.

They'd done all the touristy things like visit Hollywood, Disneyland, Sea World, and the beaches before heading to Mexico. They'd spent time with her father and his girlfriend, and Lily was so pleased Rick and her dad had hit it off. She'd found a beautiful hiking spot and once Rick's leg and ankle felt better, they'd taken several strolls together. Though it wasn't the Vermont woods, Rick had seemed to absorb west coast nature just fine, and Lily felt stupid for ignoring it for so long.

"I believe you accomplished a lot more than just getting Rick to relax," Hope said as she brought coffee to the corner table in Rick's store. "I heard him humming all by himself in the sugarhouse this morning."

"Humming?" Sage and Joy said at the same time.

"Humming." Hope nodded. "You've got some skills, Lily."

"To Lily." Sage held up her mug as did Hope and Joy. The three women saluted her and they all took a sip of their coffee, including Lily.

"Oh, wow," Lily said. "Rick said this maple coffee was good, but I had no idea."

"Best around town, sugar." Joy winked at her.

"So what's next?" Sage asked. "Are you really going to stay in Vermont with us?"

Lily loved how by deciding to stay, she wasn't just getting Rick, but a wonderful set of sisters and a mom. A truly magnificent package. One she wasn't sure she deserved, but was going to accept anyway.

"Yes, I'm staying. I quit my job at Utopia, which didn't go over too well. Now they don't have me… or Drew." She swallowed more coffee to give herself a minute. The news of Drew's behavior and death sent a shockwave through the company. Corporate had worked overtime to bury any bad publicity the whole ordeal would put on Utopia Resorts. "The vice president and president accepted my resignation thinking I was leaving because of Drew. They offered me a sweet package to keep me from taking any legal action against the company, not that I would have. I wasn't leaving because of Drew anyway."

"You were leaving because our Ricky stole your heart," Hope said, clapping her hands.

Lily grinned. "I don't even know how it happened." She still couldn't believe she'd made plans to box up her belongings, leave her beloved California, and move in with Rick.

In Vermont.

In the woods.

It was crazy, but she couldn't imagine not being wherever Rick was. Speaking of which…

"Where is Rick?" They'd flown in from California late last night, crawled into bed, and this morning he'd said he had a few things to take care of. She had assumed he meant syruping things, but she hadn't seen him anywhere on the property.

"Haven't seen him since first thing this morning," Joy said.

"Yeah, and in addition to the humming, he was acting weird," Hope said.

"Weirder than usual," Sage added.

Lily shrugged and finished her coffee. "I'm heading over to my grandmother's place. If you see him, tell him that's where I am." She hadn't been over there since Drew had smashed her laptop against the fireplace and she wanted to clean up and move on.

She bid the women good-bye and hopped into Rick's utility vehicle. It was a far cry from her sleek Lexus, but the ramped up golf cart was fun to drive through the woods.

I'm having fun driving through the woods.

She never could have predicted this. Finding love in Vermont had turned her into someone else entirely. Someone she liked a lot more.

The utility vehicle skidded to a stop in front of her grandmother's place. Rick's pickup truck was in the driveway too.

"Found you," Lily said as she hopped out of the vehicle and jogged up the front steps. The door was slightly ajar and she pushed it open. "Rick?"

Soft, saxophone music floated out to her.

"Rick?" She stepped inside.

"In here," Rick called from the great room.

Lily walked deeper into the house, the scent of lilies reaching her nose. Big, beautiful white blooms filled tall, hammered copper pots and lined the perimeter of the great room. Rick stood in the center, wearing a… a tuxedo? He held a single lily and motioned with his finger for her to come closer.

She nearly tripped on the step leading into the sunken room. Rick in a tuxedo was a sight to behold. The man knew how to fill a pair of jeans and a flannel shirt, but holy cow. What he did to a tux should have been illegal. Add to that the slight tan he'd gotten on their vacation and he was the sexiest thing she'd ever seen. His eyes were an electric blue against his sun-darkened skin and the streaks of lighter blond in his hair brightened up his entire face.

And it was a perfect face. One she could look at for the rest of her life.

"I suddenly feel very underdressed." Lily gestured to her gray yoga pants and purple hooded sweatshirt. Her hair was up in a sloppy ponytail.

"You're breathtaking," Rick said. "Just like always." He reached out his hand and took hers, tugging so her body pressed up against his.

"What's this all about?" She scanned the room, taking in the flowers, the music, the two wrapped presents on the coffee table, the fact that Rick must have cleaned up Drew's mess.

"I have two ideas I'd like to share with you and get your approval. You ready?" He guided her to the couch and gently pushed her to sitting.

"I guess so." Her heart drummed in her chest with a little more force as she waited to hear what he had to say.

"Okay, idea one involves this." He sat next to her and presented the larger, rectangular gift. "Open it."

Lily took the present onto her lap and slowly removed the paper. She was both nervous and excited at the same time. What was Rick up to?

When the last of the wrapping paper had been torn away, a beautiful carved sign lay in her lap. Lily swiped her palm across the rustic wooden finish and fingered the lettering. "Hinsdale Inn?"

"I think we should turn this property into a bed-and-breakfast inn in memory of your grandmother. You can still use your hotel expertise, but in a scaled down capacity that's right for this area. I can still tap the trees and you'll build barns with me. We'll both win." Rick looked at her with such a hopeful expression in those blue eyes.

"Rick, it's a wonderful idea! I love it." She threw her arms around him and dropped kisses on his cheek. "Let's do it."

"I'm glad you like the idea. I wasn't sure, but it sounded right in my head."

"That's a smart head you got there, handsome." Lily fingered his bowtie. "I don't know that it required such formal dress though."

"Actually, the tux is for this gift and idea number two." He leaned forward and plucked the remaining gift off the coffee table—the small, box-like gift.

When he slid off the couch and got to his knee in front of her, Lily squealed and yelled, "Yes!"

Rick laughed. "How do you know there aren't worms in this box and I'm just going to ask you to go fishing at Cassie's Pond?"

"If there are only worms in there, I will hurt you."

Smiling, he ripped the paper off to reveal a velvet jewelry box. He took her hand in his. "I thought I had it all, living here in the woods. I didn't realize what was missing until you stormed in on impractical boots and showed me. Now I can't live without you, Lily. I love you."

He opened the box and Lily gasped at the shiny, square-cut diamond that stared back at her.

"Oh, Rick. It's beautiful."

"I bought it in California, so you'll always have that La Jolla sunshine with you. Even here in Vermont." He slipped it onto her finger. "I'd ask you to marry me, but you already said yes. I'm not giving you the chance to change your mind."

"I'd never change my mind. I love you, Rick."

She leaned forward, cupped his cheeks in her hands, and kissed him. She'd enjoy kissing him like that every day for the rest of their lives together.

If you enjoyed *More Than Pancakes*,
please consider leaving a review
on Amazon and Goodreads
and recommend my books to your friends.
Thank you!

If you have a book group,
I'd love to interact with you!
Email me at cdepetrillo@yahoo.com or message me through Facebook for options.

Check
www.christinedepetrillo.weebly.com
for release dates on
Books Two and Three
in the Maple Leaf Series

More Than Cookies (Book Two—Sage's story)
More Than Rum (Book Three—Hope's story)

Read on for a peek at
More Than Cookies!

More Than Cookies Sneak Peek

Chapter One

A solo guitar captivated the entire room. Sage Stannard watched her cousin, Rick, as his fingers deftly strummed the strings to accompany the band's lead singer as she sang "Angel Eyes," by Jeff Healey.

So tonight I'll ask the stars above,
How did I ever win your love?
What did I do? What did I say,
to turn your angel eyes my way?

Sage glanced to Lily, Rick's brand new wife, sitting in a chair right in front of the band, her wedding gown spilling white and lace and pearls all around her. Red-gold curls were piled high on her head, a sparkly tiara-type headpiece nestled in all that hair. She looked like a real-life princess, and Sage wondered how the hell her hermit, formerly grouch-tastic cousin could have ever snagged such a woman.

It doesn't add up.

Lack of logic aside, Sage was happy for her cousin and his bride. Rick had gotten Lily over her fear of the woods due to a bear attack, and Lily had pulled Rick out of the solitary existence he'd prescribed for himself after suffering a heart attack at such a young age. The sassy Los Angeles hotel designer had managed to bring the quiet Vermont maple syrup maker back to a semi-human level.

She'd even gotten him to wear a tuxedo.

It was a nice story all around. So nice, it made Sage gag a little. Nothing too major. Just a slight difficulty swallowing all that perfection, all that ooey-gooey sweetness.

All that happily-ever-after bullshit.

Not that Sage didn't want a slice of that sunshine for herself, but her track record in that department… well… sucked. Big time. Not only was the pool of available men in their thirties back home in Vermont no bigger than a goldfish bowl, but the fish in that bowl were super huge yawns with a capital Y. She'd given them a chance, but how many hayrides can a girl go on before it just isn't romantic or cute or fun anymore?

Forty-three. That was how many. Sage knew firsthand, and she was totally done conducting research on the matter.

"Hey." A sharp jab to her side made Sage turn to face her sister, Hope, sitting next to her. Both of them sported bridesmaids sheath dresses Lily had picked out for the wedding. Dressed alike, they resembled identical twins though Sage was a year older than Hope. "I never thought we'd see the day our Ricky was so… so…"

"Happy," Sage said with a sigh.

"Yeah. I mean, look at him. He usually closes his eyes when he plays as if he's hiding or something."

Hope was right. At the moment, Rick's big blue eyes were staring right at Lily. He had an expression on his face that clearly said he'd never get tired of looking at his wife, never get tired of waking up next to her. God, he loved her so much.

Something stung in Sage's eyes and she squeezed them shut.

"You okay?" Hope slid her arm around Sage's shoulders.

Sage nodded and folded her arms across her chest. The time to get out of her bridesmaid dress was fast approaching. She was about done with this wedding, happiness for Rick and Lily aside. A foul mood lurked around the corner, waiting to pounce, to seek and destroy.

"Why wouldn't I be okay?"

Hope studied Sage's face for a few uncomfortable seconds then shrugged. "I don't know. You seem—"

"Look, I'm fine. You're fine. Rick and Lily are extra-fine." She caught sight of their mother, Joy, whooping it up with Lily's father, Robert Hinsdale, the famous actor, and his actress girlfriend, Jeri Kappen. "Even Mom is fine. Let's just finish this night up and get on with things."

"Someone needs more wine." Hope tapped a finger against Sage's empty glass. "Turn that frown upside down, girlie, before I have to officially classify you as Downright Pissy." She attempted to poke Sage in the cheek, but Sage slapped her hand out of the way.

"Knock it off." Okay, now she sounded downright pissy to her own ears. *Dammit.*

She focused on Rick stepping off the stage and pulling Lily out of her seat. He dropped a light kiss on the back of her hand then slid his arm around her. The two of them slow danced to the next song and soon the dance floor was full of couples. Hope had already trotted off to stand next to their mother. Neither of the girls had brought dates to the wedding because it was in California. Not that both of them hadn't tried, but summer in Vermont meant every able-bodied male was outside nearly around the clock growing, cutting, building, or digging something. They were permanently attached to their John Deere tractors. None of them were willing to hike across the country, especially to Los Angeles, the direct opposite of small-town Danton, Vermont.

Usually being alone didn't bother Sage. Today, it was getting to her. She needed a break from all this mushy stuff.

Wedging her small purse under her arm, she got up and marched out of the ballroom. She hunted down the bathroom and pushed open the door. Standing under the air conditioning vent, she let the cool air wash over her face. She walked to the sinks and the wall of mirrors behind them. Giving herself a once over, she had to admit Lily had chosen well with the bridesmaid dresses. An electric green that made Sage's eyes a deeper shade of emerald, the dress showed off curves and emphasized legs toned from tons of hiking in the woods, running around Rick's store baking cookies and other confections during sugaring season, and zipping to catering jobs in between. The dress also showed that though Sage liked to cook and adored eating even more, her size six ass was in top shape.

She angled herself a little to check out her own butt in the mirror. *Why doesn't someone want a piece of that?* Well, she supposed men existed who wanted a piece of that, and several she'd already given it too, but none that she wanted to say "I do" to.

And she was bored with the search. So bored.

She used the bathroom, washed her hands, and finger-combed her straight blonde hair before applying more lip gloss and heading back out to the reception. She paused in the doorway of the room and spotted Lily's cousin—whose name she'd forgotten—making his way toward her. He'd rubbed up against her "accidentally" three times when they were taking part in the actual wedding ceremony, and Sage was certain she didn't want to allow him a fourth "accident." She couldn't be responsible if her hand "accidentally" made contact with his face.

Deciding to go outside instead, she turned on her three-inch high heels and made her way down a stairway with a pearl-topped railing. When the jewel-embellished doors slid open, Sage stepped onto the sidewalk in front of Gems Utopia Resort, one of the themed hotels Lily had designed before she left it all to come to Vermont to be with Rick for as long as they both shall live.

Craning her head back, she took in the impressive exterior of the hotel. All cut angles and shiny surfaces, the entire structure screamed extravagance and creativity.

Creativity. That was what Sage needed in a man. She didn't mind the roughened, lumberjack look—hell, who would?—but she was looking for more than muscles encased in flannel. She wanted someone with a spark.

Or someone who could light a spark in her.

****

The July sunshine filtered through the maple trees and white pines, casting warm, golden streaks on the lush greenery beneath Orion Finley's booted feet. He absolutely loved summertime in the Vermont woods. Everything smelled fresh and alive. Huge dragonflies hovered in place as they checked on a leaf here, a branch there, landed on a rock bordering the path leading deeper into the woods. A few hawks circled overhead, letting loose a screech every now and then to make sure Orion knew they were keeping an eye on him.

Only two things were missing to make this trek into the forest perfect. His dog, a Greater Swiss Mountain dog named Ranger, and his six-year old daughter, Myah Rose. Both were currently held captive in his fire-breathing ex-wife's lair.

Temporary.

He had to constantly remind himself that it wouldn't be this way forever. He would get both of them back. Soon. Orion didn't care what he had to do, but Ranger and Myah belonged with him and he wouldn't stop until everything was as it should be. He had plenty of room at his farmhouse for a small girl, a large dog, himself, and his father, Ian Finley, a retired fisherman who Orion now took care of. He could handle it all. He knew he could. Proving it—when his opposition was a she-beast lawyer he used to love—was turning out to be the biggest challenge of his life, but he wasn't one to shy away. Especially not when the reward was getting to see Myah every single day.

Damn, he missed her blue eyes and her black hair—two features she shared in common with him, only her eyes were bigger and her hair longer. Her smile was definitely better than his too, because she still remembered how to smile. His lips, on the other hand, were reluctant to take on that shape since The Divorce. Since Adriana Whitfield-Finley, his once true love, decided being married to a chainsaw artist and living in the woods of Vermont wasn't what she was "put on this stinking planet to do." She wasn't supposed to be "wasting her time and intelligence on someone like him." Her words. Her razor sharp, dice-a-man's-heart-into-pieces, fuck you words.

Whatever. He never should have gotten involved with her in the first place. He knew as well as his father did that sophisticated women didn't settle down with men like them. Men who liked to spend their days outdoors, making things with their own two hands. Men who were more comfortable wearing sawdust instead of cologne.

Men who weren't rolling in money.

Orion's mother had skipped out on them when he was ten. Adriana hadn't made it to Myah's tenth birthday before she had to get away from the "stifling squeeze" Vermont—and apparently he—had applied to her metaphorical throat.

He hated metaphors.

He also wouldn't be getting into any situations remotely resembling a relationship with a woman. They were all sweet smiles and passionate kisses… until the claws came out.

No thanks.

Sighing now as he continued farther into the woods, Orion pushed aside thoughts of Adriana, Myah, Ranger, and his father. This morning was about finding the perfect trees to make his next sculptures. The order was for three, life-sized black bears—one of his most favorite things to carve. A zoo in New York had requested the carved critters for a display to be erected near the Christmas tree at Rockefeller Center in December. They wanted them now so they could build the rest of the display around his bears. This one customer would bring in some good money. Hopefully it would be enough to convince a judge that he could, in fact, support his daughter.

After taking a swig from his water bottle, Orion followed a brook toward a grove of suitable pines. Tall, straight, and healthy, they were perfect for this project. He reached into the pocket of his cargo shorts and produced three lengths of bright orange rope. He tagged three trees to mark them for his buddy, Adam Rouse, who would come in with the heavy equipment, cut those babies down for him, and tow them to Orion's workshop. Then he'd get to hack away at the logs until the bears emerged from the shavings.

He couldn't wait.

Carving always made him feel… free. As if he could give birth to absolutely anything he wanted out of that wood. As if it were just waiting for him to breathe beauty, creativity, and art into it. As if, without him, the wood would not have fulfilled its true purpose in this life.

He ran his rough and scarred hands over the trunk of the nearest pine. The bark scraped across his fingertips—except for the pinkie fingertip on his left hand. He'd lost from the first knuckle up to the tip during one carving project where he was making the entire cast of The Wonderful Wizard of Oz for an obsessed Frank L. Baum fan. If Orion had "only had a brain," he would have been extra careful carving around the lion's mane, but he'd been still developing his techniques. Still experimenting with which angles created the right effects, which tools did the job best. He'd made a rather important note to self on that job. Under no circumstances should one's pinkie finger come into contact with the grinder's blade. Not good. Lots of blood. Lots of swearing.

Looking at that abbreviated finger now, he shook his head and pulled out his cell phone.

"Hey, Adam," he said when his buddy answered. "I'm west of the brook, about two-thirds of a mile in. Tagged three trees."

"Got it," Adam said. "I'll grab those tomorrow for you."

"Thanks, man." And that ended their conversation. Vermont men didn't need a lot of words to get jobs done. Orion liked it that way.

Carrying his phone, he turned to retrace his steps back to his workshop. As he walked, dog barks and a few gunshots echoed somewhere closer than he would have liked. Damn hunters were always parading through his land with their bloodhounds, cornering bears and calling it a sport when they put a bullet into the trapped creature.

Pointless.

As far as Orion was concerned, there were much better ways to spend one's time.

He continued on his way, but stopped when a deer bounded across his path. Its big brown eyes connected with his for a moment then the animal was gone. While Orion stared down the path the deer had taken, another shot rang out.

Something hot and fucking painful bit into his right thigh. He immediately clamped a hand over the aching area and his stomach did a sick flip-flop when his hand came away wet and red. His vision got spotty. His ears rang and not in the this-is-an-awesome-rock-concert way. No, definitely more like the I've-been-shot-and-am-going-to-pass-out way instead.

This was so not the morning he'd planned.

Check www.christinedepetrillo.weebly.com for release information!

Other Available Titles
by Christine DePetrillo

Alaska Heart
Firefly Mountain
Kisses to Remember
Abra Cadaver
Lazuli Moon
Dive (mermaid anthology with Joseph Mazzenga, Heather Rigney, Rachel Moniz)
Night Eternal (gothic poetry with author Joseph Mazzenga)

Young Adult Romance
writing as Christy Major

Run With Me
Sail With Me

Co-writing as Goodwin Reed

A Less Perfect Union

About the Author

Christine DePetrillo tried not being a writer. She attempted to ignore the voices in her head, but they would not stop. The only way she could achieve peace and quiet was to write the stories the voices demanded. Today, she writes tales meant to make you laugh, maybe make you sweat, and definitely make you believe in the power of love.

She lives in Rhode Island and occasionally Vermont with her husband, two cats, and a big, black German Shepherd who guards her fiercely against all evils.

Find Christine's other titles at
www.christinedepetrillo.weebly.com.
Connect on Facebook at
www.facebook.com/christinedepetrilloauthor,
on Twitter at @cdepetrillo,
and at The Roses of Prose group blog
on the 4th and 14th of every month at
www.rosesofprose.blogspot.com.

Made in the USA
Middletown, DE
13 December 2019

80622990R00215